G488

‖‖ ‖‖‖‖‖‖ ‖ ‖‖‖‖‖‖‖‖‖‖‖‖ ‖‖‖
☑ **W9-BDP-236**

CHECK INSURANCE
MEDICA

Also by Don Harrison

The Spartan

The
Alexandrian
Drachma

Don Harrison

 Knights
Press

Stamford, Connecticut

Designed by Able Reproductions, copyright © 1984.

Published by Knights Press, P.O. Box 454, Pound Ridge, NY   10576

Library of Congress Cataloging in Publication Data

Harrison, Don, 1941–
    The Alexandrian drachma.

    I. Title.
PS3558.A666A78   1984   813'.54   84–7933
ISBN   0–915175–00–2

Printed in the United States of America

The Alexandrian Drachma

1.

"Aieee, no, no, young sir, effendi. Please come back, the rocks are dangerous." Ali, our English-speaking guide, waved his whip and with surprising agility for an old man jumped down from the seat of the open horse-drawn carriage. "Please sir, stop!" Ali ran shouting and grabbed Alex by the sleeve of his linen shirt. His broken English was insistent. I had just opened the carriage door preparing to step out onto the sandy ground. Only moments before the energetic Alex had simply leaped over the door, his boots hitting the sand with a thump, and bolted for the ruins. Alex stopped, looking down at the coffee-colored guide with dismay.

"I was just going up to the ruins . . . ." Alex seemed annoyed and puzzled, brushing the guide's brown hand away from his shirt sleeve.

"You don't understand, sir. The rocks are warm from the morning sun, and deadly snakes sometimes crawl on them to bask. Most dangerous. Cobras and asps. One bite and you're finished, young sir."

"I didn't realize," Alex said, grinning. "Like the one that did Cleopatra in? I remember the old jokes about her when we studied her life in school. There was some question as to where she may have placed her asp."

"The very same, effendi. Please now, follow me, and watch where you place your hands." The bent Egyptian guide started to walk slowly up the sandy path.

Alex watched while the guide trudged up the path littered with broken stones and drifts of sand. Towering above the shattered landscape was the ninety-foot base and column of Pompey's Pillar—the morning sun reflecting off the polished sheen of the shaft of red granite. I caught up with Alex, who turned and looked at me with smiling gray eyes. He had removed his tall felt hat and waistcoat and faint signs of perspiration dampened his linen shirt. A soft breeze coming in from the sea ruffled his blond hair. "I cannot believe it, Edward. Tomorrow is the first of January, and it's the middle of winter. It should be freezing, but it's warm, almost balmy."

"Yes, it's quite warm," I replied. "The snow at Caerleon Castle was piled high against the walls when we left. Alexandria, at last. Are you happy?"

"Oh, yes, very. But there's nothing here, except sand, broken stones, and snakes. I had expected so much. There's nothing left. Where is the Tomb of Alexandros, the temples, the palaces, and the splendid buildings?"

"Gone, I'm afraid." Alex and I had expected so much, each rebuilding the ancient city in his mind. A beautiful city founded by the Macedonian conqueror Alexander the Great, a city where Cleopatra had once ruled, a city that had known the Caesars and the Romans. Now there was nothing but rubble and Pompey's Pillar.

"Effendi, hurry please. The day grows hot and it will be time for morning tea. There is nothing to see here. We go now, sirs."

Alex and I walked the short distance up the low hill, carefully watching for snakes. The guide seemed annoyed by our slow pace. To him the ruins were nothing, but to us they held a fabulous history of ancient empires and legendary heroes. The splendor of ancient Alexandria had once rivaled that of Rome. In the near distance the waters of the Mediterranean Sea sparkled in the morning sun, a sea that had once known the fleets of Greece and Rome.

"We go now, sirs." The insistent words of our guide brought us back to the dusty, grimy town that Alexandria had become.

"Would it be possible to visit the underground crypts and vaults beneath the Serapeum?" I asked. "The vaults of the temple are said to connect with the Tomb of Alexandros."

"The crypts? On, no, gracious sir . . . not possible. They have been closed for many years. It is dangerous." Ali shook his wrinkled head.

"The crypts, Edward? I had forgotten about them. The storerooms used by the priests of Serapis. . . ."

"Not possible. They are dangerous and haunted by ancient afreets, ghosts of the old gods driven there by the Prophet Muhammed, a thousand blessings on his name, when he came to Egypt to drive the heathen evil away. Most dangerous, effendi."

"Do you know where the entrance is?"

"It is near, but I warn you. . . ."

"Nonsense, my good fellow. Should I report you to the hotel?" I spoke harshly, shocked by the words of the superstitious guide.

"Oh, no, great lord. I have many mouths to feed, several wives, and many children. It would be possible to go there. Some men would be needed to lift the slab of stone covering the entrance, and we would need torches. If that is what Lord Caerleon wishes. It would take money . . . ah, much baksheesh to hire the men, ahhh. . . ."

"Much baksheesh? Well what of it? Hire the men!" The guide scurried off down the hill, shouting and madly waving his whip. "Excitable lot, these Egyptians. Damn, it is getting hot."

Alex smiled, wiping beads of perspiration from his brow and helping me remove my heavy waistcoat. The thought of some action seemed to lift his crushed spirits as he watched the guide collect men to raise the stone guarding the mysterious crypts.

Alexander Saint-Hilaire. Had it been two years since we had first met? That day would stay in my memory forever. . . a cool and misty day. I had come in from the Welsh Coast and Caerleon to conduct some estate business with my London solicitor and having the afternoon free took a cab to the British Museum to view the Elgin marbles, those masterworks of Grecian antiquity saved from the lime kilns and destruction by the quick action of Lord Elgin. The statuary had created a sensation and the "mode à la Grec" swept England. After a long wait in the rainy mist, I was admitted to the great hall where the marbles had been carefully placed.

Even in their ruined, battered, and dismal state the noble marbles were beautiful, speaking of an elegant age long passed. Here were the gods, and goddesses that had once adorned the Parthenon. There was a lovely caryatid that had once held up the roof of the Erechtheion, and a tall, fluted Ionic column taken from the same building. Along one wall of the room were placed yellowed marble slabs depicting the Panathenaic procession of men, maidens, and sacrificial animals brought to the Acropolis for the splendid festival of Athena Parthenos, the guardian virgin goddess who had raised her city to greatness. I paused for a moment, looking closely at the Parthenon frieze. Surely the master hand of Phidias had carved this once white marble. Two nude young men sat astride their rearing stallions. Tiny flecks of paint still clung to the recesses, showing that the marble had once glowed with color, but it was the nobility of the youths that held me entranced — the broad shoulders, the beautifully modeled muscularity of the chests, the strong yet slender athletic waists, the curve of a leg muscle. I must have forgotten where I was for suddenly I felt a bump and a shove. It was then I first saw Alexander Saint-Hilaire. His beauty took my breath away. It was as though the ancient carvings had suddenly sprung to life and, mumbling apologies, stood before me. . . .

"Lord, effendi! The men are ready!" Our guide came tromping across the sand, followed by a group of shouting robed Egyptians carrying bundled straw.

The coffee-colored men and boys stood around while I bartered for their services. Friends who had visited the Nile Valley had told me that there were no fixed prices and that haggling was expected. Never pay the first price, they said, as you can always get it down lower. But I wanted to get on with it and gave the guide his first price. He seemed surprised, eagerly taking the coins. "Let's open the crypts, and then we can go back to the hotel for tea." Our little processional started out with the guide in the lead, Alex and I following, and the natives bringing up the rear.

We circled around Pompey's Pillar, passing beneath its great shadow cast across the sands like some giant sundial. A little beyond, a partially covered sphinx stared at us, its leonine body showing through the sand, its smile . . . an enigma. "It is here." The guide stopped. "Beneath the sands." He spoke some Arabic words to his men, who began to sweep the accumulated debris away with the straw torches and their hands. He came over to us. "Lords, effendi, again may I warn you against exploring the crypts. Sometimes it is not wise . . . ah, but I can see you are determined." He scowled, muttering some no doubt unpleasant Arabic words to himself, then turned to his men as they uncovered the entrance to the Serapium.

"Jumping Jove, Edward, our first excavation in Egypt, our first dig for the Tomb of Alexandros. Do you suppose it's down there?"

"Have no idea, but might as well have a look. After tea we'll check in and talk with the British consul general about transportation to Cairo and getting permission to dig from that old Albanian, Pasha Mehemet Ali. Permission is difficult. My agent in Cairo wrote that we may be prevented from taking my little obelisk from Philae home to England. The pasha has decided to keep his treasures in Egypt instead of giving them away. We'll see. Look, they've uncovered the stone block!"

A few feet of debris had been cleared, revealing a stone set into an ancient pavement. It was about three-feet wide; an iron ring had been imbedded in the center for lifting. Brown hands grasped the ring, and with much grunting and groaning the stone left its bedding and was gradually lifted up and placed to the side. The dark hole was at first misted by dust, but as it settled a stone step came into view. What lay below? We paused, perhaps awed by the enormous age separating us from the builders who had first constructed the vanished temple. There was a sudden rush of air from the hole, causing a moment of dread. We stepped back startled. "Don't worry, just escaping air from the crypts. Light the torches, and we'll go on down," I said. A spark from a tinderbox set the dry straw aflame, and we were ready for our descent into darkness. "Come on, Alex, follow me." I took the lead as Alex dropped his coat and hat, and with flaming torches in hand, we gingerly placed our boots on the first stone step. The rest of the hole fell away into gloom.

"Holy Saint Pete, it's dark down here. Golly. . . ." Alex muttered his usual youthful euphemisms, but as we descended he quieted. To our right was a cold stone wall; on the other side of the three-foot steps was an empty void. Placing our torches in our left hands, we laid our right hands on the wall for support. The bottom was no-where in sight. The flickering torches cast our shadows along the wall, and our footsteps echoed throughout the chambers.

"I think I can see the bottom. Yes, just a few feet more," I shouted, as my boots hit a pavement of stone. We gathered for a moment, looking up and around. Stretching into the distance was a series of rounded arches supported by granite pillars. The floor was littered with dust and debris. "The vaults seem to go on forever. Let's look around." Passing beneath a row of several arches we could see side rooms leading off to somewhere. "It is vast."

"Sacred bulls of Apis, think of the treasure this place held. Piles of gold and silver! The treasure of Serapis, enough to buy all of England, I bet." The dim light flickered off Alex's face as he spoke, his words ringing around the stone vaults. "Let's see what is in the side chambers." He wandered toward a gloomy door, sticking his torch inside, but suddenly stepped away and let out a scream of fear. I ran over. The empty eyesockets of many skulls gazed vacantly out at us. Yellowed gauze linen wrappings, the shrouds of the ancient dead, lay scattered among pieces of bone and dried flesh. We turned our eyes away from the horrible sight. Suddenly, there was a whirring, a buzz-ing, a screeching. The ceiling was alive with a dark mass of something that began to fly at us. In dread terror we ducked down, trying to escape the horde of great black bats. In their fright they bumped against our faces, clinging to our hair and clothes. We struck out with our hands, waving our torches. In what seemed to be a macabre nightmare, we had come face to face with mysterious Egypt.

In a few minutes the black mass had crossed overhead to find another more peaceful roosting spot. We stood up, shaken but grin-ning at each other, sharing our silly fright because of harmless bats. "Now we know why we were warned not to come down here," Alex said. "The place is strange."

"Eerie. Reminds me of the old Roman vaults beneath Caerleon Castle. Spookier, though. Want to take another look in the mummy room. You don't have to look . . . if you're scared. . . ."

"Me scared? Never. It was just the first sight. . . . I was startled."

The guide and his men seemed to have gained their composure and watched as we stuck our torches into the grisly room. "Poor devils, ripped apart in a treasure search. There was a big market for the bodies a while back. They were ground up and sold for medicine; truly a ghoulish practice. In 1828 a dead Italian carpenter was buried in the desiccating sands and sold for a very high price to one of our gullible countrymen. It was the only known mummy with a beard. There are fools born every day, eh, Alex?"

"Let's get out of this room." Alex turned and I followed, leaving the ancient dead to whatever peace they had left.

"Lords, effendi. Surely we will disturb the afreet of Serapis. He lurks in dark, forbidden places waiting to claim victims that he takes to hell. We go now!"

"Nonsense. Let's go on. Perhaps we can find where the passages go; there seems to be no end to them." Alex and I turned, passing beneath another archway. A hot wind rising from the depths of the endless corridors began blowing, slowly at first, but soon increasing in strength. There was a smell, a foul odor, of something in the wind. The torches began to flicker, the flames blowing here and there. The wind moaned and howled, whipping our faces and hair. Sand and debris stirred up by the wind swirled up around us, blinding our eyes. We covered our nostrils to keep the smell away. What was it? Musty and rotten, the smell of the grave and the long dead rushed through the vast corridors. A thousand demons seemed to pursue us.

"It is the afreet of Serapis who has come to take our souls. Run! Run!" Our faithful guide and the workers dropped their torches and fled toward the staircase. An awful howling pounded our ears, and it was difficult to stand against the terrible wind. We almost gagged surrounded by the nauseous odor of the place. Catching Alex by the arm, I pointed my thumb at the dim shaft of daylight that seemed so far away. Dropping our torches, we ran toward it, scrambling up the staircase with every ounce of our strength. As soon as we popped out of the hole the workmen placed the stone block back into the pavement. The guide stood smiling at us, wearing an "I told you so" expression.

"What was it? The wind and the smell, ugh, horrible."

"The afreet of Serapis, of course."

"Yes, Alex, I think our wise guide might be correct. It was something. We should be getting back to the hotel; it's time for morning tea." We walked silently back to our carriage, wondering.

With a smart crack of the guide's ready whip the old nag started up with creaking bones, and we began our return to the hotel. The dirty, narrow streets were packed with Alexandrians. Some wore European suits, their heads topped with bright red Turkish tarbooshs, whose jaunty tassels hung to the side of the tall caps. Other men clung to the Eastern style of dress, wearing dark robes, their belts carrying ornate swords and daggers. They led or rode camels or slow donkeys. Carts of every size blocked the streets; they carried farm produce, pottery jars, or animal fodder. Here and there we saw black-robed women, their entire figures veiled from the sight of men in the Moslem custom. The many shops advertised Egyptian coffee or tobacco, their signs lettered in English, French, or German, along with the beautiful flowing Arabic script. Alexandria was a cosmopolitan city, her harbours berthing sailing vessels arriving and leaving from every port in the world. There was a strange, exotic charm about the city, so very different from the small, staid town of Caerleon.

We had just passed a large mosque, whose minaret, covered with blue-and-turquoise tile, glittered high into the sky. The morning sunlight filtered into the narrow streets misted with the smoke of household fires and dust. The light caught the ornate woodwork of the latticed windows of the tall houses that stood along the street. We were looking up at them when suddenly the carriage stopped. The guide raised his whip to spur the nag onward, but the horse's harness of gold and silver, which shimmered in the dusty light, was firmly held by a brown hand. A robed man sitting astride a dappled Arabian stallion gazed at us with intense insolence. Only his black piercing eyes were visible, for his face and head were veiled and voluminous black robes enfolded his commanding figure. From his waist hung a jeweled scabbard and a dagger. But it was the fierce gaze shooting out between the folds of his blue veil that held us. His eyes locked into mine and then shifted to Alex's. For a long moment the two men stared at one another, two men from different worlds in a strange meeting in a crowded street. What did he want? I was about to shout out in fear, for the scabbard looked to hold a powerful sword, but the Arab dropped the harness, turned his stallion, and quickly rode away. He was soon lost from sight.

Alex shook his head, as if trying to break a spell that the blue-veiled man had put him under with his almost hypnotic gaze. "Great Pompey's Pillar, who was that?"

"The man should be arrested for such brazen action. We should report it to the police."

"Lords, effendi, it will do you no good. The man is lost to sight."

"Who was he?"

"Oh, effendi, a most feared warrior of the desert, a Tuareg. They hide their faces in blue veils, for it is a mark of their tribe, and if I may speak frankly, they would split you from ear to ear without cause. They are vicious slave traders with markets from Damascus to Khartoum. Beware of all such men." The guide snapped his whip, and we drove on.

"You would not find me taking tea with such a wild-looking creature. One does not take tea with a barbarian."

"No, I think not, Alex. But perhaps we looked as strange to him as he looked to us."

"Englishmen do not look strange. Perhaps it's because I didn't put my waistcoat back on. Breaking the rules of etiquette. I hope you don't mind, Edward. Even in the shade my shirt is damp."

"No, Alex, it's fine." I was glad he had left his coat off, for the soft linen cambric clung to his chest and back, impressing his hard, youthful muscularity into the damp cloth. He had the vitality of a frisky colt, his wide eyes darting about from object to object as we passed through the streets. As he turned and twisted in his seat, the fibers and sinews of his muscles stretched the cloth into fine taut lines that caressed his body. His was an unconscious grace of movement, quick and smooth, the elegance of a young animal, lean and fit for whatever life might throw in its way. Was it that I was growing old and had forgotten how exciting life could be?

My thoughts drifted back to the British Museum and my first meeting with the beautiful boy. I had been flustered while he stood there blushing, stammering his apologies, and I had failed to notice my uncle standing near until I heard my name being called. "Edward, old chap, blasted good to see you again. I see you've met my son, Alex. Alex, this is your cousin, Edward, the fifth earl of Caerleon." The boy and I shook hands.

My uncle, Phillip, the marquis Saint-Hilaire, tall, lean, and almost too aristocratic of bearing, was a man of great wealth and fame. The newspapers constantly reported his many activities. He had become involved both with the excavations at the Roman city of Pompeii and with the notorious Lady Hamilton and her affair with Lord Nelson. He had helped Lord Elgin bring the precious marbles to a safe haven in England and had aided the Greeks as they fought for liberation from the Turks. The poet and writer Lord Bryon, at thirty-six years of age, had given his life for that noble cause in 1824. Phillip had fallen in love with Greece. My father read me an account of his marriage to a young Greek woman whom he had given the name of Olympias, the same name as the mother of Alexander the Great. It was a romantic notion that reflected his love for that ancient civilization. He brought his beautiful bride to England where she became an attraction in the British court. While in the past he had come to Caerleon Castle bringing odd gifts from unknown places, he never brought his wife, always rushing back to his beloved Greece to search for some new rediscovered ruin. As we drove along, these things came quickly into my thoughts, though they had meant very little to me as a youth.

One afternoon I had just returned from classes, and my father's butler called, saying that father wanted to see me. The great hall of Caerleon Castle was always a place that struck me with awe. Its Gothic vaulting towered above me; the stained glass gave the room a churchlike feeling, and paintings of my ancestors looked down at me with grave and solemn expressions. Father sat at the far end of a refectory table, a pile of boxes and wrapping paper cluttering the highly polished walnut table. My father, in his usual gruff way, told me that my uncle had sent a gift from London and that he was uncertain as to what to do with it. Brushing away the paper he showed me the gift. It was a small Greek statue, about two feet high, of a youth, perhaps a god or athlete. The arms and legs were missing, but the head was finely modeled. Its expression had a pensive, poetical quality, and the marble torso, while pitted and chipped, was gracefully wrought. A note from the marquis said he had found the statue in Greece and that he must return to Europe and would not be able to visit us.

Father did not care for the statue, saying that it was a heathen idol and shameless because the youth wore no breeches. He said that he would find a dark corner of the castle to put it in and thus out of sight of polite society. I told him that I liked it and wanted to put it in my rooms. He picked up the "heathen idol", as he called it, by the black marble base and shoved it into my arms. It was heavy but I lugged it up the grand staircase into my bedroom, placing it near a window where the morning light would catch the surface, highlighting the faint sheen of polished marble. Throughout my youth I would look at the Grecian boy, wondering who he might have been and what his life in such an ancient age might have been like. I found that I was falling in love with him, wishing he were alive so that we might touch.

So were the unresolved yearnings of my youth, and as I think of it now, although it was odd to fall in love with a chunk of marble, it was an expression of an unnamed desire I felt as my hands caressed the marble athlete. Paul, beloved Paul. One summer when I was going on sixteen that hard marble turned into living flesh and blood. Paul would go out of my life in the autumn to become a soldier of His Majesty's Royal Dragoons in keeping with the noble traditions of his family. But until then . . . He was taller than I, more rugged, given to hunting and fishing, while I read my beloved books. However, there was an unspoken bond between us that had existed since we had played together as boys, and as young men the bond had strengthened. But now we were at a crossroads—he would take his path and I had yet to find mine.

We were to spend our last days together. I saw him pull into the courtyard from the high window of my room. With a jaunty air he drove his pony-drawn cart through the crumbling walled bastions of the castle, across the useless filled-in moat, and beneath the useless portcullis, stopping before the grandeur of the Norman portico, as without ceremony he shouted my name, "Edward, you silly ass, get down here!" His voice was loud and demanding, quite in keeping with his military ways. He would make a good officer in His Majesty's Army.

As we left the castle I could feel its looming presence. Part Roman, Norman, and a good deal Gothic, its towers and spires, its walls and fortifications were built for a different age but yet had survived. It was drafty and cold in the winter but cool and pleasant in the warm summers. With a lurch and a snap of the whip Paul and I were off to the sea that lay some six miles away. The pony clopped along over the familiar stones of the Roman road, past the remains of the Roman amphitheater, following the River Usk. We soon passed through the town of Newport and could see the shimmering blue-black Bristol Channel. Rather than take the low road to the sea Paul turned the pony and took the upper road that led to the sea cliffs.

The ride had been wordless, and we did not look at each other as we sat in the bone-rattling cart. Sometimes our knees or legs would touch, but neither of us seemed to want to draw away and so I often felt the warmth of his leg next to mine. He drove on through the waving tall sea grasses as flocks of gulls cried above, screeching and fighting against the buffeting, stiff winds that blew in from the sea. We were alone in an empty world as he drew up the reins, stopping the pony. He sat silently for a long while, then suddenly turned and looked down at me with soft brown eyes, his brown hair whipped by the wind. "We've meant a lot to each other, haven't we, Edward?"

"Yes, Paul," I said. The gentle softness in his voice was unexpected, and I stammered. His usual gruff ways vanished, and I realize now he may have built his strong, rugged facade as a protection to hide a more sensitive inner self.

"Want to walk a bit?" he asked. "It's going to be a long time before we see each other again . . . a very long time." I nodded. I also felt the growing mood of sadness that had taken hold of Paul as he realized that he was going away, parting from kin and home, making the break necessary for young men if they are to fulfill their goals. He jumped down from the cart, and I followed, watching as he tied a hobbling rope around the legs of the pony. We stood almost touching, watching the tiny fishing boats far below. Perhaps without thinking his hand closed around mine, holding tightly to my fingers. I looked up at him, but his eyes were set on the distant horizon. Hand and hand we turned and walked through the grass. He stopped some distance away from the cart and faced me in the blowing wind. His eyes were moist from tears. He broke his tight grip and cupping my face with his hands he kissed me.

My mind swirled as our lips met. I wanted to bolt away and run, but I could not, realizing this was the thing I had longed for, the unknown element, the fulfillment of my secret yearnings as my fingertips had caressed the cold marble of the Greek youth. Paul had brought my secrets out of my inner soul with his sudden, rash, but magnificent kiss. My entire soul cried out with joy as he drew me closer, folding his strong arms around my waist, pressing our loins together. I could feel his hardness pressed against mine through the cloth of my trousers. Halting, tentative, almost afraid of what I was doing, fearing that I would do the wrong thing and break the enchanted moment, my fingers ran across his hard muscles, feeling the strength of his back and his broad shoulders as we remained locked in the kiss.

He drew away and my heart stopped. I had done the wrong thing. But then he looked down at me smiling as he unbuttoned my shirt, pulling the cloth out of my trousers. It whipped madly around my thin chest as his mouth touched my nipples. I could feel his tongue, watching his head, his long brown hair blowing in the strong wind, as he knelt before me unbuckling my belt, pushing my trousers down. My manhood was fully aroused as he touched his lips to it. Suddenly he plunged his mouth around the shaft. What ecstasy engulfed my confused, bewildered mind. I had never known that such physical contact could be so exhilarating. I could feel the surging passion gather in my loins and I wanted to jerk away before I shot, but he held me close as I exploded into his mouth.

After a while he rose from his knees. I knew what I must do, what I wanted so much to do as I unbuttoned his shirt. His chest was covered with a growth of fine brown hairs. Still afraid, but with more daring I ran my fingers down over his broad chest, exploring his beautiful body. He stood tall and handsome, his back against the wind. He sensed that it was my first time at love, and he guided my hesitant fingers down his belly. He fumbled with his belt until his trousers fell. He closed my fingers around the hardness, jerking off with my hand in his. I wanted more, I wanted to taste him, to feel his manhood, my lips around it as his had been around mine. I knelt.

I touched my lips to the moist, swollen head, my heart pounding for fear that I would turn away, my bold act alien to my senses and my being. But it was not so. It was natural and good, a thing that I did not fear but wanted to do with all of my heart. I ran my fingers up around his loins, feeling the manly strength, down around his strong legs that tensed under my touch. There was a marvelous smell about him, of sweat, sweet to my lips as, unable to wait any longer, I eagerly took his rearing manhood full into my mouth. The rigid shaft was almost too much for me to take, but desire filled my heart. Boldly my fingers touched the base of the shaft, and I felt the loose sacs of warm skin, hairy and round. What an ecstasy of touch and smell. My surging, overwhelming emotions were so new and vital to me that I wanted the windy moment to last forever, but very soon Paul grabbed my head and tenderly held me against him as he emptied himself with an animal groan. It was the climax, the height of masculine expression, of a deep-rooted and primitive passion that was more animal than human. In a way we were sharing, a boy and a youth, that unknowing urge, uncomplicated really, that simple desire that brings two men together for shared love, timeless and a part of the natural ways of the universe.

The moment was poignant as we embraced on the high cliff, the wind rushing and whipping around our half-naked bodies. The sea grasses whispered their timeless songs and the gulls and seabirds struggled against the wind, their sharp cries disturbing the peace of our new-found love, but we barely noticed as we kissed, our arms hugging tightly a moment that must soon end. Evening was approaching, and we had to return before darkness fell. There was a last long and lingering kiss before we walked hand in hand back to the cart.

Paul entered my life again when he returned on leave from the Army, but he never again mentioned our brief affair on the sea cliffs. Whatever emotions or feelings had given rise to his passions had vanished; his eyes were hardened under the severe cloth of the military. But for me it had been a magic event, a time of awakening to new desires, an experience that engraved its memories on my every thought for a long time . . . an experience that engraved its memories on my life forever after.

2.

"Lords, effendis, the hotel." The guide reined up the slow-moving nag and opened the carriage door, which tinkled, decorated as it was with camel bells. HOTEL TRAFALGAR. The faded sign hung over the main entrance, and, if one squinted one's eyes, the faint outlines of the word NAPOLEON showed through the paint, reflecting the vicissitudes of shifting political power. A doorman stood ready, and we walked into the cool foyer. The small, dark, and plump levantine proprietor bowed deeply, his many finger rings, gold watch chain, teeth, and military medals sparkling in the soft light.

Smiling, he patted his little hands together. "Lord Caerleon and young sir. I hope your morning was pleasant. Tea will be served on time. I should imagine you'll want to freshen up." He then called white-robed servants to take hot water to our rooms and to bring us fresh shirts for the ritual of tea.

Separated from the rest of Alexandria, there was a musty feeling about the café as we walked in. There was no hint of the Orient here. The starched white table cloths, the bud vases holding a fresh cut flower, the potted palms, the polished tile floor, all might have been found in any English hotel. Dominating the room was a large framed lithograph of the mad king George III; his dour features looked down at us. Two bright Union Jacks were draped around the portrait. The fact that good King George had been dead for ten years had failed to make any impression on the Levantine. It was something British and apparently that was all that mattered.

Few persons occupied the tables as we walked in. Servants, almost unseen, stood quietly waiting our pleasure. Since breakfast there had been an addition to the room, a large sign, freshly painted, now hung above King George. HAPPY NEW YEAR 1831. There was to be a party that evening to celebrate. Tea was served from a silver samovar and brought to us in cups of hand-painted china.

Alex had ordered toast, which looked quite unlike any toast I had ever seen, but he gobbled it up. Alex was always hungry. Except for the usual clatter of china and silver the room was quiet. A young couple sat at a table next to the paneled wall. I assumed them to be newly married, for they held hands, whispered, and were oblivious to everything about them. Five others, all men, sat sipping tea. I wondered what had brought them here. Were they minor government officials or tourists like us. As my eyes roved, I noticed a tall, heavily bearded man, neatly dressed in the dark cloth of the clergy. His long black beard was combed down over his starched collar; he read a well-worn Bible. There was a nervous energy about him. His eyes darted around as though he wanted to talk with someone, and he smiled as he saw me looking at him. He got up, coming over our way, bowed and introduced himself. "Reverend Zedediah Perkins of Baltimore, Maryland," he said. We returned the introduction, and the big man sat down, carefully placing his bible on the table. He asked if we had seen the Great Pyramids; we explained that we had just arrived the night before.

The reverend drew his bearded chin in against his chest and in a low sepulchral voice spoke, "The Great Pyramid hides the tomb of the Great Lawgiver, Moses. I have been sent by my church in America to find it." I expected a crack of thunder so grave was his tone of voice.

· "The Tomb of Moses?"

"Yes. The Great Pyramid was built by the Israelites, not by the ancient Egyptians. What blasphemers the historians are. In his tomb were placed the Tablets of the Ten Commandments. In the tomb will be the bodies of Joseph and Abraham."

"It is current thinking that the Pyramid was built to protect the body of Pharaoh Cheops, a king who lived centuries before Moses . . ."

"Nonsense. The stone blocks contained in the Pyramid could not have been raised without God's help . . ."

"Herodotus says . . ."

"A heathen author. The Bible is the revealed word of God and none else can be trusted. I shall find the Tomb of Moses if I must dismantle the Pyramid stone by stone. Then I shall find the cities of Pithom and Rameses. That will prove once and for all time the existence of the Israelites in Egypt." The good reverend's voice had risen and by now all of Alexandria must have known of his mission in Egypt. "When that is done I shall find the secret meaning of the hieroglyphs. They obviously contain messages left by the Israelites telling of God's holy works in Egypt. How glorious will be the day when God reveals his secret symbols telling us how he created the universe and Adam and Eve."

"But the works of Thomas Young and the Frenchman, Champollion, they have broken the language of . . . the Rosetta Stone . . . ," I stammered, becoming slightly irritated by the American.

"False, all false. The code has not been broken. The glyphs are secret and arcane symbols of a higher power. God will reveal the meaning to me, and the world scholars will recognize me. . . . But I've said too much, pride goeth before the fall. May I bid you good gentlemen a fine morning. I must go off to pray. Perhaps God will reveal a way for me to convert the heathen Moslems." He got up, bowing, taking his bible, and strode out of the room.

"Certainly a man of strong opinions . . . and a strong voice," Alex said, ordering another plate of toast.

"A man gripped by his passions. Egyptology is a young science, and there are still many things about the ancient Egyptians we do not understand. It has been only thirty years since Napoleon opened the country to outsiders. Have you had enough toast?"

"Enough to keep me going until lunch anyway."

"I say, sir, I heard you mention Young and Champollion. Are you familiar with their work?" I heard a voice behind me and turned. A pleasant looking fellow in his mid-twenties sat at a table near the draped window. He had sandy-colored hair and a fashionable chin beard, and wore thick glasses, which he removed and placed on top of a stack of books and a writing tablet. He had the air of a scholar about him – bookish, you might say.

"Only vaguely, I'm afraid. I am aware of the contribution to the 1819 edition of the *Encyclopedia Britannica* by Thomas Young. And of Champollion's letter to the French Academy in 1822. But I've not studied the subject in any great depth."

"Allow me to introduce myself. Charles H. Rhind of the British Museum. My second season in Egypt. Been doing some epigraphy work. The ancient inscriptions are disappearing so fast that the museum thought something should be done to copy them. The natives hack out pieces of inscribed stone to sell, and the Europeans are carting off objects that, I fear, will be lost forever."

"Sounds as though you face a very big job. You can read the glyphs?" Alex asked with some amazement. In order to prepare for our long voyage we had made various attempts to learn the language of ancient Egypt, but had failed.

"Yes, just like English. The loud American is a fool; they are not a secret code of arcane wisdom. The Nile Valley is overrun by fanatics, religious freaks, mystics, and occultists of every kind." He stopped and looked at us quizzically. "Why have you come to Egypt? Everyone comes here to find something – a tomb, a belief, or even to find themselves. All things are possible here."

"Well, we. . . ." I stammered a bit and looked at Alex. Our originally pure motives for coming to this ancient land seemed to have degenerated into greedy and dastardly treasure hunting, and I decided I was not going to mention we were planning to take an obelisk back to England. Rhind's goal of saving the antiquities was both good and noble. Perhaps our own motives were a little less lofty. "Egypt is the fashionable place to come for winter," I said, deciding to keep silent about our real purpose. "We came to see its legendary monuments."

But my poor attempt at camouflage was immediately overthrown. "We have come to look for a tomb, and if we are able to locate it, well, it could be the greatest find ever made. I get dizzy even thinking about it." Alex's words came in an enthusiastic rush.

"Ha, I knew it." Rhind said, smiling. "Gold fever strikes almost the instant one touches the shores of Egypt. Whose tomb are you seeking?"

"Alexander the Great. I'm named for him. Golly, just think."

Rhind smiled with a trace of scorn. "Ptolemic Period. A bit late for my interests. Could be an interesting dig, though. Do you know where it is?"

"In Alexandria, we think."

"Hmn," Rhind said, thoughtfully. "A lot of Nile water has passed by since he was entombed. Too much destruction. I don't think you've a tinker's chance of finding it, anymore than the blustery reverend has of finding the Tomb of Moses. But good luck." Rhind lit his pipe and gazed at us with soft hazel eyes.

"The last historical mention of it occurs during the reign of the Roman emperor Caracalla, who is said to have taken the Macedonian's sword. Then, it was lost. But I know it still exists," Alex exclaimed excitedly.

Rhind looked approvingly at him. "This young man certainly has courage," he said. "Of course, you're discounting the terrible destruction of Alexandria in the late third century A.D. The heathen idols were smashed, the books were burnt, and the palaces and temples were torn down, destroyed along with the rest of what constituted the Classical world. I don't see how the Tomb of Alexander the Great could have escaped the general destruction, but perhaps, with extraordinary good fortune, you'll find it. I must be off. The museum party has already gone on ahead up the Nile; a death in the family detained me in London. Don't give up hope, for Egypt still holds many unsolved mysteries." The young Egyptologist smiled brightly as he gathered up his books and then left the room.

"Interesting chap. Seems to know a lot," Alex said, taking a last sip of tea. "Suppose we're too late and the Tomb of Alexander was destroyed?"

"It may have escaped destruction, but it's a very small chance. Anyway, your motives go beyond mere treasure seeking. Your father, before the terrible tragedy . . ." My words trailed off, for I didn't want to upset the young man who sat opposite me.

"I've come to accept the fact, though it's very difficult. His goals are now my goals. I will search for the Tomb of Alexander the Great." Alex's voice was firm, though there was a trace of tears in his grey eyes.

"I admire your determination, Alex. The odds against you are very great."

"I know that, but I'll be satisfied with having searched, of knowing that every possibility has been exhausted before we have to return to England."

"Cheer up, good lad. This is only our first day and the search has only begun. Perhaps my Cairo agent can help. He's been in Egypt for many years. We've talked of this before. The first thing to do is to go to Cairo and get permission to dig and afterwards get on down to Philae. We must get the obelisk and return to Alexandria before summer arrives with its blistering heat. We should be back here by April and that will give us at least three months to search for the tomb. We'll dig up all of Alexandria if we must, though the natives might object." I smiled, hoping to brighten the conversation.

"Edward, you've been so kind to me during the last year, after Switzerland. How can I ever thank you?"

"There's no need. I've enjoyed your company. Your zest and enthusiasm cheered up the Gothic halls of Caerleon Castle. We do get along rather well, don't we?"

"Yes, Edward, we do." Alex reached over and touched my hand in a gesture of friendship. While we had come to Egypt to escape the English winter and to rescue my obelisk from Philae and to find, impossible as it may have seemed, the Tomb of Alexander the Great, I was, in truth, preoccupied with the handsome young man who now touched my hand. In my heart of hearts I wanted to be near him until the day he would come into his inheritance as the Marquis Saint-Hilaire and perhaps leave my life forever. True, I had other thoughts but these I had pushed out of my mind. Yes, I knew I wanted Alex as a lover. I wanted him as a man wants another man in the sweet passion of love. I did not know his desires or his wants, but I knew that I would not force him and face the possibility of his rejection. I could never bear that. I was quite willing to have him only for a good friend, and, if we were never to become lovers, I would accept with joy being near him for the several months of our stay in this ancient land. "Yes, Edward," Alex's voice interrupted my thoughts, "we do get along very well. We've a long and difficult journey ahead, but I know we'll make it."

"I think we will. We'll have our vacation, see Egypt, get the obelisk, and you'll find the Tomb of Alexander. It must be around here someplace. But first things first. We must go to Cairo and get permission to dig. We should be off to the British consul general's office to arrange for transportation. Come on, Alex, the adventure begins."

The consul general's office bore the trim, no-nonsense look of the military. Bright regimental flags, neatly stacked rifles, brisk boots, shiny marble floors, and whitewashed walls. Overhead fans worked by brown boys pulling on ropes kept the place cool. We were met with snappy salutes from several neatly trimmed young officers. The British consul was a short, rather florid man, sporting a full set of muttonchops. He got up from his desk and greeted us. "Colonel-Major James J. Pettigrew, at your service. We received word of your arrival last night after the H.M.S. *Argos* dropped anchor. The comings and goings of all Europeans are carefully watched. There have been clashes between the strict religious Moslems and the Europeans who violate their customs. What brings you to Egypt?" The colonel's manner was brisk as he stood slapping a riding crop against his knee.

I told him of our plan to take the obelisk back to Caerleon Castle and to begin a search for the tomb. And there was the matter of transportation to Cairo some 130 miles to the south.

"Ah, Lord Caerleon, I see. A *laissez-passers*, called by the Turks a *firman*, is needed to do any digging, but once you have a *firman* signed by the pasha you can do most anything you want. Pasha Mehemet Ali rules Egypt with an iron and sometimes brutal hand. He has given the antiquities of Egypt to anyone who asked for them, but of late he has realized they might have value, though he is not entirely certain what value the non-Moslem items might have."

"I have letters from the British government. They are anxious to have the obelisk in England. My agent in Cairo, Robert Arundale, has payed the Pasha ten thousand pounds for the object, and he has worked for several years with the locals at Philae, winning their friendship."

"You search for the Tomb of Alexandros?"

"We do not know if it still exists."

"Finding the tomb would have enormous historical importance, and for the English to take credit. . . . There is much competition in Egypt for significant finds, especially between England and the French, who are most anxious to build their collections. It is a matter of national pride. Unfortunately, it has become a cutthroat business and dangerous . . . murder is not unknown. If it becomes known you are on a treasure find, or if you have a statue or a piece of papyrus, you could place your very life in jeopardy. Do you understand?"

"Man's greed is an understandable vice, but surely you exaggerate the dangers."

"I think not. But there are other dangers. The climate is not kind to Europeans; some have died of plague and sickness. Some have met a bad end at the hands of the natives who do not care for the white Christian "devil," as they call all foreigners. Frankly, Lord Caerleon and young Alex, Egypt is a dangerous land, and I do my best to dissuade our people from making the trip. But my warnings have little use, I'm afraid. Well, since you are already here, it will be my job to make the trip as pleasant as possible. The British have considerable influence with the pasha, and you should have little trouble obtaining your *firman*. I will arrange a military escort as far as the Rosetta mouth of the Nile. The voyage through the Delta is a welcome relief from the heat and dust of Alexandria. I hope you have a pleasant stay." Colonel-Major James J. Pettigrew gave us a smart salute, and we left his office, returning to our rooms at the Hotel Trafalgar for a rest and to escape the heat of the day.

I am afraid our room was in a state of disarray; frankly, it was a mess. Besides six big steamer-trunks, there were wooden boxes of all sizes on the floor, containing a small library for reading on the long journey upriver, a good supply of spirits, canned food, notebooks, drawing pads, sets of watercolors for painting and sketching, surveying equipment, telescopes, compasses, various medicinal treatments and bandages, rifles and several pistols for defense, boxes of shot, and cleaning rods for the guns. Whenever I leave on a trip I always have the feeling I've forgotten something, but this time I think I brought everything—except the family dogs and my butler. My crest, the Capricorn, that strange half-goat and half-fish, was imprinted on everything, reminding me of my Welsh heritage. Caerleon, a derivative word, comes from the Latin, *Castra Legionis*, the "Camp of the Legions." The Second Augusta occupied the site of our family home for 300 years before the Romans left England forever. Certain ancient authors say Caerleon marks the spot where the crowning of King Arthur took place, but I secretly doubt it.

Both Alex and I had doffed our street clothes, putting on the more relaxed *"robe de chambres"* of Indian silk that gave us a decided oriental appearance. Alex sat on the floor pretending to smoke a hooka. He had tied a veil across his face and wound a towel around his head for a turban, trying to look like a pasha. He imitated our guide as he spoke, "Itt isss theee lorddd anddd thee younggg sirrr, effendiii, whooo haveee comeee tooo finddd deee losttt tombbb."

"Ha, it must be the caliph of Bagdad. Perhaps I will tell you a thousand and one tales of Ali Baba, of flying carpets, and of afreets."

"The mysterious Orient is hot, dusty, and not very mysterious at all," Alex said, smiling.

"Perhaps after we find the lost tomb we can search for the source of the Nile. It's the biggest river in the world, and no European knows where it comes from. Think what a discovery that would make for some intrepid explorer."

"Yes, let's look for the source of the Nile. Plunging into the heart of darkest Africa, fighting off blood-thirsty natives, crocodiles, elephants, cobras, we'll stumble, gasping with our last breath, on the source of the Nile. What adventure, what action. We'd be famous!"

"Well, I think we'll have enough adventure for the next three months at least. Better get some rest. Tonight is New Year's Eve, and the Levantine has planned a big party. Should be fun. I know how you like parties. I'll order afternoon tea to be sent up here, and we'll go on down about 8 o'clock."

Alex and I dressed in our best evening frock coats, vests, and trousers, the cravats of our linen shirts were properly ruffled, our gold watchchains were properly draped across our mid-sections, and the servants had polished our gold-buckled shoes to a high gloss. We took one last glance in the mirror as I adjusted Alex's cravat, and we were ready to face the world and a new year.

Glittering and pleased with ourselves, dressed as proper Englishmen, we went down the marbled staircase into the brightly candlelit room. Red, white, and blue Union Jacks hung from the ceiling, sparkling crystal vases held freshly cut roses, and the tile floor had been cleared for dancing. A military band, shining with gold braid and buttons, proper for this insular, quasi-military society, tuned their instruments waiting for the arrival of the colonel-major.

Our heels clicking against the tile we moved toward the portrait of George III where a punch bowl was filled with tepid champagne. I took a cup and poured Alex and myself a drink. A few soldiers stood chatting with the English girls, as their parents, the governmental officials, waited anxiously for their commander. We introduced ourselves, and the English guests flocked around, eager to hear recent news from the homeland. The death of George IV had brought to the throne his eldest surviving brother, William IV, a rather undignified, jovial sailor. As it usually took a month or longer for any English newspapers to reach this outpost of British civilization, they hung on our every word, hungry for any hint of royal scandal. How human of us to seek clay feet on the grand and mighty.

Around 9 o'clock Colonel-Major Pettigrew arrived with his attractive wife in arm. As he entered, the military band gave him a flourish of drum and trumpet but soon returned to the less strident melodies of popular dance music, setting the bright mood with a briskly played mazurka. The candlelight gave the room a soft glow as the couples lined up for the dance, the women on one side and the men on the other. But soon the social barriers would drop as the couples touched hands in the lively dance. The girls were attracted to Alex, and he did cut a splendid figure as he gracefully danced between the swirling patterns of the mazurka. With flirtatious fans held in petite pink hands, they gathered around him, unable to resist his dashing good-looks, looking up at him with coy smiles and suppressed twitters. I was glad to see he was having a good time, but secretly envied the girls. I spent almost the entire evening discussing British-Egyptian relationships with the florid colonel, without ever hearing a word he said.

The dinner that evening was to be a late one, and everyone kept their eye on their timepieces as midnight approached. A few seconds before the moment, Colonel-Major Pettigrew readied himself to signal the band. The crowd hushed as his hand dropped, and the band struck up the familiar, traditional refrain: "Auld Lange Syne. . . ." I stood next to Alex, and we raised our wine cups to the new year, singing the sentimental words with gusto. We brought our glasses together in a tinkling clink, smiling at each other, each perhaps wondering what 1831 would bring. I wanted to touch him, to reach out and share the moment, but dared not.

The band broke the reflective mood as it launched into the stirring chords of "God Save the King," and we raised our glasses to salute the portrait of George III. Pettigrew gave a speech and said that by this time next year the old royal portrait would be replaced. The news was met with a loud cheer and a hip, hip, hurrah.

The musicians, no doubt mellowed by the champagne, played the familiar waltzes of Strauss and others. And I must confess I had become a little tipsy. So had Alex, who still swirled around the room with a young lady lucky enough to have been asked to dance with him, though the floor had nearly emptied, the guests calling for their carriages. Torch-bearing servants ran along outside to protect the departing guests against the night.

Alex was flushed with excitement as he returned to my side; laughing, his eyes bright, he bumped slightly against the table holding the punch bowl. With a quick movement I reached out and caught him. "Alex, be careful," I said, grinning. "I think you've tied one on."

"Oh, what a night. I've never had so much fun. Did you enjoy yourself, Edward? I never saw you dancing." Alex plunked himself down into a chair, smoothing out his rumpled hair.

"Yes, I got a wordy lecture from Pettigrew about Anglo-Egyptian politics. Rather dull. I never really liked dancing. To confess, I've two left feet and never learned how. But you were wonderful. I watched you, you cut quite a dashing place for yourself with the English girls of Alexandria."

"I love dancing and music, Oh, my head is spinning."

"Want to call it a night? I think we've greeted 1831 with the proper ceremonies. It's going to be a difficult day—we must prepare for the trip to Cairo. I've written Arundale to expect us. I hope he received the letter."

"Yes, Edward, we'd better get to bed." Alex got up, slightly weaving, and in friendship I offered him my arm. What joy it was to feel his hand on my arm as we staggered tipsily back to our rooms.

It was good that we had mutual support as we stumbled into the dark room. Faint moonlight cast a ghostly light on the turned-down bed with its livid white linen sheets and pillows. We could vaguely make out the threatening and looming steamer trunks and the wooden boxes that now presented a lopsided obstacle for our unsteady legs. I led Alex to his side of the bed, offering to help him undress, but he said he could do it himself. He reached down to remove his shoes, struggling with his drooping cravat. I went around to the other side of the bed, doing the same.

Alex was a strange duck, personally fastidious and curiously very shy about his person—modest to a turn. This would be the first time we had shared the same bed. He had had his own room back at the castle, so this night would bring a new intimacy to our friendship. I knew his schooling had been religious and strict, but how the boy learned to dance so beautifully was a question that popped into my head. Perhaps it was natural instinct. I turned slightly to watch him. He had placed his nightshirt over his head before removing his clothes. Who knows what lies he had learned at school. Perhaps, as some taught, he thought his body shameful. I pondered.

I had given up the church when I came of age, finding little there to fit my ways of thinking. I supposed myself to be a freethinker and liberal for my times. I harkened back to the period when my ancestors ran naked against the invading armies of Caesar with zesty screams of blood lust, their bodies painted with blue woad. Had not my remote ancestors built Stonehenge and Avebury, those magic circles of stone, for secret and unknown rituals? There was nothing about the modern age with its rigid credos of ceremony and custom that I liked at all. I was a heathen and a pagan, but even I was faced with the conventions of daily life imposed by the suppressive moral codes of the church and the state.

Glancing around, I saw that Alex was ready for bed. I too had put on my nightshirt as my thoughts rambled. "Good night, Alex," I said, looking over. "I hope you'll not have a splitting head in the morning." Alex mumbled something that I didn't catch before crawling into bed. He must have fallen asleep at once as I heard his deep breathing. The hour was very late, and I was very tired as I snuggled beneath the covers. I could feel Alex's body heat and almost touched him. Alex, dear Alex. Was I falling in love with him? His very being consumed my thoughts. It was true. I was a pagan, and I knew I could love only men. What was their attraction? The thoughts in my numbed mind tumbled over and over as I searched for the answer . . .

Finally, I must have fallen asleep, but woke, hearing a muffled cry. Was Alex having a bad dream? My thoughts stirred as I felt the bed covering being yanked away and heard the sound of bumping and something crashing to the ground. The muffled cries were louder, and I jolted up only to have a hard fist slam against my head, knocking me against the pillows. What in hell was going on? "Help! Help!" Alex screamed as my fists shot out against the formless black shapes that swirled around the room. My fist plunged into the darkness, the moonlight catching it as it slammed into the shape hovering above me. The dark shape of a hooded man fell away, but there were other invaders. Instantly I was on my feet while Alex screamed horribly. Two hooded men were dragging him out of the bed, trying to wrap him in the blankets. What outrage was this? I lurched over the bed and tried to grab him but was knocked down, falling back on the bed. Quickly I jumped over the bed by making a headlong dive, catching one man by the waist who started to pound my head with his raw fist. Something glinted in the dim light. It was the sharpened edge of a dagger that now rose against me as I fought desperately against the dreadful intruders.

Grim fear gripped my heart as the dagger-bearing man forced me backward. The other had gained his feet and was now dragging Alex out of the room into the hallway, his arm around Alex's throat as he struggled in the blankets. I fumbled for the feel of steel . . . a pistol. Where in the hell had I laid the damn thing? My hand searched the tops of the cases until I felt my fingers wrap around the cold barrel. I had never been very good at using one of the things, but the blood of my ancestors flowed through my veins, and I let out a frightening war whoop. I cocked the pistol and with a shattering blast and booming explosion it went off . . . somewhere. God knows, so bad was my aim that I might have shot Alex. I ran out into the hallway where the hooded men were dragging Alex down the back stairs. I let go with another volley, nearly knocking myself down, but it was enough to frighten the intruders. Dimly I saw Alex struggle free of his bindings, free enough to send a fist into the face of the man who was dragging him. He was a brave lad, but his arm caught the edge of the dagger though I yelled a warning. It was too late. The hooded men took to their heels, fleeing down the stairs in a mad tumble.

I fired again, and the flash caught the veiled face of one of the attackers as he momentarily turned. His black, burning eyes gazed out at me and Alex through the blue cloth. It was the Tuareg. He shot a hard look at the wounded Alex, turned and fled out of the servants' entrance.

By now the entire hotel was aroused from their sleep. They came running down the hall and up from the servants' quarters with lit candles. "Quickly, my friend has been hurt. Call a doctor and the police!" They scurried away, and the Levantine ran up the marble stairs, his eyes tearful, and helped me carry Alex back to bed. Tying a tourniquet around Alex's arm, I was able to stop and slow the bleeding. He was shaking with fear and shock, his skin had paled and he was almost in tears. "It will be alright, don't worry and don't be afraid. We've driven them off. The doctor will be here soon." I was anxious for my friend for he groaned with terrible pain. But it was not too long before the doctor appeared, rushing into the bedroom where we had laid Alex against the pillows, his nightshirt covered with drying blood. The doctor quickly applied an antiseptic and bandaged the wound, a deep and jagged slit across the top of his forearm, though luckily the blade had not cut through any vital veins. I felt a presense behind me and heard my name being spoken. I stood up and looked around.

A tall man, dressed in military garb, stood in the doorway talking to the sad-eyed Levantine. A red tarboosh sat on his head. There was a strangeness about the man as he stood there, slapping his riding crop against his hand. The high acquiline nose and piercing gaze of the man as he watched me and Alex reminded me of a bird of prey — a falcon, a hawk. The picture of some ancient god of Egypt came to my confused mind . . . some hawk-headed god of the old Nile. He relaxed his steady gaze and the vision was gone. He bowed as he came into the room. His voice was low and he spoke English. "Lord Caerleon, my apologies. I hope the wound is not serious. I am Roumer Ibrahim, captain and police chief of Alexandria. What has happened?"

I explained the nature of the unexpected attack and mentioned the blue-veiled Tuareg. "I cannot imagine what they were doing, nothing of any value was taken, though they almost got away with Alex. Very odd, really." I was puzzled. Were they trying to kidnap Alex, perhaps to hold him for ransom, having learned that I was a man of means? I would have given all that I owned to have gained his freedom.

"May we speak in the hallway. The attack was not as strange as you might think. The Tuareg are known slave traders. . . . How can I put this to you? Your friend is a very beautiful boy. How old is he?"

"Eighteen."

"A most desirable age for the slavetraders."

"What are you saying?"

"If the boy had been captured he would have been placed on the slave market and sold . . . for sexual purposes. . . . There have been several cases where young blond boys have been taken, never to be seen again."

My anger seethed, and I stuttered, "Th . . . tha . . . that is unspeakable, barbaric, and un-Christian." I was shocked and shaken by the horror of the terrible thing the police captain was saying.

"You are not in a Christian land, Lord Caerleon! Here it is you, a European, who is the barbarian. Your kind drink to excess and carouse in public. You rip the veils from our women, and you violate the sanctity of the mosque. Go back to England while there is still time. I think your journey bodes evil for you and your young friend if you were to continue. The boy will be in constant danger. The tribe of the Tuareg is widespread. He could easily be taken and sold for his weight in pure gold. A most valuable possession for someone of great wealth. Mark my words, Lord Caerleon!" The imposing man, whose words cut with the sharp edge of a dagger, suddenly turned and walked down the hall.

3.

I slumped back into a chair, my body tired and soaked with perspiration, my eyes weary, and my head throbbing. Realizing dawn was filtering through the latticed windows I tensed, my fingers closing around my pistol as the horror of the night before rushed into my confused brain. Yet only the faint trace of gunsmoke remained in the air and a few overturned boxes lay strewn around. I was about to raise my pistol at the sight of two blurred figures hovering over Alex. "Ah, Lord Caerleon, you're awake," the white-haired doctor said in a thick Scottish brogue. "The lad is sleeping peacefully. He's a stout boy. He's lost a bit of blood, but two weeks of rest should see the bloom back in his cheeks. I'll leave my nurse here and check again this afternoon. Infection could be most dangerous." He indicated a tall woman who stood by his side. I pushed myself out of the chair and walked over to the bedside. Alex looked very pale against the white sheets, a clean nightshirt gathered up around his chin. His breathing was deep and regular. I watched him with thankful eyes. Taking his departure, the doctor shook my hand and left.

Later in the morning the colonel-major arrived in an angry huff. He had pressed the local authorities for a full investigation of the terrible deed. Apparently, his efforts were to little avail. The Egyptians were quite willing to see the Christian white devils stew in their own juice. Worried, Pettigrew placed an armed guard at our door.

As the days passed, Alex recovered. The wound was clean and would leave only a slight scar. The deeper wounds were inside. I had a cot brought into the room for myself and lay awake on it each night, pistol in hand for as long as I could. Sometimes Alex would cry out as he remembered the horrid invasion of the slavers. Our first day in this strange city had been a delight, a fantasy of color, charm, and exotic pleasure, but now Egypt was threatening, a dark menace full of unknown terrors. As soon as I could I brought up the possibility of our returning home, but the brave Alex would not hear of it, saying that nothing would stop our journey.

Day by day he regained his strength. The time was not unpleasant —our co-patriots would bring flowers, sweets, and homecooked meals; I would read from the classics, from Herodotus, who had seen Egypt in its days of glory, and from Homer, who told splendid tales of the Trojan War and of the adventures of Odyssus. I had grown fond of Keats and Shelly, and now read their poems aloud, while Alex had brought several dogeared novels of Sir Walter Scott from which I also read.

It was good to be near him, and it seemed we had never been so close as we were at that time. As he lay against the pillow, his eyes bright, his laugh cheerful, I thought that I had never seen a man of such beauty. The light would catch his tawney golden curls, moist from the warm air. His nose was classically Greek, forming an almost straight line from the brow to its tip. His mouth, curving in a graceful line and ending in dimpled hollows like the ones so often seen on ancient statues, might have inspired Phidias. His chin was strong, though a bit fleshy from youth. His face was clear, as yet untouched by the cares of the world. We would often touch hands, he smiling trustfully at me. My heart melted. Could it be that I was falling in love with Alex? At the time all I knew was that it was good to be near him and for the time being to share in his life.

I had written Arundale about our plight, giving the approximate dates for our arrival at Cairo. I received a letter saying he would watch for us. Meanwhile, Alex was eager for us to be on our way and anxious to see the wonders of the Nile.

The week at the Rosetta mouth was uneventful. The Nile Delta was a garden of Eden with farmers working the land. The gentle, slow movement of the boat as it was pushed and pulled along the canal enhanced the impression of a timeless land where men and women knew only the good earth and its fruits. It was a time before civilization – before pyramids and cities.

Our small sail boat finally came to Bulak, the port of Cairo. The wooden bow hit the earthen bank with a loud screech. Boatmen leaped out, securing the boat to the dock. We walked down the narrow gangplank. The harbour was a colorful chaos of donkeys, camels, carts, and carriages. Swarthy dark men rushed here and there, loading and unloading the many boats. Through the melée of languages and the confusion created by braying, snorting, and wheezing animals, I thought I heard my name being called out. Alex and I stopped, seeing a native man coming out of the crowd, his hand extended in greeting. His tall figure was hidden by the bright and gaudy robes worn by the natives, his head covered by a draped turban. Several white-robed boys followed close at his slippered heels. "Lord Caerleon?" His English was perfect.

"Yes?"

"Robert Arundale Bey, your Cairo agent. I've been watching for you. Glad to see you're both safe and sound," he said, bowing.

We were both astonished as we had expected someone dressed as a European. "You look just like an Egyptian, with the robes and all," Alex said, shaking the man's hand.

"Ah, you must be Alex. Sorry about your brush with the slavers. A nasty event, to be sure. I can now understand why. . . ." Arundale looked at Alex sharply. "Well, let's load up your baggage. It's a long trip into Cairo." The boys scrambled to grab our possessions, placing the trunks inside the waiting carriage and hoisting the rest of our belongings atop several donkeys. Arundale continued, "Much easier to get around here. Some say I've gone native, perhaps that's true. Ha, even got myself a Turkish title. Those heavy frockcoats and tight trousers that you're wearing are difficult to find in Cairo. Been here six years now, and I guess I've become a part of the place. You'll be staying at my diggings in the European section. What do you think of Egypt?"

We followed Arundale and his boys to the carriage. Clearly, the

robed man was one of those strange breeds of Englishmen, a true eccentric. Men who have shucked off the commonplace, becoming part
and parcel of places far distant from home, pursuing their own odd
dreams in bizarre landscapes.

Lying a mile to the northwest of Cairo, the port of Bulak offered us
a distant view of the city, and from the carriage it looked like an
Oriental dream, a fantasy vision of domes and minarets rising in
romantic splendor above the smoky mists of haze and household
fires. Here was the strange and mysterious world of the *Arabian
Nights*, of Saladin and the Crusades, of Omar Khayyam. The entire
view was of great charm and beauty, but beneath it all I had a chilling
sense of unknown terrors.

We slowly passed through the crowded streets. The vision vanished, as do most romantic illusions, and in its place was the city of
Cairo: dirty, squalid, and a jumble of slums. Sitting next to a young
driver who took a mean lash to the horses, Arundale turned and said,
"The European quarter is isolated from those of the natives; the big
wooden gates are closed at sunset for our protection. Westerners
sometimes have a bad time in Cairo." Later, as we passed through the
narrow streets, he would point a lean finger, "This is Khan Khaleel,
the street of the goldsmiths; the leatherworkers have their own section, as do the potters and stonecutters. You can find just about
everything here; caravans come from all parts of Africa and the Mid-
East. Anything you want is here . . . even death." Arundale spoke
with a hint of bitterness.

The sun was high overhead as we drove past the thick walls of the
European section, passing beneath a towering gateway and through
the opened thick wooden doors. Guards stood on silent sentry duty,
their weapons at rest, but smiled as they recognized Arundale. Our
carriage passed them, the donkeys laboring under the weight of our
baggage. After the noisy streets of peddlers, vendors, and shouting
merchants, the European quarter was strangely quiet and, as Arundale had said, isolated. The Europeans lived in a walled fortress, a
white Christian society surrounded by a hostile Islamic culture.

The carriage stopped before a gate of ornately carved wood with bronze insets. Slowly the gate swung open, and we drove into a spacious courtyard. A fountain with cool splashing water stood in the center. As we drew up before a dazzling whitewashed entrance, a number of houseboys came running out to take our heavy baggage. After we had alighted Arundale led us into his beautiful house.

A tiled hallway entered onto a central room which was circled by Moorish arches supported by slender columns. Rising from the graceful columns was a jeweled dome. From tiny windows set with colored glass, light caught the colored tiles in flashes of brilliance. Our reflections gleamed in the polished marble floor as we walked around a fountain of white marble that sprayed perfumed water, cooling the warm air and filling it with the scent of roses. Through the opened doors at the other end of the hallway, I could see a gracious and lovely garden. Several blue and green parrots sat on perches, yawning and screeching. Stunned by the ornate splendor of the room, I nearly stepped on a peacock in full plumage. Arundale smiled. "The Islamic dream of paradise, of heaven and earth." He studied Alex, who had wandered off, and was now playing with the parrots, tickling them as they nipped at his fingers. "Ah, paradise. This is an old palace; originally it belonged to a wealthy Mamluk. He kept his harem of young boys here."

"What?" I asked, unsure whether I had heard the agent's words correctly.

"The Mamluks were lovers of beauty as you can see. Much given to hashish and opium, and notorious boy-lovers, devoted sodomites."

"Such things are not mentioned in polite society, Arundale!" I said, turning several shades of deep crimson.

Arundale's eyes were hidden in shadow, but there was a mocking tone to his voice. "Have I shocked your delicate English sensibilities, Edward? Egypt is not England, dear Edward, and as soon as you learn that fact you'll preserve your sanity. The Mamluks were converted white Christian slaves taken from the Caucasus by the Ottomans. They were *ahl as-sayf*, "people of the sword," trained and effective fighters. Napoleon faced them in 1798. The Pasha destroyed their power when he took Egypt in 1811; however, their love of beauty still lives in this glorious palace, an earthly paradise if ever there was one. Alex was very fortunate to escape the slavers. Others do not escape. The young man is very handsome. One could easily fall in love with him. Is that not so, Edward?"

"I suppose. I don't know." The frankly blunt words caught me off-guard, and I had no defense as I tried stammering out an answer.

"Do you love Alex, Edward?" Arundale pressed his disturbing inquiry. My mind swirled as I tried to find an answer to this second and bolder question. Luckily, the arrival of a servant momentarily diverted my host's attention. "Ah, Hamid," Arundale turned and I saw a white-robed Egyptian boy coming down the hallway. "Hamid, my chief-houseboy. Some things about this palace have not changed since the days of the Mamluks, dear Edward." "Hamid, these are my distinguished guests Lord Caerleon and the Marquis Alexander Saint-Hilaire. Show them to their rooms. Have you prepared the baths?" Hamid nodded and smiled, revealing a row of very white teeth set into a handsome light brown face. He blinked wide and heavily lashed eyes, watching us closely as he bowed. Pleased that everything was ready Arundale said approvingly, "Hamid is a very good boy. I taught him English. Get settled in and when you have bathed and changed we'll take afternoon tea or coffee in the study. I have a large collection of antiquities that I want you to see. Your rooms are upstairs, it's cooler at night and you can see the Great Pyramids from the roof. *As-salaam alaykum*, "peace be upon you," as the Arabs say. He bowed, turned, and walked away.

Alex turned from the parrot, having heard Arundale's parting words, and watched as our host left the beautiful domed and columned room. "Arundale lives like a Persian prince."

"Yes, he does. Apparently, dealing in antiques is a lucrative business."

"If my masters are ready I'll show the way to your quarters. Please, effendis, this way." Hamid gracefully swept his arm out, indicating we were to follow. He led us outside into the sunlight of the walled garden and from there to a flight of stairs leading to the upper stories. The air was heavy with the scent of flowers and a soft breeze per-

fumed the warm air. The boy led us up the stairs and opened a paneled wooden door as we crossed a small marbled terrace and stepped
inside the room as he opened the ornate latticed windows. Our large
and spacious rooms were carpeted with rugs of lush design. Perforated brass lanterns hung from beamed ceilings; divans covered
with exotic furs stood against the carved wooden wall that was
covered with busy arabesques of inset ivory, mother-of-pearl, and
gold. Motioning that we were to follow, the boy opened double-
doors leading onto the roof. All of Cairo seemed to be at our feet as
we stepped out; below us the Nile was a bright ribbon of sunlit
water. In the distance, rising from a violet haze in awesome majesty,
sat those great triangular piles of ancient stone, all that remained of
the seven wonders of the ancient world. We stood speechless.

After a few contemplative moments, Hamid beckoned us back inside. "My master has given you these to wear. He does not like European clothes worn in his house. These caftans are of the most
precious materials." The boy opened a closet and held out two robes;
one of a soft peach and the other of a pale blue, with embroidery of
gold and silver thread, each with matching belts and slippers. "The
bath has been prepared. Do you wish the water to be scented with
rose, jasmine, or oil of sandalwood?"

Alex gave me a confused glance, "I think rose would be nice, eh,
Edward?"

"Oh, yes, very nice. Where is the bath?"

"In the west wing. Other English who have been here have com-
plained the water was too hot. I will look to the fires and return.
Here are towels and slippers are over there. The servants will collect
any soiled clothing you wish cleaned. I will return very soon." Hamid
bowed and left.

"I suppose we'd better undress. I'll get a pile of towels." Grabbing a
handful of the big, heavy linen towels, I threw some to Alex. With
his usual painful modesty he stepped behind a screen to remove his
clothing, and in a moment he stepped out, his entire body covered by
them. "You look rather like a wrapped mummy," I said, grinning, but
was immediately sorry for my words had caused Alex to blush. I had

wrapped one towel around my middle and flung another around my shoulders. Alex gave me a quick glance, obviously noticing as he did, my naked chest and legs.

"Let's take a bath, I'm dirty. Probably the usual brass or porcelain tubs filled with tepid water." Alex threw a corner of his towel over his shoulder, looking rather like an ancient Roman with a toga, and strode gracefully toward the door just as Hamid came in. With slippers flopping and towels flowing we retraced our steps.

Going through several hallways, Hamid came at last to a small door and a hazy cloud of fragrant steam greeted us as we passed through it and entered the bath. It was quite unlike anything we had expected. The Romans had known such luxury, but to the dulled mind of the modern Englishman the bath was a shock, a dash of Oriental debauchery hinting of the dark sins of the flesh. The room flashed and dazzled the eye, its walls and dome covered with tiles of exotic and exquisite designs of deep lapis blue and rich turquoise. A pale light streamed through windows of patterned alabaster, catching the surface of the fountain and the pool which stood in the center of the room. The reflected light danced across the tiles as the steamy water bubbled and cascaded from marble lion heads. The pool itself was not deep and there was a ledge running around it for sitting. The entire room smelled of roses. "Do my lords find everything to their satisfaction? The water is not very hot, but it is heated from beneath the floor. I could go down and put more wood on the fire if you wish. There are scented oils, ointments, and unguents if you wish a massage after the bath. It is very relaxing and will sooth the skin." The boy indicated the marble tables against a far wall. Without another word he then doffed his white robe and stood naked, his arms outstretched, waiting for our towels.

Poor Alex froze, blushing and looking uncertain about this unexpected assault on his modesty. I took the towels from my shoulders and waist, giving them to Hamid. The Egyptian was hairless and smooth, his body rather girlish in its adolescence. He waited for Alex to hand over his towels. Alex hesitated. Suddenly, he took a deep breath, ripped the towels away from his body, and bolted for the pool of steaming water. I rather pitied Alex being thrown into such an uncomfortable situation, but, on the other hand, there was a touch of the lecher in my pagan soul. I wanted to see his naked body and to somehow liberate him from his cocoon.

Walking across the slippery tiles, I watched his huddled form as he sat down in the water, his hands and arms firmly clenched in front of him. I crossed to the other side and with a languid hand scratched my naked belly, "How's the water, Alex?"

He looked up, "Oh, fine, a little hot." He smiled weakly at the sight of my naked body.

"I'll remove some of the wood used for heating," Hamid said, anxious to please.

"No, it's alright, don't bother." The bubbling water covered Alex's broad shoulders, lapping against his square chin.

Stretching out my arms I took a deep breath, "Ah, it's good to be naked and out of those heavy woolens. I think I'm putting on a little weight, but you look slim and fit. Alex."

"Do you think so? I know I eat a great deal but I never get fat." Alex seemed to relax a little, removing his arms from the front of his body.

"Yes, you do eat quite a bit, but you're energetic and burn it off easily." Casually I sat down, sticking my feet and legs into the swirling water which, though hotter than I was accustomed to, was soothing. Trying not to appear obvious, I studied the tiles and the marble fountain that splashed the water on me with a playful hand. Purposefully, I aimed some at Alex, who, when hit, flinched. I laughed and he gave me a quick smile in return.

"Damn you, take that!" With a hefty hand he shot a handful of water back at me and I returned the gesture. Soon the pool was a raging sea as we tossed the water back and forth. At last, completely forgetting his shyness, Alex stood up and with both hands gave me a complete dousing. I rubbed the water from my eyes. Alex's body was as beautiful as his handsome face; finely modeled, the muscles firmly cut across his rather pale skin. His chest and belly were covered with a downy growth of golden hair which, catching the light, softly glowed and sparkled from the droplets of water that clung to his fair skin. His manhood arched out strongly from a tawney cluster of hairs circling his muscular thighs, his manly sacs fell from the base full and rounded. Realizing his nakedness, he quickly sat down.

"No, no, Alex, stand up. You've a very fine physique. I wish I were in such good shape."

"Do you really think so? I've always thought of myself as being too pale and thin. I've hated to show myself; besides, the human body is a shameful thing."

"God certainly didn't bring us into this world with a pair of breeches."

"Oh yes, the young master is very beautiful and manly." Hamid grinned, his eyes gleaming with unknown thoughts as Alex stood up. "There's no shame in the body. I think Allah made you very well, young effendi."

"Hamid speaks the truth. Don't be such an odd duck, always creeping behind a screen to change your clothes. Look at me. Do I worry about being naked?" Apparently, our words seemed to assure Alex that his naked state was not something ugly, because he now gingerly rose a little more out of the water. "See, God didn't strike you dead or anything."

"Nobody has ever told me I had a good body. The nuns at school were very harsh about, well, showing yourself."

"You're not in school now. Forget those days. You're a fine, handsome young man and you've nothing to be ashamed about." My eyes lingered on Alex for several moments as he stood up dripping water and shining like a young god. There was a quickening of my blood, and I felt the surge of warmth in my loins. I changed the subject. Turning to Hamid, I asked, "How long have you been in Arundale's service?" The agent had been mischievous with his words, implying that he and the Egyptian were lovers, and, that perhaps his entire staff served in this dual capacity as well.

"Only for a short time. He is a very good man . . . see." With one hand Hamid yanked up his testicles, along with his circumcised penis, an unmanly fate that both Alex and I had not suffered. "O yes, the master is a very good man. I still have a man's rightful possessions. I forget, it's a Moslem custom for a man to take many wifes, if he can afford them, quite unlike the English who take only one. The husband fears his wives will wander and buys a cut-man to guard them. Oh yes, effendis, they were ready to be lopped off. My parents ordered it, however, the good master says Hamid is a good boy and buys me at a high price and I am saved from the knife. Isn't that a good thing for the master to do?" Hamid's smile stretched from ear to ear as he dropped his "rightful possessions."

"Yes, Hamid, that was a very good thing to do, eh, Alex." I had found the boy's account amusing, but Alex only blushed.

"Arundale Bey is a sad man, I think. It was good when he called for me at night, but he does it no longer."

"Why is that, Hamid?"

"I do not know, noble lord. He has taken to drinking and hashish. Sometimes he is a crazy man, no doubt an evil afreet has possessed him. Perhaps a massage with scented oils. . .?"

"Why don't you let him massage you, Alex." The young man seemed to have recovered from Hamid's shocking display and, with some masculine fortitude verging on bravado, he had lifted himself out of the water, permitting Hamid to briskly rub him down with a dry towel. Indeed he looked more assertive as he stood straight and tall, his shoulders back and his belly tucked in, as if feeling a new strength and pride. I realized my move had been bold and daring; there was a chance Alex might have bolted, becoming more withdrawn and shy. But here he was stark naked and feeling rather good about himself, I thought.

Hamid's rubbing slowed, turning into a caress as he ran the towel over Alex's fine body. "Perhaps the handsome effendi would wish, how do you say it in English way . . . bugger me?" Alex failed to understand the word, but I knew. . . .

"No, Hamid, no! I . . . think Alex only wants a massage with oils."

"What did you ask, Hamid?" Alex turned, looking down at the boy, who saw my stern look and shaking head and seemed to understand.

"Nothing, young master."

I felt like an old mother hen protecting her brood from life. For all I knew about Alex he may have enjoyed "buggering" the boy. He seemed so pure and innocent that I assumed him to be virginal, but in truth I had no way of knowing as such things were never openly discussed in polite society.

It was to be a pleasant afternoon. Hamid's expert fingers worked magic, relaxing our bodies as he rubbed the scented oils into our skin. Finally, as it was nearing teatime—a sacrosanct moment—we returned to our rooms. Alex's oiled muscles ripped in the sunlight when we passed through the garden. Brazenly, he had only wrapped one towel around his loins and seemed to have lost his shyness as he boldly walked up the stairs. Once in our rooms he did not hide himself as formerly, but merely unwound his towel, which slipped down around his sturdy legs onto the patterned carpet.

The young Egyptian helped us slip splendid floor-length garments over our heads; he showed us how to wrap our belts and to slip the golden slippers onto our feet. "Ah, you are indeed princes of the East. Most grand. The master will serve tea in his study. Follow."

Walking behind Hamid, we both felt a bit odd in our ornate robes. Alex grinned. "Princes of the East! Great blocks of pyramid stone!" He spun around, enjoying his new role in life.

"You do look princely in pale blue," I said.

"And you look kingly in pale peach. Edward, you are a handsome devil."

Arundale's study was a large whitewashed room filled with Egyptian antiquities. Stiff, hieratic statues of stone and wood, lined the walls. Garish painted coffins with great black eyes stared vacantly; cases held scarabs and small statues of rich blue faience, golden jewels, and wide collars of inset enamel, bracelets, and finger rings. The wealth of a vanished age permeated the room. Arundale was sitting at a large desk, his back to an ornate paneled wall; getting up, he walked toward us.

"Lord Caerleon and young Alex. I see you've changed. Now you look like natives, true Egyptians." Arundale was a tall man, and since he wore a robe similar to ours, I could see that he was lean, almost skinny, his hands slender and bony. His face was gaunt and sunburnt; the patch of untanned skin very white. His lank brown hair grew very long, and he had tied it back at the nape of his neck with a string. He was freshly shaved, but his square chin was dark with stubble. His eyes had a strange intensity, no doubt from staring at the burning desert sands. At the moment he kept them trained on Alex, looking at him with a certain curiosity. "Yes, the antiquities are beautiful. Loot. Simple plunder. The best collection of Egyptian artifacts in the world." Arundale paused, staring at his collection. I had the feeling that his mind had left the room and was wandering somewhere else. There was a long moment before he spoke again. "Well, it is for sale. Wealthy collectors come from all over Europe to buy a little souvenir to add to their collections." He paused again and shot a strange glance at Alex. "Alex, good friend, do you see something you like? Your face has intrigued me ever since I first saw you at Bulak, and I have been staring at you, I know. I am reminded of . . . Edward said in his letters that you hoped to find the Tomb of Alexandros . . . a noble goal. I too have an interest in the subject. Who were your parents?"

"M . . . My father was Phillip, Marquis Saint-Hilaire, and my mother was called Olympias but that was not her real name . . ."

"Yes, I knew it . . . there is a connection. Phillip and Olympias, the parents of Alexandros."

"What are you saying? I asked. Arundale was shaking with nervous intensity.

"These things are only expensive baubles, second-rate material, but I have more. Follow." Arundale turned, looking at the ornately carved wooden wall that covered the far end of the room and walked towards it, and we followed. "This was the private prayer room of the former owners; the carved wall faces the East toward Mecca. This recess is called a 'mihrab,' and there is a little room behind it called a 'maqsura,' a private chapel that I've converted for my own use." He touched a certain part of the paneling, and a small door swung open. Behind it was set a heavily barred iron gate. After Arundale opened the various locks and slid back an iron bolt, we entered the small room. "These are my true treasures." Light from the tiny overhead windows caught the dull glow of ancient gold, priceless gems, and, alone against the far wall, a jeweled box sitting on a marble pedestal. "Some day when I leave this accursed place these things will buy me the finest estate in England . . . but, here, look, this is the proof. My most priceless treasure." Arundale spoke with a certain awe as he took the box and slowly opened it. "The Royal golden tetradrachm of King Alexandros." The coin of about three-inches in diameter lay on a bed of purple velvet, its bright gold catching, in a radiant flash, the dim light. Impressed into the gold was the profile of the young king. Golden locks of hair circled around ram horns, the horns of Jupiter Ammon, a symbol of the king's divinity. The priest of Jupiter Ammon in the far oasis of Siwa had made the conquering boy a god on earth. The coin held us with hypnotic fascination.

"See here, the words in Greek, *Basilikos Alexandros*, that King Alexander impressed around the rim of the coin. It is in mint condition and priceless. The other side has even more interest, for it is the only known representation of the "Soma," the lost Tomb of Alexandros."

"Soma?" Alex asked.

"The title of his tomb; it refers to his body."

Arundale sat the box down and slipped on a pair of silk gloves. "I never touch it with my bare hands," he said, gingerly turning the coin over. The reverse side showed a Greek temple, with cornice and pillars. Between the pillars was a covered, golden catafalque, a likeness of the one apparently used to carry the enbalmed body of the young hero from Babylon to Memphis, where the first Ptolomy had placed it before building the great mausoleum at Alexandria. "There is an inscription, but see how engraved in the cornice of the temple is the star-burst emblem of the royal Macedonian dynasty. It must be the Soma, the royal tomb."

"It cannot be anything else," I said, examining the tiny detail on the coin.

"Look between the pillars, there you will see in minute detail the fabulous funeral car. It matches exactly the description given in the histories of Diodorus Siculus in which it was reported that gold Ionic columns supported a roof of gold scales set with jewels, topped with gold olive wreaths. According to his histories, at each of the corners stood statues of golden Victories holding out a trophy. Ibex heads embossed the cornice. The open spaces between the columns were filled with a golden net to shade the golden sarcophagus from rain and sun, and golden lions guarded the entrance. The royal catafalque was drawn by sixty-four mules, their harnesses and collars of gold set with gems. See, here on the coin are the tiny Ionic columns, the golden Victories, the net, and the lions. In my opinion this cannot be anything else than an ancient representation of the royal Soma. To find the treasure tomb itself would surpass anything so far found in Egypt."

"Yes, it would." My tone of voice—that of almost religious awe— matched Arundale's. "If the tomb still exists, but I fear it does not."

"Do you believe in the supernatural, Lord Caerleon?"

"I've never thought about it, but I do not think so."

"It exists. Egypt is a strange land and you cannot live here as long as I have without feeling . . . forces at work. There are forces at work here, now, in this room. I can feel them. I knew it when I first saw young Alex. His profile matches exactly that of the Macedonian."

"What are you saying?"

"There is a bridge unbroken by the passage of millenia that connects the Macedonian with Alexander Saint-Hilaire!"

"What?"

"Alexander is the reincarnation, the living image of the ancient Macedonian. He has come back to us, don't you see. The coin proves it."

Alexander stood a little distance from us as we spoke. A shaft of sunlight caught his golden hair, shimmered through his curls, but did not cross his features, which were in shadow. Arundale gasped and fell to his knees.

"Alexandros Helios."

"Get off your knees, Mister Arundale. I . . . I'm not the reincarnation of anybody. Edward . . ."

"Come now, fellow, get off your knees. Old Alex is just a normal everyday English schoolboy. The Egyptian climate has gone to your head."

"No! There is a bond. Communication with the other side must be made. We must call on the spirit of the Macedonian."

"You are mad!"

"Mad, you say. Leave me now. I must think on this. Go. Hamid will serve tea and sweetcakes. Go!" Arundale pointed a long finger at us, and we backed away from his wild-eyed stare and into the study. The door closed and Hamid stood smilingly ready with cups of hot tea and a plate of sweets.

". . . well, it is quite plain that Arundale is as mad as a hatter, crazy. The drachma is beautiful. I wonder if he wants to sell it. It is true, Alex, you do look a great deal like the hero. I have always thought you resembled an ancient Greek."

"The man was out of his mind. But the coin did show the tomb. Oh, Edward, this place is strange. I think we should go home and forget about the obelisk and about ever finding the tomb. This place is getting on my nerves in the worst way."

"I am sorry, Alex, I did not realize your feelings. Are you home-sick?"

"Yes, I suppose. I just don't know. I do miss England . . . and home."

"Your parents?"

"Yes, most of all. I haven't quite got over their . . ."

"Don't think about it, dear Alex. I know it is hard. Stiff upper lip, old fellow." I smiled at my young friend, trying to lift his spirits. "The cakes are very good."

"I suppose," Alex said, smiling in return. "A stiff upper lip and three cheers for William IV."

"That's the boy. Everything will be alright. *Esprit de corps.*"

Arundale came out of the treasure room wearing a contrite ex-pression. "I am sorry, Edward . . . Alex, please forgive me. I've been in Egypt too long. I don't know what I was saying."

"Don't worry about it, old man. The coin might have magical

powers. It does show the tomb and Alex does look like an ancient Greek. In this place one could almost believe anything. The obelisk, I'd almost forgotten about it, this firman that we must get from the pasha . . ."

"Pasha Mehemet Ali and the Egyptian court. The court of the Italian Borgia's could not have been more rife with intrigue and political double-dealing. It will be necessary to arrange an appointment. But I've not stayed here all these years without having some influence. We'll see. Like most visitors to this antique land . . ."

"I met a traveller from an antique land,
Who said: Two vast and trunkless legs of stone."

"That's the Shelly poem," Alex said. "Stand in the desert . . . ah, I've forgotten the rest."
I took up the poem.

"My name is Ozymnadias, king of kings,
Look on my works, ye Mighty and despair!
Nothing beside remains. Around the decay
Of that colossal wreck, boundless and bare,
The lone and level sands stretch far away."

Arundale sighed. "Yes, Edward and Alex, it is true that there is ruin and decay, but it is magnificent rubble. While I'm dealing with the Egyptian court, you two can go out and have a look at the pyramids. Go in the morning before the heat of the day. I'll arrange for a dragoman, an English-speaking guide. Again I'm sorry. Egypt can do odd things to your thinking."

Our host bade us goodnight! As we left his house, he stood, waving goodbye to us. I couldn't help thinking how ghostly pale he looked in the hall-light, his eyes burning as if they held some knowledge almost too dreadful to bear.

Early the next morning Alex and I found ourselves near the base of the Great Pyramid. Arundale had provided a big, husky dragoman to translate and to clear away the packs of young beggars who clustered around the tourists. Hamid also trotted along, carrying a large picnic basket, and several other boys carried blankets. Alex insisted that he should ride to the Giza plateau on a camel. These imperial "ships of the desert" are actually mean, groaning, and rather stupid animals. Feeling embarrassed about his Egyptian clothes, Alex had worn his coat and trousers, as I had. Dressed in such attire he looked like a silly Englishman on a lark when he had mounted the beast, which, in turn, did its best to bite his arm. Mounted on the high, ornate saddle, Alex was jerked into the air as the dusky-looking camel rose, back first, nearly spilling him into the sand. But good old Alex was in his glory; waving his topper, he told the beast to charge. The camel was in no hurry and slowly plodded along through the sand until we reached the base of Cheop's pyramid. Alex turned his topper sideways, stuck his hand into his waistcoat, and looked up at the vast pile of stone blocks. I knew before he said it that he was going to say those immortal, if shopworn words, spoken by Napoleon when he invaded Egypt thirty years ago, "Soldiers, forty centuries look down upon you!"

"Bad, really bad, dear Alex. I rather expected your greeting to the Great Pyramid to be more original."

"It's the only thing I could think of. It is big, and it looked so small from the river. I've got something better: The Ode to the Pyramid.

Oh, great pyramid, mighty monuments of old,
Built in twenty years, so we're told.
Cheops, antique king, swathed in stone.
Pray tell, where have your ashes blown?

"A good poem, eh, Edward?"

"Shelly could've done it better." My words were lost in the hot breeze that blew across the plateau of Giza.

It was a fair morning for trudging through the sand, and then for exploring the pyramid's mysterious dark passageways, behind a torch-bearing guide. At mid-morning we had tea and lunch in the great triangular shadow cast by the pyramid. Our meal finished, we followed the some 755 feet of sand-covered blocks that marked the baseline of the north side. There, in the distance, we could see the *Great Sphinx*, partially covered by drifting sand, its recumbent leonine body some 240 feet long and its majestic human head nearly

66 feet high. No measurements, however, can convey the awesome feelings that one has upon looking up into that ancient, battered face, strangely smiling out at the world.

"Repent, The kingdom of God is at hand." A loud voice carried over the sands. Standing near a great paw, and waving a bible in the air was the American preacher whom we had met in Alexandria. Since we had seen him there had been a drastic change in his person. His black hair and beard were wildly frazzled and uncombed. His frockcoat was torn and dirty and he was perspiring greatly. "Repent. I have come to save you from your sins," he cried, having seen us. Directly, he ran toward us, shouting agitatedly, "A voice that criest in the wilderness. God's plan has been thwarted in this evil place. It's those Moslems in the palace. The pasha would not let me tear down the pyramids, and I cannot move the heavy stone blocks by myself. Everything has gone wrong. I cannot get permission to dig up the cities of Pithom and Rameses, and God has not revealed to me the secret meaning of the glyphs. Everything has gone wrong. They've stolen my money and without it I cannot go home. But I shall not fail God. He has set me a great task and I shall fulfill my mission. Repent your sins." The American reverted to his preaching.

"Do you really think he would tear down the pyramids?" Alex asked incredulously. It's ludicrous."

"Yes, Alex, I think he would. By his bare hands if he could move those heavy stones. The desert has made him mad. We should be getting back to Cairo. Arundale should have some word by now from the palace. It might be fun to do a little shopping."

It was nearly sunset before we arrived back at the European quarter. We had spent the afternoon delightfully exploring the labyrinthine shops of Cairo. Arundale had indeed spoken the truth, for they were filled with exotic goods of gold and ivory, skins of unknown beasts, and unknown aromas. I bought some pipe tobacco, and Alex purchased some perfume that the proprietor said was made from the crushed petals of the sacred blue lotus, the very scent that Cleopatra had used when she greeted Mark Antony so long ago. It was probably so much sales gibberish, but the perfume did have a lovely, musky scent.

The soft evening was upon us when our party, including the dragoman, and the servants, returned to Arundale's beautiful house. As we
entered there seemed to be an air of excitement. Servants rushed
about on mysterious missions. The perforated brass lanterns were lit,
and the scent of incense filled the arcades. Arundale stepped out of his
study. "Good news, Edward. The pasha has agreed to see you in two
days. Much *baksheesh* passed into the hands of his officials. Took me
all day."

"Good. Once I get the papers I can get on down to Philae and get
the obelisk. If I had known that it would be so much trouble . . . the
house seems unusually bright this evening."

"I've invited a most interesting guest whom I want you to meet."

"Oh."

"Yes. He is an *imam* — a kind of teacher, a holy man. He has access
to the library of the al-Azhar, the Moslem University. His name is
Abad al-Jalil and in Cairo he is considered to be almost a saint. Met
him some years ago down in Nubia, of all places. He is widely traveled and has been in England and other European countries. He may
remember reading about the tomb in some old books. I told him
about Alex."

"You are not going to start on that again are you?" I said.

"No, no. Abad al-Jalil is a most learned man, a mystic. You'll see.
Wear your Egyptian clothes, and we'll dine in the manner of the
bedouin, the nomads of the desert. Hamid will call you. Go on now,
throw off those restricting English things, breathe deeply of the
fragrant air of Egypt. Put your cares away. Tonight we shall seek
. . ." Arundale smiled, his gaunt face alive with a strange excitement.
His eyes sparkled, and he looked at Alex before returning to his
treasure room.

"What was that all about? I hope he still doesn't think I'm the Macedonian."

"He has something up a sleeve of his caftan."

The excitement of the evening was infectious, and Alex and I
rushed upstairs. Hamid brought a kettle of hot water and gold
enameled bowls for shaving. While I honed my razor and whipped
the shaving soap into a lather, adjusting the mirror to fit my six-foot

frame, Alex and Hamid selected the caftans that we were to wear. Alex seemed unable to come to any decision, holding the gaudy robes against his naked body, smoothing down the heavy silk and ornate embroidery. It was good to see him relaxed and at ease. I turned to the chore of shaving.

I squinted my brown eyes searching for wrinkles on my thirty-six-year-old face. There were some around the eyes but only a few. I was not quite ready for age, but knew it would come one of these days. Ah, the golden days of youth were long since past. I realized my body was not as strong as it had been. There was a slight sag in the muscle tone, and I had developed a detectable paunch around my middle. The soft life of being a country squire was taking its toll. Beneath my rather hairy chest the skin looked pale. Perhaps the voyage upriver would give me a chance to get a little exercise. Wiping the foam off I stuck out my chin, still looking for signs of aging. I realized my worries had become a problem. Alex's youth had made me more aware of my age. I was almost, but not quite, old enough to be his father. I brushed my longish brown hair into place and waxed my mustache. Alex grinned, seeing me primping before the mirror. "Edward, you're a handsome devil. You should learn to dance. I hate to see you standing all alone while I'm out on the floor. You always get stuck with some pompous nabob, and you look quite bored."

"I think everyone I've ever met has tried to show me the steps. Just never learned, I'm afraid."

"Come on, Edward. We'll give it a whirl. Just keep to the count of the music. One, two, three, and one, two, three, and . . ." Alex grabbed me in his arms, attempting to show me how to dance, as he hummed a waltz tune. "See, it's easy." We twirled around the room, our naked feet sinking into the soft pile of the lavish carpets. Hamid took up the beat and clapped his hands. "One, two, three, and one, two, three, and . . ." Alex continued.

Being so near to him, my hands resting on his broad shoulders, our legs touching as we swirled, was having its effects even in this most frivolous of moments. "I'm afraid not even your dancing feet can teach an old dog new tricks, Alex. I'm afraid I'm forever cursed to stand and watch while you dazzle the young maidens," I said. Breaking the dance hold I grabbed a towel, pretending to dry my loins. "You'd better get shaved for Arundale's party." My voice was casual and joking, but Alex's attempt to teach me dancing was unexpected, a sensual moment that had left me shaken and nervous.

I splashed some rose water around my body and dabbed a bit of Alex's lotus perfume behind my neck. Hamid helped us slip the robes over our heads, wrapped the belts, and slid our feet into the slippers. I rather liked the freedom of the loose robes. Could it be that we were going native? Antony and Cleopatra? I had sat through Shakespeare's immortal play about the Serpent of the Nile once and that had been enough.

Shining and glittering, and smelling like whores of Babylon attending the court of Nebuchadnezzar, we went down to dinner. It was a beautiful, almost enchanted evening, an Oriental dream. A new moon hung like a scimitar just above the azure horizon, which gradually darkened into a deep lapis midnight blue. Clusters of stars flashed like diamonds flung across a piece of black velvet. From our terrace we could see the spires and domes of Cairo silhouetted against the darkening sky. For a moment we seemed poised, ready to step into another world, a fantasy universe of shimmering gold palaces, magic carpets, magical jinnis who granted every wish, and hidden caves holding vast treasures. A tale of a thousand-and-one nights now seemed to be chanted as the *muezzins* called the people to prayer from the towered mosques of Cairo. The Egyptian servants fell on their knees, bowing to the sacred city of Mecca, a mysterious place, forbidden and remote in the vastness of Arabia that few nonMoslems had ever seen.

A soft, caressing breeze with the scent of the rose garden greeted us as we descended the stairs, and I noticed that even the usually nonchalant Alex seemed taken by the beautiful Cairo evening.

Hamid led us to a small gazebo of carved lattice wood on the other side of the garden. Inside, Arundale rose from a pile of pillows to greet us. A big brass serving table set on the deck of the gazebo; a multitude of good smells came from hot covered dishes. "We eat in the bedouin style by sitting on the floor. My friend has not arrived yet . . . ah, here he comes now." A tall, robed man walked out of the house and into the garden, looking over at us. His brown, handsome face, wreathed in a full beard of snowy white, reminded me of some wise prophet of the Old Testament, or of a learned monk who had just left his cell for prayers, or perhaps of old Saint Nick who arrives at Christmas. There was nothing of our century about him at all. I perceived that his robe was black, his turban stark white and, though he carried a walking stick, his stride was brisk and firm.

"Arundale Bey, greetings. I had forgotten about the guards at the gate. I convinced them that I was not here to steal or murder a foreign devil." He spoke perfect English. "Ah, your two English friends." He smiled a dazzling smile as we were being introduced. I could not guess his age. He bowed, touching his chest, mouth, and forehead with a graceful fingertip. " 'A good heart, good words, and good thoughts.' A Moslem greeting. I am not a Moslem but it is a fine greeting." Alex and I bowed, mouthing the Arabic words as best we could. "Ah, soon you will speak Arabic words like a sand dweller. Have you studied our language?"

"No, just the usual schoolboy stuff, some Greek, Latin and French," replied Alex.

"England has fine schools. I studied at Oxford as a youth and in France after Napoleon's invasion. Ah, it is so good to have English friends. In that way my pitiful efforts in speaking the language are always kept fresh. The food smells delicious. I have always said Arundale Bey keeps the best kitchen in Cairo."

Alex and I sat down awkwardly, half-sprawling on a pile of pillows. Hamid uncovered the dishes, and we looked around for knives and forks, but none were in sight. "We eat as the men of the desert eat, with our fingers . . . and a good supply of napkins." Arundale took a slice of thick bread, using it to scoop up a mess of something. "Lamb and rice, just dig in, fingers and all." After we had all consumed large amounts of Arabic food, Hamid brought strong, black Turkish coffee and brandy. Contentedly, Alex rubbed his stomach, wiping his fingers in a perfumed bowl of water, then leaned back, touching his head against my shoulder, his eyes gazing into the night sky. At this point the servants gathered in the garden, and with flutes, drums, and hand-cymbals, began to play the soft melodies of Egypt. Hamid danced, swaying and moving to the exotic rhythms of the desert. Was there ever such a moment as this? I felt Alex's head against my shoulder. I wanted to tell him that I loved him; I longed to take him in my arms on this most romantic night. I . . .

"Arundale tells me of your interest in the Macedonian and of your search for his lost tomb. My aide at the library mentioned that there has been inquiries about the same subject. Perhaps there are others who seek the same prize."

The Egyptian's words brought me back to reality. "Who?"

"I do not know. My aide merely mentioned the fact. Did you know, Lord Caerleon, that Alexandros is a favorite subject in Arabic folktales? His exploits and conquests have never been forgotten. Yes, he is called Silandar Dhulkarneim, the Two-Horned. But, of course, the fact that he was Greek and a pagan, is forgotten. In our tales he becomes an Islamic warrior fighting the infidels, the enemies of the Prophet Mohammed. He rescues Egypt from the horrible Zangs, drinkers of blood and eaters of brains, he is seen in Persia and India. There is no feat of heroism that Silander cannot do . . . but that, alas, does not get us any closer to finding his tomb. Arundale Bey has told me of the golden drachma and that young Alex bears the same profile as that of . . ."

"No, we are not going to get into that," I interrupted. "Arundale, good fellow, I think that you have been in the hot sun too long."

"I must have seemed rather mad, but the fact is that Alex looks like the ancient Alexandros. Look!"

Alex, hearing his name being called, aroused himself out of his lethargy, his dreamy eyes looking around. "Did someone call my name . . . Alexandros." We looked at him, startled. "Ha, I'm not him at all, had you fooled." He laughed.

"Ah, Alex is playful," Arundale remarked "but his face is the same as the one on the coin. You cannot deny it."

"Yes, it is the same," the Egyptian spoke softly. "Perhaps, if you would be willing, Lord Caerleon, Alex, we could see if a time-connection exists. Such things are known."

"What are you saying?" I asked.

"We could send Alex back in time, if he is willing."

"Would it hurt?"

"No, it would be perfectly safe and harmless. You would drift back to the time of Alexandros and see with his eyes the events that constituted his final days. We could follow the funeral carriage to Alexandria and perhaps witness its final fate."

"You are speaking nonsense, sir!"

"No, Edward," Arundale interjected. "It is possible to send the mind, free of the restraints of the body, back in time. I have seen Abad al-Jalil do it. There is no harm and it could answer many questions."

"I would like to do it," Alex spoke. "Who knows on this night of nights what could happen."

"I wouldn't do it, Alex."

"Oh, Edward, you are such a fuss. It's harmless. What do I have to do?"

"Relax."

"I'm already quite at ease."

"Arundale believes the coin has mystical power, and will provide a connection with the past," the Egyptian continued. "Do you have it?" Hamid brought in the jeweled box containing the drachma and placed it on the floor where the brass dining table had been before he had removed it. We all watched as Hamid opened the box and the bright yellow of gold flashed in the starlight. "Ah," the Egyptian exclaimed, "the royal, golden drachma; it is beautiful. See how it gleams in soft light; it is as though it has an inner fire. Amazing that it has come down to us in such fine condition. Perhaps it has been preserved for this moment. Who can say? Alex!"

"Yes."

"Alex," the Egyptian explained, I want you to look into the coin, not with your eyes, but with your mind. Do you understand?"

"I don't know."

"Look into the coin, feel the gold, feel the great age of it. Let your thoughts and your mind drift into the gold. Go back into ancient times, to those vanished times and gods. Think of Alexandros." The words of the Egyptian seemed as soft as the wind and whispered around us. Alex stared into the gold as he was told. I must say, while I thought the entire thing to be silly and a waste of time, there was a strangeness about the moment: three grown men staring at the golden drachma, listening to the words of Abad al-Jalil. I wondered how such a precious object had survived. Into what hands it had passed since it was cast two millennia ago? I confess that at this instant I, too, felt my mind being drawn into the gold . . .

"Aieeee. Aieeee!" Alex cried.

"Bring him back!" I shouted.

"No, he has fallen into a trance. It would be most dangerous at this moment."

"Aieeee."

"Alex, what has happened? Where are you?"

"I am lying in bed and I am dying. My eyes are weak, and I can barely see my soldiers as they file past my bed. I raise my hand in salutation and blink my eyes. Where is Hephaistios? He should be here. Where is he?"

"Hephaistios?"

"My friend, my lover, my adored one, my beloved. Where is he? He should be here to comfort me in my dying hour. What's that? You say that Hephaistios is dead? Dead? Yes, yes, I remember. The great funeral pyre. No! Leave me alone. I want to die. What in this world is not mine? I am king of Persia, the lord of lords, the king of kings, and master of the entire world. Nothing, without Hephaistios at my side sharing my glory . . . and his. The darkness is gathering in around me, my eyes grow dim, but wait, I can see him, my glorious friend. Hephaistios. Hephaistios."

"What are you doing? I demand that you bring him around . . ."

"Ease your thoughts, Lord Caerleon, of the house of Capricorn, your friend is sleeping deeply. He has become Alexandros who has died. We must call him out of Alexandros' body. Come away Alex-

ander Saint-Hilaire! Fly up from the dead shell of the king of Persia.
Hover. Float above. What is happening?"

"The great and rich city of Babylon is in tears. My troops cry out
with grief, but they already fight among themselves for the crown of
Persia and my conquests. To the victor belong the spoils. I have
ceased having any interest in their affairs."

"Do you see your former body, that shell of former life?"

"Yes. It is being embalmed and covered with precious scented oils
and balsams. My general, Ptolamaios, claims the body, wishing to
take it to Egypt. It had been my wish to be buried at Siwa in the
Temple of Zeus Ammon and to be with my divine father forever."

"Go forward in time. What do you see?"

"I have been dead for a long time, but my features still show the
breath of life. There is no decay. The tomb is filled with rich
treasures and gifts given in behalf of my immortal memory by the
world rulers who emulate my conquests. Ptolemaios and his descen-
dants lie about me in gold encrusted coffins . . ."

"Where are you? In what city? Memphis?"

"Alexandria. My city, no longer a tiny port, it is filled with won-
drous palaces and temples."

"Come forward in time. Has anything happened? Has anything
changed?"

"No . . . but wait. There is something. I can hear the sound of men
fighting; they are destroying my beautiful city. My city is burning."

"The Soma, the tomb, are men in the tomb?"

"No. They are afraid to enter. They have no respect for our gods,
but they remember and respect my name."

"Go forward in time. What do you see?"

"Nothing."

"What?"

"Nothing. The place where I lay in death is vacant. There is no
gold. My body has gone. They have taken me . . ."

"Where! Where!"

"The star of Macedonia. Where you find it you will also find
me . . ." Alex slumped over, his face wreathed in perspiration. Heaving a deep sigh, he fell backwards into the pillows.

Abad al-Jalil rushed to his side. "Alexander Saint-Hilaire! You are released from your mission in time. Put the golden drachma out of your mind. Catch the winds of time. Float. Alexander, return."

Alex shook his head as if awakening from a deep slumber. "I must have eaten too much and drifted off. Is something wrong? You're all looking at me so oddly."

The Egyptian smiled. "No, no, good Alex. Everything is fine. Have a sip of brandy; it will clear your mind."

"The hour is late, and I am very tired. I think I'll go up to our rooms. Coming Edward?"

"In just a moment. You do look tired. Hamid will help you. Hamid!" We watched as Alex and Hamid crossed the garden.

"What did it all mean?" I asked. "He clearly saw the tomb, and then the treasures and the body vanished. What does it mean? Was the tomb robbed?"

"It is difficult to say," Arundale answered. "From his words it would seem that a friendly force took the body. He mentions great violence outside the tomb, but also that men were afraid to enter."

" 'The star of Macedonia. Where you find it you will also find me.' "

"It could be that friends, those who were not fanatical Christians or Moslems, bent on destruction, moved the tomb to a place of safety, and that it still exists."

The Egyptian spoke. "That was my impression. After so many centuries it could be that the tomb still exists. A faint glimmer of hope, Lord Caerleon. All you have to do is to find the star of Macedonia."

4.

The court of the Egyptian pasha can only be described as comic. I had the sensation of being onstage during a production of an exotic *opéra bouffe* by Mozart or Rossini, and half-remembered tunes from *The Abduction from the Seraglio* did in fact come to my mind. The huge Nubians who stood guard were dressed in brilliant livery, cloth-of-gold turbans, flowing pantaloons of gaudy silk, slippers with up-turned toes. Behind them great plumes of ostrich waved in the perfumed air.

Our appointment with the pasha was early in the morning. Arundale said that this was because the Pasha liked to complete the business of the day early in order to have more time with his harem, but I had the feeling that Arundale was not telling the whole story. We had dressed in our very best frockcoats; even Arundale had worn European clothes. Looking as if we were going to tea at Buckingham Palace, we entered the carriage. Not long after our hired four-in-hand pulled up before the Egyptian palace. We were greeted by The Very High Lord Chamberlain of the pasha, who led us through a succession of ornately decorated rooms to the throne room. Pasha Mehemet Ali was short and broad shouldered, with a rounded beard of reddish graying hair. His dress could have only been described as "gaudy military," covered as it was with ropes of gold braid. Bright medals and decorations glittered on his broad chest.

The chamberlain bowed deeply and was immediately given some papers by an aide. They were the letters from the British government that we had submitted to the pasha. The chamberlain carried the papers up to the dias and gave them to the Pasha, who sat stiffly on a throne of red damask and gold. The two conferred for a while; finally the Very High Lord Chamberlain turned back to us. "His Excellency welcomes the distinguished guest from Great Britian. He has seriously considered your plan to remove the obelisk of Ptolemy Euergetes II from the island of Philae. But, unfortunately, the French have also made claims on the obelisk."

"Dominique Jomard. I knew he would get into this business," Arundale whispered. "He is the French consul general and a real bastard, if you know what I mean."

The chamberlain continued. "His Excellency has been most generous with foreign powers and has been very liberal with his gifts. However, now he thinks that it would be best for Egypt to preserve the antiquities herself and to keep them here. A new museum to house newly found artifacts will be built in Cairo."

"Excellency," Arundale spoke directly to the pasha, who now darted glances at each of us. He seemed nervous, perhaps he was thinking of his harem. Undeterred, Arundale went on. "The British government and Lord Caerleon have made generous gifts to the pasha. The permission for the removal of the obelisk was given over a year ago."

The chamberlain shuffled through his papers. "Yes, the sum of ten-thousand pounds has been deposited."

"This venture has been very costly for my client. There will be the additional cost of transporting the obelisk down the Nile to the port of Alexandria and then to England. The Egyptian government made a definite commitment to Lord Caerleon long before the museum was planned . . . a definite commitment. The British government will not take it lightly that one of her citizens has been, shall we say, robbed." Arundale let his words sink in.

"A strong word, Arundale Bey, very strong," the chamberlain protested. "The British consul general will be informed of your slur on His Excellency." The chamberlain and the pasha now conferred for several minutes. "The pasha is aware of the commitment," the royal advisor said slowly. "His word is of course good. You will understand, however, that His Excellency wishes to maintain a relationship with both England and France. In order to grant Lord Caerleon's *firman*, the French claims must be denied, an insult to that country and an embarrassment to the Pasha, a very great embarrassment. The pasha tries to improve the life of his countrymen by building canals for irrigation and by sending students to Europe for an education, but such projects are very costly, very costly."

"What sum does His Excellency feel will compensate for his embarrassment?"

"He feels that the additional sum of ten thousand pounds would cover his embarrassment."

Arundale turned to me, whispering. "His Excellency is bleeding you dry. Can you raise the sum?"

"I have transferred funds from the Bank of England to the British offices here in Cairo. The government will guarantee the account."

"We might bargain," Arundale whispered. "Lord Caerleon feels that he has been very generous and offers five thousand pounds."

The Chamberlain screwed up his dark face, "Nine thousand pounds."

"Six thousand pounds."

"Seven thousand pounds."

"Eight thousand is Lord Caerleon's final offer."

"The sum is acceptable."

"See, I've saved you two thousand pounds."

"On receipt of Lord Caerleon's cheque the *firman* will be granted."

"The cheque will be transferred from the British office." Arundale, Alex, and I bowed, leaving the costly presence of the pasha of Egypt. "You know, Edward," our friend remarked, "this expedition could be very expensive. Once you have your *firman* there will be the locals to buy off, the kashifs, the aghas, the omdehs, and the sheiks who will provide the labor force for the removal of your obelisk. I hope you can afford this junket."

"I can afford it," I said decisively. The acquisition of the obelisk of Ptolemy Euergetes II had become an obsession with me, a strange passion of the very rich. After all, if an obelisk could stand on the grounds of Kingston Lacy House in Dorset, why not on the grounds of Caerleon Castle?

The next few days were anxious ones as we waited for the Egyptian court to grant my *firman*. If it were granted there would be much work to do in preparation for our trip up the Nile to Philae. One morning while we waited I rose early! Alex was still bundled up in his covers. For all of his physical charms, he snored quite loudly at times. Leaving him, I went downstairs to check on some details with Arundale. I stopped just outside his study, for I thought I heard a familiar voice, and I had. Entering, I ran into my first cousin, Carlotta, Countess von und zu Rietberg and her tall, arrogant Prussian husband. Together with Arundale they were peering at a stone statue from which they looked up when I entered. I had not seen my cousin since late spring of the previous year when we had attended the state funeral of George IV. I had hoped it would be our last meeting, but no such luck was to be mine, for here she was in front of me, dressed in the latest fashion, and looking as if she were about to step into the throne room of Buckingham Palace.

"Edward, of all people. Count, you remember my cousin?"

"Carlotta! What are you doing here?"

"The same as you, dear Edward, escaping the cold and looking for treasures. I heard you and dear Alex were coming to Egypt. You could have dropped me a note, at least."

"I am sorry, there was so much to do. . . ."

"I suppose that I do understand. You're looking well. How is young Alex?"

"In good spirits."

"Such a dear, good boy. He was so hurt when he lost his parents."

"He thinks of them often."

"Phillip was such a dear man and his lovely Greek wife. . . . I don't think you ever met her; she had an exotic beauty and was the rage of London society . . . she spoke so quaintly. But they are both gone now, buried beneath the snows of Switzerland. Their bodies were never recovered from the terrible avalanche. Such a pity. Thank God, Alex was in school in Italy. They were on their way to take him on a spring vacation. The Alps can be so very dangerous in the spring. Poor Alex. Arundale Bey has such lovely things and so very old. Imagine! They are even older than the British monarchy. Speaking of the Court, His Majesty has appointed me lady-in-waiting to Princess Victoria, such a vivacious child. Imagine, she's only twelve and someday she will be a great queen. I am so excited, but you know how much the Court means to me."

"Yes, I know. I am glad for your appointment." Carlotta rambled on. I put her words out of my mind. I had found English court life to be stiflingly dull and artificial, but my cousin doted on every aspect of it—the parties, the minor scandals, the fashions.

". . . Cairo is so fascinating, quite unlike London," she was saying now. "We were thinking of going on down to Luxor, but we will return to Italy, via Brindisi, and then on to Rome. Arundale has such a lovely house. The Moorish style is all the rage. Perhaps I'll have a room built onto the manor house. I saw the gardens, perhaps we could take a stroll. The Count has such a difficult time making up his mind when he wants to buy something."

"Of course," I said, taking Carlotta by the arm and escorting her into the gardens.

"It looks almost English. Edward, there is something I wanted to talk to you about."

"Yes."

"Young Alex . . . I know we have gone into this before . . . but I still think that he should come and live with us."

"I am his legal guardian until he comes of age at twenty-one, and I refuse to discuss the matter any further."

"Edward, you can be so bullheaded at times. Listen to me. Alex needs both parents, and it is unnatural for him to live with a grown man. You should be married. God knows you are old enough. A man of thirty-six should have a wife and children. It's the proper thing."

"I'll marry when I am good and ready. Alex and I get along very well, and there is nothing unnatural about our relationship."

"He would have a home if he came to live with us. A mother, a father, and sisters and brothers, who are his own age . . . not as his companion some wildman, running around the sands of Egypt looking for an old obelisk and an old tomb. Such useless, silly things! I have never understood you, Edward."

"I think I understand you, dear cousin. In three years Alex will inherit his father's considerable fortune and his titles and estates. Your husband, the Prussian count, is known to be a heavy gambler. His losses at Monte Carlo are legendary."

"Edward! How dare you suggest such a thing?" Carlotta's mouth flew open at my accusation, and I secretly smiled, for I must have hit the proverbial nail on the head.

"Hermann has enormous wealth, enough to buy and sell Monte Carlo," she said, her eyes sparkling with anger. "Mark my words, dear cousin, I mean to take Alex from you and give him a decent home and the love of both parents, a love that he needs, before he is corrupted by your insane life. The way things are now, as any sane person can see, is unnatural!"

Carlotta stomped off in a huff, and a few minutes later I heard her carriage rattle out of the courtyard. "Unnatural?" The question rang in my ears. What did I feel for young Alex? And what did he feel about me? Carlotta's harsh and threatening words had the effect of bringing my hitherto secret feelings to the surface. It was true I was falling in love with Alex. What was the meaning of that love? Moreover, whatever the nature of my own feelings, I really had no idea what his were for me; in the year we had been together after the death of his parents, we had grown close, in a brotherly relationship—friends, it seemed, and nothing else. True, we had touched, but for me it was a touch of fire, inflaming my very soul with desire, a need to take him in my arms, to embrace . . . dare I say it . . . to kiss him and to reveal I loved him, and, to have him, hope of hopes, say he loved me in the same way.

Loneliness can be a terrible burden. Was I, as Aristophanes suggested in that ancient discussion of the power of love, Plato's *Symposium*, seeking my other half? Was I oddly split from myself? Was Alex the other self that I had searched for, someone who would complete my life as I would his? There were questions but as yet no answers. Certainly the Greeks had exalted love between men, seeing it as noble, courageous, and perfectly moral. Unfortunately, modern England was not ancient Greece. A veil of shame had closed in around the noble and good, and a free display of my true feelings and emotions would have brought my downfall in this evil age.

I would keep what I had with dear Alex, a sense of friendship that had grown up between us. I would settle for a smile and a touch. In time he would receive his inheritance and seek his own ways and fortunes in a difficult world. I would wish him well as he departed Caerleon Castle. My only hope was that from time to time he would think of me, remembering the pleasant times we had as he passed from boyhood to manhood, a time he had shared long ago with a man who had loved him with a passion that could never be expressed.

In the days that followed my exchange with Carlotta, we busied ourselves in preparation for our trip up the Nile.

Our search for a suitable *dahabiyeh*, or sailboat was to take considerable time. These were not very safe vessels, for their shallow drafts, necessary if they were to avoid the numerous sandbars lying just below the surface of the Nile waters, made them easily sinkable in a strong gale. In these boats the cabins and the dining salon for the traveler were aft, and the kitchen and the crew quarters were forward. They had, in addition, two sails: a patched triangular sail near the bow and a smaller sail astern. Since only Alex and I would be on the boat we would require a crew of four and a captain, the *reis*, who would guide us through the Nile waters as we traveled upstream.

To obtain such a vessel, we bargained seemingly endlessly with the Egyptians. Rentals were not cheap, running from six hundred to fifteen hundred pounds a month. Moreover, equipping the vessel with any measure of comfort would cost extra. Five days passed, and had not Arundale and the British consul general come to our aid, we would have been still floundering on the Nile waterfront. In the end our fortune was the result of another's misfortune. The young couple we had casually met in Alexandria had returned to Cairo. The bride had come down with severe adbominal problems, known as "Cheops revenge," and they had been forced to go upriver for treatment. The husband was only too happy to give his houseboat over to us and to get out of Egypt. He had only praise for his crew and the English-speaking reis, a dark, sprightly man of good reputation. In this manner Alex and I obtained our *dahabiyeh*, and a few days after our *firman* also arrived. The Turkish crest was sealed in red wax, and the illegible name of Pasha Mehemet Ali scrawled below. It read:

Decree

In conformance with the explanation and request made by the English traveler Lord Caerleon, who wants to go as far as Philae, to satisfy his curiosity, make researches, and excavate certain ancient buildings, the present order is issued and transmitted to him, so that he may be able to travel without fear for the aforementioned purpose, and so that, without presenting any obstacle to his researches, the governors of the provinces and the other officials attached to the administration of the land shall give him aid and protection.

If Allah is willing, let there be conformance to these dispositions. Given on the twentieth day of the month of Rabiay-at-Tani, 1235.

"Well, Alex," I said, carefully folding up the precious document, "we'll soon be off down the Nile."

"Jumping riverboats, after so many days, I thought permission would never arrive . . . and finding a good boat . . . we must be doing something right. Down the Nile, golly." He had been at my side in all these affairs, enlivening the tedious negotiations with his boyish enthusiasm and sense of high adventure. I suppose taking Alex to Egypt was mad; he should have been in school like any normal youth of his age. But then, his youth was anything but normal. When he came to Caerleon Castle a year ago he was a sad and unhappy boy, utterly shattered by the death of his parents whom he had loved dearly. He spent the days moping around the Gothic halls, rarely speaking or eating. Yet what a change had come over him when he found out about my trip to Egypt. The journey had become his entire life, and he rapidly forgot his sorrow and misery. He began eating and he rarely stopped talking. His excitement was boundless, and he would not hear of returning to his stuffy old school. And so here we were on our adventure in Egypt.

The days in Cairo were coming to an end, at least for the time being. We had received an invitation to attend a reception at the British House for the new consul general. A certain major E. P. H. Browning, lately of India and South Africa, had been appointed to the post. It promised to be a glittering affair. While we dressed in our best evening clothes, blue dress coats with gilt buttons and velvet collars, fancy-colored vests, black breeches, and the obligatory white ruffled carvats, Hamid came to the door begging Arundale's pardon. He had come down with a touch of fever and would remain at home. Thinking nothing of it at the time, we entered our carriage and were off to the British House.

It appeared that the entire European community in Cairo had turned out for the reception for the major. Alex and I slowly made our way down the line of guests and dignitaries, until we came to a small, dark man, sporting a neat goatee, an "Imperial," as it is called. It was the Frenchman, Dominique Jomard. "It seems that you are going to take our obelisk from us, Lord Caerleon. How sad," he said smoothly, waving a scented silk handkerchief beneath his nose. "It was such a pretty little thing. Of course it cannot compare to our obelisk, the one we took from Luxor last year. Ours is much bigger, much, much: 227 tons and 90 feet tall. Such a fine red granite needle. It will be erected in the Place de la Concorde next year as a graceful addition to the city of Paris. Sad to say, dear Lord Caerleon, your obelisk is only half the size and weight of the one in Paris. Better luck next time." Jomard smiled sweetly. This was clearly a case of "my obelisk is bigger than yours," and had not the British government been so slow about the affair the great needle might be standing in a square in London rather than in Paris.

We must have met everyone of greater and lesser importance, and our hands were tired from shaking so many other hands. Alex enjoyed himself and was dazzling, his handsome face breaking repeatedly into a charming smile, his dashing figure tall and spendid. There was an almost audible flutter among the young women as this scion of aristocratic stock bent down to brush his lips against their soft gloved hands. Gowned, perfumed, and bejeweled, their dowagerlike mothers pushed them near to the titled young man.

A small orchestra struck up a slow waltz, and with Alex's urging I asked the not unattractive Mrs. Browning for a dance. It had been years since I had taken a woman in my arms and that my feet had tried to master any involved dance steps. As I fumbled with my patient partner, trying to place my feet in the right direction, Alex, with astonishing skill for one so inexperienced in such matters, swirled in quickstep beneath the crystal chandeliers, holding the waist of a tightly corseletted young woman. Recognizing the skill of the dancers, the orchestra picked up the tempo; Alex and the girl took to the floor once again in a flurry of her ribboned velvet and his highly polished slippers.

Rather glad to have escaped Mrs. Browning's jeweled arms, I retired to the sidelines to watch the glittering crowd as the speeded up waltz ended. Alex bowed to his partner. There was a patter of applause as he returned to my side. I handed him a cup of the rather warm punch, and he took a piece of cake into his gloved hand, smiling and happy.

"Dear, dear Alex. You are astounding. I think you've stolen every female heart in the place."

"It was fun. Such things as dancing were frowned on in school."

"I'm afraid you're in great demand." Alex put down the cup and again took the floor. But even he was breathless, when a few minutes later, he returned to the punchbowl.

"Ah, Lord Caerleon and Alex Saint-Hilare. How good it is to see you both again." Turning, we looked into the kindly eyes of the Egyptian, Abad al-Jalil. He seemed out of place in his black robes and white turban, and I, for one, was surprised to see him. Correctly interpreting my look, he said, "You do appear surprised, but no matter. The pasha and I are very close, and so the Europeans invite me to all their parties and social affairs. Who knows when they might need the ear of the pasha." He smiled, lifting his eyebrows in a bemused expression. "I hope there were no ill effects from your sleep, Alex?"

"No, none at all. Edward told me what happened. Do you really think I saw the Tomb of Alexandros?"

"The human mind has a wealth of undiscovered possibilities. It is said that a man who can control his mind can control the world. The mysteries of the mind remain."

"But I could not see the tomb after the treasures had disappeared. I saw it quite empty."

"It is strange. Something blocked your mind. It could be that either you or your spirit really did not know what happened, or perhaps your spirit was unwilling to disclose the location, especially, if the body and the treasures were removed by friendly agents."

"I would be willing to go back."

"No, it could be dangerous for you. It might force a mental state that would be difficult on you. In any case I have been meaning to call on you; I've found a book which might be of some use. Where's Arundale Bey? He is so very fond of these state occasions; he meets new customers."

"Hamid said he had a touch of the fever," I explained.

"Sad. The climate of Egypt is sometimes bad, even for those who have become accustomed to it. Arundale Bay is rather an odd chap. We met some years ago in Nubia at the great colossi at Abu Simbel. Perhaps you are familiar with these giant figures of Rameses II, towering some seventy feet, and cut entirely out of the living rock. They have only been recently uncovered from drifting sand."

"Yes, I have heard of them; it's as if the Cathedral of Notre Dame were carved out of a single block of stone. If it is possible we'll sail up and see them."

"Certainly worth the trip, yet as I was saying, Arundale is an odd chap. I think he should go back to England, for he is at times moody and depressed. But do give him my best, and say that I will call in a few days."

"He has been a great help to us. The Pasha has granted our *firman*, and we will soon be on the Nile."

"Yes, I know. I told the Pasha to grant it with a slight price increase. Oh, please, do not be angry. It was my idea to construct a museum here in Cairo. Your money will be used to build the museum."

"Eight thousand pounds should build a very good museum," I said, not without some irony.

"The situation demands it. Very soon Egypt will be stripped of its antiquities. I wonder what would happen if an Egyptian demanded that Westminster Abbey be dismantled and taken to Cairo. I reminded the pasha that without antiquities to lure them no foreigners would bring any money into Egypt. Tourists are very wealthy and Egypt is very poor. So you see the situation. But, excuse me, I wander. Thinking that you and your friend would be here tonight, I borrowed a book from the al-Azhar library to show you; it might be useful in your quest. Perhaps we could talk in private. Shall we take coffee in that small salon? Good." The three of us walked across the marble floor, sidestepping the dancing couples, to a small room adjoining the ballroom where it was quiet.

"I have the book here," the Egyptian took a small leather box from the inner folds of his robe. "Books are very precious and if I were to lose this one. . . ." He drew his finger across his throat. "The record and personal diary of Jabir ibn Hayyan; he was a scholar of note and also an alchemist. He entered Egypt in 639 of the Christian calendar with the forces of General Amr ibn-al-As, who took the city of Alexandria in 641. To read from this description it was then a lovely place: 4,000 palaces, 4,000 baths, and 400 theaters."

"In order to understand his writings, we must remember the times he lived in. The desert followers of Muhammad coming as they did, out of Medina and Mecca, were semibarbaric and bent on conquest. Their enemy, on the other hand, representing Greco-Roman culture, was far more sophisticated and urban."

"A strange meeting for both parties," I mused aloud. "Christ meets Allah. It would be the Arabs who would conquer, and the old world of Athens, and Rome—the world of classical learning—that would be ground to dust."

"Do not entirely lay the blame for the downfall of the Classical world on the Arabs, dear Lord Caerleon. Is it not true that the Christians in the year 400 murdered that beautiful woman, Hypatia, the head of the Neoplatonic school of philosophy? She was ripped apart by fanatical Christians."

"Shall we say then that the destruction of the ancient world was a joint venture?"

"Yes, let's leave it at that. The book of Jabir ibn Hayyan." The Egyptian reverentially turned the flap of the leather case and slowly opened the old book. The script was in flowing Arabic, with numerous charts, maps, and diagrams, which covered the parchment pages. "Jabir ibn Hayyan was a man of learning, but deceived by his time. From his notes we learn his chief passion was trying to turn base metals into gold; nevertheless, he had a fine mind. He was much taken by the Pharos lighthouse, the clever pulley system, and the Serapeum . . ."

"We were there, a hellish place filled with mummies and a horrible wind. The afreet of Serapius," Alex exclaimed.

"It may have been the afreet of Serapius that you heard. No, I do not speak superstition. It is known that certain ancient temples had oracular devices that would enable the priests to speak through the mouth of the statue of the god and in this manner to produce magical effects. Look closely at this diagram. Do you see the system of pipes and tunnels running to the destroyed base of the great statue of Serapis? Evidently, it interested ibn Hayyan enough to include it in his sketches. But these things have only an interest to the scholar. But, I have been waiting to speak to you of a matter of far greater importance." The Egyptian's eyes blinked with excitement. "I have found the Tomb of Alexandros!"

"What?" Both Alex and I shouted simultaneously.

"Fantastic," I added, still stunned.

The Egyptian unfolded a page of the crinkled parchment. "As you can see, a map. Look at the drawing of that little building; it matches the one on the golden drachma. It too has pillars and the star of Macedonia in the cornice, and written over the drawing is the word, 'Sikandar'."

"That proves the building still was standing in A.D. 641, anyway," I said, peering intently at the map.

"There is more, I translate:

I came to the place of Sikandar Dhulkarnein, he of the Two-Horns. In reverence for the destroyer of heathen temples the General has marked this as a holy shrine. The holy body and treasures of Sikandar given to him as a gift from Allah have been taken by the magic of powerful afreets to the House of the Double-Horns. Beneath the sign lays the body of the beautiful blond avenger, Sikandar.

"The House of the Double-Horns? Where is that at?"

"Clearly, it is at the oasis of Siwa and in the Temple of Jupiter Ammon; the symbol of the god was the ram's double-horns."

"Are you saying that someone moved the body to Siwa?" I asked.

"Yes. A great mystical aura had formed around the figure of the Macedonian; even the Roman emperors paid him homage. It is possible devout persons, seeing the destruction, moved the body to Siwa for protection. Sometime later, the original site of the Alexandros Tomb was converted into a mosque. A mosque stands on the very spot today. It is in the older section of Alexandria and rather shabby, but the name is a hint: el Qurn Mosheh . . . the Horns of Moses."

"Moses, the Hebrew prophet?"

"Muhammad respected the Old Testament prophets. They were men of the desert as he was, and gradually the symbol of the horns became associated with Moses, not Alexandros."

"Yes, the names could have gotten mixed up," I said, thinking of the name, Caerleon, and its origins. "You are saying, then, that the mosque marks the site of the Soma . . . but the body and treasures of Alexander the Great may have been moved to Siwa."

"Exactly. It's an interesting speculation. The location of the tomb is extremely hypothetical, if it still exists at all. And I fear it does not. There have been inquiries made at the oasis of Siwa, but to my knowledge nothing has ever been found. And the tomb may or may not be in Alexandria. We have only the writings of a man long dead."

"When we return to Alexandria we can explore this mosque," Alex said. "At least it's something to go on, a clue."

"Yes, Alex," The Egyptian said thoughtfully. "There's some hope, a chance. You've set yourself a very difficult quest, but you've the will and the mind to find the tomb, and somehow I think you will. See, here is the Pharaos lighthouse, a wonder of the ancient world, rising to 400 feet, but toppled in an earthquake in 796 of the Christian year." Alex and the Egyptian studied the old map with delight. For my part, I wondered what the faith of the Egyptian was, for he drank brandy and a circle of smoke rose from his old, yellowed pipe. Perhaps in his travels he had broken away from the rigid customs of Islam. It was a pleasant moment in the quiet room, just the three of us—a youth, whom I loved, an almost middle-aged man, and the old wise man—our lives and thoughts for the moment bound together. Perhaps there was a connection that had brought three dissimilar men together in one room: the quest for the Tomb of Alexandros. I hoped against hope that it might still exist . . . somewhere. I wanted Alex's dream to come true, though I must confess I thought the quest would be fruitless. Alex and the Egyptian finally came to the last page of the book of Jabir ibn Hayyan. The Egyptian looked up and smiled. "Ah, the hour grows late, and I must go," he said, carefully placing the wonderful book back into its case and returning it to the folds of his robe. "Perhaps it would be possible to talk again when you return from Philae. The Nile is a holy river; it has flowed long before the existence of Egypt, Greece, and Rome, before Moses, Christ, or Muhammad. It will still flow when we are dust. Have a good journey." Together we rose and opened the door; immediately laughter, and other sounds from the party filled the small room. Europe had imposed itself on us again.

Almost instantly, the young women rediscovered their handsome hero. With a soft rustle and a swish of velvet, *crepe de Chine*, and taffeta, they swarmed about Alex, like bees around honey, or, perhaps, they were more like flowers, for they seemed in their billowing gowns to be pale, delicate blooms. Their gowns *décolleté*, cut more to reveal than to conceal, their throats sparkling with cut-stones, jets of lustrous black, emeralds of dazzling green, rubies of glowing crimson, and set in ornate gold and silver, their hair swept back off the forehead in the fashionable *chignon*, they fluttered about with sparkling eyes and coy gestures. With sweet voices that showed their breeding and manners learned at the best schools for ladies of a certain class, they stood, with dainty, gloved hands closed against their lily-white bosoms, hoping the dashing Alex would ask them for a dance.

So the evening went. I was quite glad when the party ended. Alex was rather tired, too, having spent the entire evening on the marbled dance floor with one or another of the English girls. When we finally got in our carriage to return to the European quarter he slipped off his glossy, black pumps, rubbing his sore feet, still giddy with laughter.

The streets of Cairo seemed to have taken on a sinister look. As the moonlight cast ominous shadows across our path, servants ran alongside carrying torches. An armed guard covered both the front and the rear of the long line of coaches and open carriages. There was a wait while the wooden gates were opened by the guards, and the processional of laughing Britishers passed through. Hamid met us when we returned to Arundale's house. The boy was upset for some reason, but said his master was sleeping. The house appeared silent and empty. Hamid led the way with a candle and in this manner we passed through the moonlit garden to our rooms. Alex and I were very tired; we had danced the night away and were a little drunk. The hour was very late. I must have fallen asleep very quickly. Suddenly, a loud crash awoke me and I saw the door being flung open. Arundale stood in the doorway, his back to the dawn, then stumbled into the room. His eyes were wild and staring, his mouth hung open, his thinning, long hair hung matted around his head; he was half-dressed in trousers and a coat. There was the rank smell of liquor about him. "Arundale! For God's sakes what has happened?" But he ignored my words and ran to Alex, who sat up in his bed.

"Alexandros! Divinity! I worship at your feet. See, I have brought your drachma. It is yours, holy one." He opened the jeweled box, and the golden coin fell out onto the bedcovers. "I am leaving this evil place! My mind crawls with evil things, diseased things. Black snakes rear their heads, spiders crawl over my body, maggots eat at my guts. Oh, God protect me. Take the drachma, holy one. Remember me." He jerked to his feet and, howling at the dawn, flew down the stairs. We got up quickly and followed but were stopped by white-robed servants and Hamid.

"No! You must not follow my master. It is only the fever that has made him this way. It will run its course and he will be himself again."

"Your master is sick and needs help."

"We have sent for a physician," said Hamid. "Please return to your rooms. Everything is being done for the master." There was almost a threat in their manner, and Alex and I returned to our rooms.

"He was just roaring drunk, if you ask me," I said.

"He was crazy. The drachma," Alex said, looking down at the tiny gold coin. "I wonder why he gave it to me?"

"I don't know. Put it back in its box and we'll give it back."

It was dawn and tomorrow we would cast off and begin our 600 mile journey upriver. There would be much to do moving our trunks and boxes to the boat. After morning coffee we took the carriage to the river front. Our five-man crew was already at our little *dahabiyeh* bringing aboard fresh produce, and when we arrived they began loading our baggage. The boat was named *Star*, referring to the star of Islam; Alex and I liked to think of the star of Macedonia as the inspiration for its name. Our quarters, the bedrooms, and the outside dining salon, would be cramped for space; yet they were pleasant enough. Alex had found some material for curtains, a curious floral chintz, which he had made for the windows; we had also brought new mattresses. There were bookcases running beneath the window casements, and a small desk was tucked into a corner. During the days of preparing for our trip, we had come to love our little houseboat. True, it did creak a little, but the wood seemed sound enough. The last day was spent placing our books on the bookshelves and storing our gear. The Egyptian crewmen were at our sides helping, and it was nearing sunset before we were ready to return to Arundale's house. Our host greeted us at the door.

"Well, tomorrow is the big day." He seemed very normal. He was shaved, his hair brushed into place, and he wore a dark suit. "I rather wish I was going upstream again. So many things to see, temples and tombs half as old as time. I have made up my mind to return to England. I'll sell out and buy a grand house in the country. Won't that be keen? Egypt . . . I must leave Egypt."

"Last night you gave me the golden drachma," Alex said. "It's in our rooms; I'll get it."

"No, no, the coin is yours to keep. I half-remember last night; oh, you must have thought me mad. Please forgive me. These dark moods come over me, and I began to drink and have crazy visions. That's why I'm leaving—to escape from my madness."

"Thank you for the coin. I shall keep it forever."

"It is in good hands . . . never touch it. The gold is very soft and the marvelous detail will wear off. Even though I'm sober, I still think there is a bond between you and the coin." We went into the study. The room was dark, the statues and the mummy cases lost in the gloom. Arundale lit a candle. "Very soon I'll be a rich man. My possessions have become a weight around my neck. The statues are alien. The coffins stare out at me with their black-painted eyes. These are things that belong to the dead. I wish I had left them in their tombs where they belong. Unhealthy thoughts. Graves, mummies, ruins, the ancient dead. I'll be rid of them once and for all. I've prepared a farewell party for you tonight; I do not think I will be here when you return."

As if in anticipation of his homecoming, Arundale had given up his Egyptian ways, and our farewell dinner was served in the formal dining hall. We sat on chairs and ate from silver plates. He had invited several of his friends, fellow dealers and traders in antiquities to whom he planned to sell his large and valuable collection. And over dinner and brandy they talked of old times. The stories held our attention. The traders told of harrowing escapes from villages after they had stolen some artifact, of newly opened tombs, of ripping open mummies in a search for jewels or a papyrus scroll, of fraud and fakery. Apparently, because of the demand for antiquities, entire villages supported themselves by producing fake scarabs and the like.

The gullible traveler would be taken to a dig and after a moment of scratching in the sand a "valuable" find would be made, which he would buy, thinking the object was ancient. There seemed no end to the lengths of human skullduggery and greed, both by the European dealers and by the Egyptians.

The hour was growing late, and we made our apologies, saying that we must get up early to begin our journey. We went up to our rooms, and the loud laughter and voices faded away.

Our sleep was broken by loud pounding at the door. Groggy and annoyed by the noise I crawled out of bed, noticing the unperturbed Alex curled up in his blankets, and opened the door. It was Hamid. "Good effendi, come quickly, the master has gone crazy!" Hamid's normal complexion had paled and he wrung his hands in grief. His large brown eyes betrayed fear and were wet with tears.

My dull thoughts sharpened as I heard the sharp sound of breaking glass and the dulled roar of gunshots that managed to awake even the sleeping Alex. He sat up in the bed, rubbing his eyes, asking what the noise was all about. "Something is wrong with Arundale. Hamid says he's gone crazy. We'd better get on down." With our nightshirts flying behind us we followed the candlebearing Hamid down the steps, taking them two at a time. We ran through the marbled foyer, the screeching parrots and peacocks frantically trying to get out of our way, and came to the open door of Arundale's treasure-filled study.

The candlelight revealed the destruction. The heavy granite statues were overturned; the mummy cases smashed; the glass cases broken and their precious contents scattered. Arundale stood in the middle of the large room waving his gun at us. His gaunt face was strained by madness, his long hair was once again matted against his skull, and his dirty shirt and trousers were soaked with sweat. His long, skinny hand brushed something from his clothes. "They're all over me. God in heaven, help me!" The crazed agent shouted as he grabbed at his shirt and trousers.

"Arundale! What's wrong? What's all over you?" I shouted back, pushing Alex behind me to protect him from a stray bullet. "Hamid, you and the servants run for help. Get anybody. Get the old Egyptian. Run! We'll try and see if we can't calm Arundale Bey!" Hamid ran out, giving us his candle. The light flickered around the room, glancing off Arundale's crazed face. "Stay calm. Arundale. I've sent for help."

"Ah, Caerleon and Alex. Beautiful Alex. You are Alexander the Great. You think I'm crazy, don't you? I'm not! It's just. . . ." The agent screamed, tearing wildly at his clothing.

"What's wrong? We don't see anything. Stay behind me, Alex."

"It's the death-beetles. They live on the flesh of the dead and they want me!" Lurching and stumbling, Arundale fell against several standing coffins, dislodging the brightly painted lids, which clattered to the floor. Alex and I drew back in dread as the ancient dead fell down on the crazed man. The mummies, some wrapped in linen, some with exposed skulls and bones, tumbled out of their coffins, forming a horrible pile. The warm air was filled with the scent of the balms and the perfumes used to anoint their dried bodies. Arundale had fallen to the floor, while the smoke of mummy-dust rose up in a dull grey haze around him. The bones, wrappings, and dried flesh clung to him. He looked like a person in the grips of a dread and macabre disease. The sick man lashed out, knocking the skeletons this way and that in a terrible clatter, their brittle remains rattling across the marble floor and tiled walls.

Alex and I ducked as an eyeless skull came flying our way. "Arundale, you've got to get hold of yourself. The doctor should be here soon," I shouted.

"See, they're here. The beetles of death." Arundale pointed to the floor. Scattered among the bones and wrappings, husks of long dead beetles glinted in the light. "They eat the dead flesh. They are born in the mummy and they die in the mummy, after the rotted skin is eaten. Look, you can see them. They're moving!"

"You're mad!"

"No, Edward. They are alive. There must be hundreds of them." Alex pointed to the floor. It rustled and appeared to crackle, as the beetles seemed to move. God in heaven! They *were* moving against Arundale. Like a living, black and evil carpet, hundreds crept across the marble floor. The candlelight reflected off their glossy shells. We stared at the agent through the dim, flickering light, and through the dust raised by the heaped up mummies. But there was something else in the room. An awful heat. It was a dry heat, the dry heat of the desert, desiccating, drawing the moisture out of the air, like a thousand suns unleashed. We backed away in terror. We were dealing with unknown forces who had made their horrible presence known.

Now drawing their spectral shapes together the mummies rose, wooden and stiff, as if remembering the human act of walking. The dead beetles moved, and the heat hovered in the room. But that was not all. A shape took form, a black mass of dense smoke floated above the room. It sparkled and flashed, a fury of shifting shapes. The horror of it! A dog? A wolf? No, a jackal emerged out of the cloud of eerie blackness. Its ears were long and sharply pointed, its nose also long and elegant. The eyes. No, I can't describe the terror I felt in glimpsing them, as they seemed to quite literally burn out of the sleek, black fur. What we were seeing was neither animal nor human, but parts of both. Gleaming collars of gold hung from the human shoulders, but the head was that of an ebony jackal!

"Alex move back," I whispered. Arundale just stood there as the forces of Hell moved against him. I shouted his name and he came to life with a lurch. Aiming his pistol at the grisly shapes looming around him, Arundale fired, the booming shots echoing around the dim room. Alex and I fell to the floor as the bullets passed through the demonic forces. Wildly, the agent threw his empty pistol at the terrible jackal. The gun also passed through it and clattered to the floor.

"Can't we do something?" Alex said, grabbing my arm. I turned. His handsome face glistened as beads of sweat covered it. With the back of his hand he wiped the sweat out of his eyes, clearing them.

"What can we do? It's like a furnace of raw heat. What in God's name is happening?" Stopped by the barrier of scorching radiance we clung to the floor, our eyes held by the horror that gathered itself against Arundale. The beetles had stopped moving. The mummies, too, held their places, their vacant eyes peering at the looming man-jackal. The ancient dead raised their bony arms, dragging' the aromatic linen wrappings up, and with grotesque fingers pointed at the agent. Their lipless skulls seemed to grin through toothless jaws. The jackal creature hovered, watching them with fiery eyes. Distantly, as if it came from another world, the room reverberated with a ghostly conversation between the mummies and the jackal. The dreadful whispering, like wind through dead leaves, came to an end. A judgement had been reached.

The stygian creature grew almost to the ceiling, scintillating with a horrible sparkle of great Energy, now contained within its force. Slowly it raised its human arm, the hand held a strange scepter of unknown design, which was pointed at Arundale. He stood there in the middle of the room, a human who now faced the terrors that rose up around him. There was nothing we could do as the forces moved with dreadful vengeance against this man who had disturbed the tombs of the ancient dead.

His end began slowly. It was the heat. It was draining him! He aged. His skin crinkled and cracked, like a drying pond in summer. Bit by bit, it fell off. Arundale was becoming a mummy. With a last desperate gesture, he raised his arm in feeble protest, but it was of little use. In a moment the drying process that turned once living men into brittle remains, husks of ancient flesh, was over. In a ghastly clunk his arm separated from his body and fell to the floor. We watched as the rest of him came apart like a shattered doll. The death-beetles moved in a shimmering horde crawling towards the pile of bones and flesh that had once been Arundale. They were eating him!

Surrounded by the horror that held us transfixed and flattened to the floor, our minds dazed and our eyes unable to take in any more of the hellish scene, Alex and I must have passed out. Once again I saw the great, looming jackal, the living mummies, the awful heat, and the horrid crunching of the beetles. And then nothing.

5.

"Lord Caerleon and young Alex! Wake up."

Dimly I perceived the form of Abad al-Jalil. He was shaking my shoulder. Alex was already awake and sat on the marble floor, scratching his tousled curls. Instantly the horror of the night came to my mind. "Arundale. He's dead! The mummies and the beetles got him."

"Yes, it was horrible. There was a big black dog that turned him into a mummy and the beetles ate him." Alex's face reflected the grisly events.

"Arundale is alive. He's shot himself. He's gone mad and out of his mind. The servants took him to his room. It was necessary to bind him. I feared he might injure himself."

"But we saw it. The black dog made him dry up, just like those mummies on the floor." Alex pointed to the pile of scented wrappings and bones lying on the floor.

"That's where we found him. Apparently the lids fell off and the mummies fell down on him. He was crazed and must have shot himself. The bullet only grazed the scalp. Arundale, however, is finished. There was a mark branded on his chest. I've seen it before on those men who have desecrated the tombs of Egypt. It is the mark of Anpu, or Anubis, the protector of the tombs and the guardian of the dead. His form is that of a black jackal."

"That's who we saw, Anubis."

"You've had some dream about the god?" al-Jalil asked softly. The roseate light of dawn caught his snowy beard, turning it to a glowing pink.

"Yes, it was a horrible dream," Alex's words tumbled out of his mouth as he recounted the events that we had thought we had seen. When Alex finished speaking, the old Egyptian rose from his kneeling position and stood up, helping us to do the same. He turned, gazing up at a window and the dawn light that streamed through it. His face was puzzled as he turned back, looking at us with dark eyes.

"It is possible that you did see something. The herbs used in the embalming process are unknown and can have an hallucinatory effect on the mind. However, there's the brand of Anubis burnt into Arundale's flesh. Certainly, the god has placed his curse on the agent. Already there's a change; Arundale has aged. His face is that of a man twice his years and his hair is stark white. He will soon die an old man before his time."

"What can we do?" I asked.

"Nothing. I will stay with him, and if he improves it's best to send him back to England as soon as possible."

"There must be something to bring him around."

"Lord Caerleon. We are dealing with ancient forces that we cannot understand. Modern science is of no use. Arundale was doomed when he first entered the tombs. The dead have taken their vengeance and there's nothing we can do."

"We can postpone our trip to Philae."

"There's no reason. You'll be back in two months or so. We'll see each other again, I hope. We've become friends and I like both of you very much. I think you're good and honest men. I'm glad you're taking the stone back to England. It'll be a graceful addition to your estate at Caerleon. The English will have a bit of Egypt. We'll meet again." There was a power about the old Egyptian that is difficult to describe, a strength lying beneath those gentle eyes, an ancient lineage inspiring confidence. He was right, there was nothing we could do, and so we left Arundale's Moorish palace, bidding a farewell to a tearful Hamid as our carriage rattled out of the gateway enclosing the European district. In the hazy light of dawn we made our way through the streets of Cairo and to the Nile where our voyage would begin.

Though the hour was early the waterfront was alive with the comings and goings of many men, loading and unloading the river boats. Brown men, dressed in their *galabia*, or long, flowing robes, shouted and chanted work songs. Here were tethered camels, horses, cows, and goats. It was the time of the low-Nile, the season of flooding; the inundation of the Nile valley would not begin until late summer. Nevertheless, even during this season, it was still a wide, great river, its surface a swirling brownish green color, as it moved along on its stately pace eventually emptying into the Mediterranean Sea. Like great birds, the *dahabiyeh* and the smaller cargo-carrying *feluccas*, with their lateen sails of patched canvas alive with many colors, caught the wind.

The *Star* sat low in the murky waters waiting, and as our carriage pulled up, the crew jumped up out of their oar-pits, put down their tin coffee cups, and ran to us. Our captain, Reis Hassan, but called Ol' Joe by us, was a sprightly man of middle-age. He had a grizzled quality, his short beard gray with age, his face and hands a network of lines and wrinkles. He had, however, enormous energy reflected in the agility with which he and his four sons ran on shore to fetch our few remaining piles of luggage.

Ol' Joe's sons were all in their twenties, lean and handsome. It was as though we were long-lost friends who had just returned from a distant trip so joyous was their greeting. Also making the voyage were three old yellow and rather mangy watchdogs, an assortment of tabby cats to catch mice, seven mottled-colored Nubian goats that Ol' Joe was taking to his family at Luxor, and a strange dog-headed baboon, with rows of sharp teeth, which spent most of its time sitting in the rigging munching dates.

Alex, fastidiously clean in his habits, gallantly ignored the smells, the barking dogs, the bleating goats and the screaming baboon as we ascended the gangplank. Once aboard, he bounded across the boat running up to the open deck above our cabins, shouting nautical expressions he had heard aboard the *H.M.S. Argo*, the ship we had sailed on from England. A crowd gathered to watch while the crew pushed the sixty-foot craft away from the shoreline with the tips of their oars. At first the *Star* was reluctant to move, but with a sudden lurch and a groan the wooden boat slid away. Manning the long-oars, the crew paddled out into the middle of the river; then raising these, they scurried to the masts, grabbed ropes, and yanked the triangular sails upward. The patched, tattered, and multi-colored triangles of canvas billowed out, catching the prevailing northwind that would push us up the Nile and against the current that now ran sluggishly beneath the wooden hull. A British union-jack was run up the tall mast, and we were underway.

Alex grinned as the wind filled the sail and nearly blew his hat away, too. "We're finally on the Nile, the river of the Pharaohs."

"Yes, Alex, we finally are on our way." I had joined my young friend on the open deck and was holding onto the railing. "We'd better get settled in. This will be our home for a month or so, and there will be much to see and much to do."

The *Star* was not very comfortable, and our quarters were cramped by our luggage. But in the days before we sailed, Alex had succeeded in making it cozy, fixing it up with curtains, rugs, and furniture. He had found two mattresses stuffed with horsehair and had bought for them linens and bedcovers. The sleeping cabin was aft, and our bunkbeds were built over bookcases. The outer room served as a dining area and a workspace. As we went down the short flight of stairs leading from the deck to our cabins, we found the crew huddled around a low shed and a charcoal stove preparing lunch, tea, and the strong, black Turkish coffee for which I had developed a taste.

Alex unpacked the last of his baggage, a small carved chest holding his valuables, cufflinks, watch fobs, and a gold frame, holding portraits of his much-loved parents, Phillip and his beautiful Greek wife, their images carefully painted on panels of ivory. Reverently touching the glass covering, he hung the golden frame above his bunk then turned, "If father and mother could only see me now. Father always wanted to sail the Nile and to search for Alexandros. He had become infatuated with the legendary Macedonian. When we get back to Alexandria . . ."

"We will search . . ."

"Father was a great man and his contributions to archaeology will be remembered. I was thinking of going through his notes and publishing his diary when I get back. He knew so many famous people and traveled all over the world."

"That is a fine idea, Alex."

"And this. . . ." Alex took the jeweled box containing the drachma out of his bag and opened the lid. The golden coin caught the mid-morning light flowing into the cabin; its reflection cast a glowing light on Alex's beautiful face as he looked down. "Alexandros, my namesake. Strange that Arundale would give it to me. He seemed convinced that I was the Macedonian, but we know that he was mad. A soul cannot exist forever and enter new bodies . . . can it?"

"I do not know, Alex. I suppose it is possible, but I've never thought much about the question. Your physical resemblance to the face on the coin is probably coincidental."

"Yes, there are hundreds of men that look like that. Ha! But it would be nice to think that I was the reincarnation of so great a man. By the time he was my age he was a king and starting out on his road of conquest with a vast army. My only kingdom is a houseboat, dogs, cats, and a snarling baboon. Well, you've got to start somewhere, eh, Edward?"

"Yes, Alex. There will be other worlds for you to conquer in time. But, now, it must be time for tea, and we had better survey our world as Egypt passes by."

"I wonder what one wears on the Nile? Since nobody will be seeing us I thought I'd wear some old things. Cleaning will be a problem. These old trousers and shirts are a bit patched, but. . . ." Alex rummaged through his clothing, finding a faded blue shirt and matching trousers, before removing his waistcoat of heavy wool, his cravat, his linen shirt, and his trousers.

While Alex was a little shorter than I, he was much broader in the chest, his arms and shoulders muscular. The sunlight caught his smooth skin as he undressed; once he was standing naked it glanced off the fibers and sinews of his strong body, gracefully playing on the fine golden hairs clustered in a rich growth on his chest and circling his low, flat nipples. His waist was athletic and trim; his stomach chiseled with firm muscularity. A thin line of hair led down it from his chest, ending in a bunch of golden hair growing around his loins. His manhood was most beautiful as it fell away from the tawny hairs, strong and vigorous, its glowing pink tip brushing against furry thighs as he moved. Beneath its arching shaft, hidden by thick hairs, the rounded sacs holding his seed caressed the inner parts of his thighs. Unconscious of his fluid movements, his elegant body, and his cleanly defined muscles, he now began to dress.

His beauty was having its effect on me, and I tried not to look at him anymore. But a flood of warmth surged into my loins, a reaction I could not stop, and, hastily, I covered myself with a shirt. By this time Alex had slipped on his trousers and shirt, and I asked him to check on morning tea. As he left the cabin I stood hard, fully aroused, and aching for relief. I watched as the thick, creamy stream jetted into the shirt, and with a groan and a sigh I arched backwards until the moment had spent. This lonely time of ecstacy only confirmed once again what I already so painfully knew: how greatly I was physically attracted to Alex. Without knowing it he was driving me into a state of conflict and self-doubt. What was I to do with my unrealized feelings, — these desires and needs — with this love that could never be? I wanted Alex as a man wants a man. Something beyond friendship that could be only consummated by sexual love. My desires for the youth remained hidden, but they were more and more a part of me now. With each moment, with each passing day I had fallen more deeply in love with Alex. Now those emotions, tinged with a new bitterness, grasped me with a fierce hand, and my soul was torn and ripped apart. I longed and yearned to tell him . . . but could not. With whispered, deeply felt words, I would gather him into my arms, and we would kiss and I would tell him. But fear held me back. He would turn away offended and unable to understand my words. He would be lost forever, hating the sight of me. No, that moment would never be. I would keep what I had and not venture into uncharted seas.

Since that first sweet moment with Paul high on the sea-cliffs, overlooking the blue black sea I knew my secret self. It was, however, to be some time before I would discover another soul-mate. In the meantime there were knowing glances, a quick touch, a brushing of bodies as I moved out into the world. In the hallowed Gothic halls I was to find others who understood my feelings, and I was anxious to join them. Yet the affairs I had were fleeting and unsatisfying, school-boy romances of exploration and shared thrills.

London was to become my home for a while. There is an anonymity in a great city, far away from the staring eyes of family and friends, that offered succor to a wandering soul. Here I was to spend, not without pleasure, the days of young manhood. There were circles—groups of poets and writers, artists and actors, who traveled outside of polite society—Bohemians, gypsies, nonconformists, and rebels. There were men who loved men and women who loved women, and no one seemed to care a tinker's damn whom one loved. Pleasure and love were the only motivations for life, they said, and I agreed, becoming lost in the wild and dissolute, the brilliant and flashy crowds.

Love affairs were easy, and I felt no fear as I took a man into my arms to share a kiss and an embrace. In my darker moments I realized a certain peril, that of whispered scandal and social ostracism, of blackmail and murder, which was the other side of the spinning coin. Several youthful aristocrats, gone through their fortunes and faced with ruin, took a gun to their heads or fled to the more friendly shores of the Continent. As they searched for a new romance, their former lovers would speak of them fondly.

It was in my late twenties when I left the submerged world, having received word of my father's death. With a sad heart I left London to become master of Caerleon and took the seal of the house of Capricorn. It was a world that I had forgotten about, one of stiff manners, righteous people, and forbidden emotions. It was to be some time before I adjusted to the quiet life of a country squire, a life composed of horses, hounds, and hunting. Gradually I grew to love the place. Somehow the villagers accepted me. At first I was the "most eligible young bachelor", with women of the village pressing their anxious daughters at me; after a while, however, I became a "confirmed old bachelor" and that ended that.

The farmers who had worked my lands for generations were my only concern, and I busied myself with their problems. Now and then I would go to London for a concert, or a play, or to attend a state function, but I would always return to Caerleon, glad to step once again through the Norman doorway.

The years passed, and I remained distant from my own problems: that of again finding a true love, and thus finally doing something definitive about my unrealized desires and dreams. Only the summers would remind me. The young farmers, stripped to the waist, their fine bodies damp with sweat as they plowed the fields beneath a hot sun, would bring to the surface the passion that I had hidden in some part of my soul.

There were times . . . one afternoon I had gone to a farmhouse rented by a young couple. As the wife was far into her time of giving birth, I inquired about her condition, telling her that my physician would attend her whenever he was needed. She was happy, and I went ouside to see how her husband was bearing up under the strain of a first birth. Seeing that he was not in the fields, I went into the barn. The sunlight entered through chinks in the roof, and standing in a shaft of light, was her young husband. He was naked, with his britches around his ankles. Groaning with pleasure, his dark muscularity tense, he gripped his manhood. Embarrassed, I blushed to have found the man in such a personal moment. He looked at me, stopped, stepped out of his trousers, and walked over. My excitement must have shown through my trousers as I watched him, standing in glorious attention, erect and breathing heavily. Smiling, and looking down, he touched my protruding member. I know that I should have fled, but, instead, I reached down and took hold of his hardness and fumbling with my own buttons, my trousers dropped. Shaking with excitement, nervous and scared, I knew that I would not, could not run away. Our lips met and parted in a deep kiss, and closing our eyes, we brought our bodies together. I had never known anything like that time. He was so hot, his body searing mine with reckless passion. It was a brief moment of lust as we were bound up body against body until we could fully express our desires. With a thrust and a sob we emptied ourselves each on the other, then stood spent, running our hands over one another. He smiled, grinning happily, and as I pulled my trousers up, stuffing my shirt in, he slipped into his. I did not know what to say. Buckling his belt, he threw his arm around my shoulders as we walked out of the barn. "A man needs it when his wife is in her state." Several times before his wife gave birth, I saw the young husband, but after it he became involved with his new family and I only rarely encountered him.

"Edward, the water is boiling for tea," Alex said, sticking his head through the door as I buttoned my shirt.

"Be right there. Might as well take it on the deck." Alex and I sat around a sturdy wooden table as Ol' Joe served tea from a rather battered pot.

"The English like their tea; now the Egyptians also take their tea." Anxious to please, Reis Hassan hurried around, adjusting our chairs and pointing out the local landmarks as the boat sailed slowly by them, paced only by the north wind that filled the great sail.

The Nilotic landscape of tall dom-palms, villages, and mosques passed as one of Ol' Joe's sons steered the *Star* down the middle of the river. Another son stood at the bow, looking out for the shifting sandbars that could easily bring our progress to a sudden halt. Children stood yelling from the banks while their mothers carried water in clay jars gracefully poised on top of their veiled heads. Nearby, other women washed the family galabias in the river, laughing and chattering, no doubt talking about the latest village gossip. In the fields one could see farmers plowing with oxen, and flocks of white heron with frogs or snakes in the beaks. As it was low-Nile we could see and hear the creaking and groaning of the *shaduf*, a leather bucket strung to a long pole which, tediously and laborously, lifted water from the Nile and poured it into irrigation canals to feed the thirsty crops.

Looming up from behind the verdant fields one could see the fringes of the great desert, the vast and barren Sahara, that surrounded the thin strip of greenery lying only a few miles along the life-giving waters of the Nile. As we watched the shoreline pass by, crops were growing which made life possible in an alien world of sand and stone. We had an impression of timelessness, of eternity. How many centuries had man tilled the fields here? No one knew. Only the creaking mechanisms of the sails and the sloshing of the rudder-paddle broke the silence. In the far distance we could see the pyramid fields of Giza begin to slip from sight.

The river traffic would stop at night; the *dahabiyehs*, the *feluccas*, and the barges with cargo made for shore before evening. The crews would buy provisions from the farmers and the country folk sitting on the ground behind their baskets of fruits and vegetables. Some farmers had eggs and butter; others, sugar canes, cabbages, barley, wheat, maize, and tobacco. The women ran around with bouquets of live poultry, hens, and geese. The goods were very cheap. A hundred eggs cost only about fourteen pence; chickens sold for five pence. A good sheep would bring from between sixteen shillings and a pound. We ate well, though at times the food was overcooked or under-cooked on the little stove, or was too spicy for our bland English tastes.

Our first landfall was to be at Memphis, the capital of ancient Egypt lying, like most spots of interest, only a few miles from the river. Alex had spent the afternoon drawing and painting with water-colors, and soon the paper had been covered with sketches of the crew working the sails, preparing lunch, or sitting around the stove talking. While Alex was not a great artist, he had developed a certain skill in rendering his subjects. Sitting cross-legged, the drawing pad on his lap, he happily dipped his brush into the pan of color and built the scene he was depicting. While Alex painted, I read aloud descriptions of the ancient sites from the several guidebooks that had been written for travelers such as we.

From a distance we could hear the call for evening prayers chanted by the *muezzin* standing in a lofty minaret, beckoning the Moslem faithful to bow towards Mecca. In holy observance our crew fell on their prayer rugs, as they did five times a day.

Apparently, visiting Europeans were not on the whole very interested in the quaint customs of the Egyptians, but preferred during the pleasant evenings, to socialize, have a brandy or two, and compare notes. The houseboats might have been sailing on the Thames, stopping at Oxford or London for the night, as servants presented calling-cards and invitations for drinks or supper. The shoreline at Memphis was soon ablaze with hundreds of colored lanterns strung from one end of these boats to the other. A few boats up the line from the place where we docked, was a large houseboat, a hundred-footer. It belonged, as her calling card revealed, to a very well-known English-woman, Lady Amelia Bradford Grenfell-Smyth. Her wealthy ship-building husband had passed away, leaving his fortune to his pretty young wife, who had subsequently blossomed into a *belle hôtesse*. It was in this capacity that she invited us to supper that night aboard her boat.

We wondered why she was still here. It had been reported in the papers that she had come to Egypt for her health, but it was whispered that she had left England under a dark cloud of scandal, all because of an affair with a young man, a ranking member of the aristocracy, who, in the grip of a romantic passion for her, had shot himself. Since her whereabouts were not covered in the press recently, we were surprised to find Lady Grenfell-Smyth still in Egypt.

Liking parties, young Alex was in a dither as he dressed for supper, for even he had heard about the glamorous lady. We could see the bright lights strung along her fine *dahabiyeh* and hear the waves of laughter coming from her party. Dressed in our best, we ascended her gangplank, and presenting our cards to the uniformed guard, sauntered on board her lavish boat, which was beautifully outfitted with gleaming brass, shining teak and mahogany, and a crew dressed in sharply creased uniforms. We were shown into the grand salon, glittering with chandeliers of crystal, curtains of silk brocade, and a table set with fine china and silver service. Roughing it was not her lady-ship's style—we could easily see that.

At the far end of the salon stood Lady Grenfell-Smyth herself, surrounded by admiring guests. She was beautiful, with fragile, glowing skin and glossy black hair arranged in curls around her face. Her neck and arms sparkled with diamonds and emeralds; her ribboned gown was of deep mauve. We bowed as we were introduced, and she smiled, gracefully nodding. "Lord Caerleon. Alexander Saint-Hilaire. How good to meet you." Her eyes came to rest on Alex. "My, Alexander, such a forceful name for such a handsome young man." Alex blushed as she took his hand and pressed it tightly in hers. "How shameful of you, Lord Caerleon, for keeping your young ward to yourself. I knew your brave father, Alex . . . such a tragic ending for so great a man. And, for heavens sake, what are you doing in Egypt?"

Alex stammered, his hands still pressed by hers, "Ah . . . Edward and I were going to Philae. . . ."

". . . such a beautiful little island, the pearl of the Nile. I was there for over two months wandering among the temples of Isis, the goddess of love . . . very romantic and lovely."

"I've been negotiating for years trying to bring one of its obelisks back to Caerleon Castle," I broke in.

"I must have noticed it, but really when you've seen one you've seen them all. But come now, it's time for supper. Alex, please sit on my right and Edward on my left," she said, smiling.

It was a pleasant meal with small talk; her wine was the best. I wanted to get back and get some rest, as we would spend the day exploring the ruins of Memphis, and morning came early to the Nile. Nevertheless, I could not help noticing that Lady Grenfell-Smyth seemed quite smitten by Alex; the poor boy was barely able to get any food down as she could not keep her jeweled hand off his. Glancing over, I tried to get his attention, but he did not see me. I was annoyed. That little green monster called jealousy was nagging at my thoughts. How protective I had become. After supper, brandy, and a smoke, the party broke up and the guests departed one by one, bidding their farewells. But during all this, our hostess kept Alex by her side, and he seemed to want to stay there, holding her hand and looking into her eyes. My mind seethed confusedly. With or without Alex I had to leave.

I could not stand to see her so openly seduce him, running her fingers through his curls, cupping his chin in her hands, their bodies touching. I would have gone over and grabbed the boy from her clutches, but it would have been a breach of politeness. Tempering my rage, I managed to walk off her houseboat by myself, though I was in tears by this time. I had lost him forever, and I must have poured a thousand curses down on the Englishwoman who had taken my Alex from me. Blindly gaining our gangplank I rushed towards the cabin, stumbling over the sleeping forms of the crew, upsetting the dogs, and coming face to face with a baboon showing a ragged row of sharp teeth. Weary and sore of heart, I fell into my bunk.

I pressed my face into the cool pillow, my mind still turbulent. Certainly by now the woman would have my Alex in bed making passionate love to her — sweet kisses, hugs, and warm bodies. I could not bear the thought, and covering my head with the pillow, I sank into deep despair. What if she would persuade him to stay with her? She was very beautiful. I would never see him again. Well, I would just have to get along without him, that was all. Callous youth. But how was he to know that I loved him? I had never told him directly or expressed in any way my love. Now he would never know because of the wiles of that scheming Englishwoman. Well, let them have their pleasure, if that is what they wanted. I should have told him . . . but I feared losing him. Yet I had lost him anyway.

"Edward? Are you here? Where did you go? Edward?" Alex's voice came through the pillow.

"Alex?"

"Edward."

"I thought you wanted to stay with her," I said, lifting the pillow.

"Why would you think that? She is a charming woman. She wanted me to stay with her, to go to her cabin, but I could not."

"I thought —"

"Thought that I was attracted to her . . . no. She is very lovely but vain. An empty woman who thinks little of her friends and only about her wealth and position. She has nothing to offer me. We have something more." Alex sat on my bed, his voice soft.

"What?"

"Yes, I realized it while she was in my arms. We share a something that goes beyond mere friendship . . . a compassion for each other that I could not betray. Do you understand, Edward?"

"Yes, Alex, I do."

"Beyond friendship there is only my love to express what I feel about you."

"Oh, Alex, you've wiped away my grief, my despair. I thought I had lost you forever, but you came back. I've loved . . . you for such a long time, unwilling and unable to voice my feelings, afraid that you would hate and reject me."

"I could never do that, Edward. Now that our feelings for each other . . . wonderful feelings . . . we can go on. I've never known such things before; it will take me time to understand."

"I too, dear Alex."

"I am sorry I caused you grief, but I could never leave you now, dear Edward." He took my hand and gave it a tight squeeze. We must have remained there for a long time saying nothing, but quietly, silently expressing our new-found love.

With what exhilaration and happiness I awoke the next morning. Turning in my bed I looked over to his still sleeping form. Alex was loudly snoring and bundled up like a babe. He loved me and I loved him. That was all my mind could take in that morning.

Two days later we landed in a port in middle-Egypt, listed in the guidebook as Antinoopolis, the city of Antinoos, the handsome boy from Bithynia, who had been friend and companion to the Roman emperor Hadrian. The site had been described in the monumental study done in the time of Napoleon, *Description de l'Egypte*, as having many fine Roman buildings, and we were anxious to see them.

Here on October 30, A.D. 130, the boy had drowned in the Nile, a tragic blow to his benefactor, the wise and good Hadrian. The death caused enormous grief for the childless Roman, who probably saw in the youth an image of the son he never had. Or perhaps he had grown to love the boy as I had grown to love Alex. Having known something like the emperor's grief, I could now understand his passion. As a memorial, Hadrian had built this city to his love, with broad streets, graceful temples, gateways, and stadiums. Hadrian commanded that his young friend be made a god, and certainly here was a temple to Antinoos. But here again was the dreadful hand of wanton destruction. When we arrived, 30 years after the French, only a few blocks of stone remained. Indeed, while we watched, the natives were dismantling and hauling away parts of a monumental Roman gateway to be used, we were informed, in the construction of a sugar factory. Nearby, a lime-kiln stood ready to burn marble fragments of the statuary that had once graced the city. Bits of statues still remained, an arm or a leg of dirty white marble. Near the bottom of a pile of shattered fragments there was a finely carved head — no doubt the head of Hadrian's friend. It was a shame that such a beautiful piece would be utterly destroyed, so I picked it up and took it back to the boat. Alex and I felt that we had at least saved something: a small chunk of Antinoos, who in dying had been raised to the level of a god by a saddened emperor.

The days passed pleasantly enough: exploring, sketching, writing, and just drifting along the idyllic Nile. Alex would look up from his drawing, smile, and we would touch hands. There was a new emotion between us, a closeness that brought joy to my heart. He was happy; I could see that.

Sometimes, before the end of the day, Ol' Joe would swing the boat into a secluded lagoon, its banks growing wild with reeds and tall grasses. We would throw off our clothes and jump into the warm water. Although crocodiles had disappeared from these waters centuries ago, Ol' Joe would stand guard while we took a bath and washed our clothes. The young Egyptians were as boyish as Alex once their initial reserve had worn off, and we would play water games, dunking, chasing, and making underwater grabs. The Egyptians were lean, almost skinny, but their physiques were finely muscled, their dark skins giving the impression they had been carved of bronze. Both Alex and I were losing our fair skin under the sun, and soon we would be as dark as the Egyptians.

After the boat had been secured at night, Ol' Joe and his sons would buy provisions, air his goats, and clean the boat with Nile water. After a light supper and coffee, Alex and I would take our beds up to the open-deck and watch the stars, picking out the constellations that hung so brightly from the Egyptian sky. The crew would curl up around the stove with the dogs, the cats, and the baboon. In this manner another week passed, our next important stop would be the temples at Abdyos.

It was to be a hot day. Ra, which the Egyptians called their sungod, rose in the eastern horizon with great brilliance, as Ol' Joe steered the boat to the middle of the river. His sons watched for sandbars, as we swung into the center, heading for a clear channel. The usual northerly wind failed, and the crew took to the oars as the *Star* moved against the current, slowly and grudgingly. In the silence we could hear the wood creaking beneath us. Something was odd about that morning. The birds who nested in the Nile reeds, and flew above us daily, were nowhere to be seen, and there was no wind. Only an oppressive stillness. Ol' Joe stood at the rudder, his sons watching for the signal to raise the sails. But the current had caught the boat, and we began to drift to the north. We were suspended between water and sky, waiting.

The river had become a stilled lake, the surface smooth and unbroken. The southern horizon began to darken, turning the bright golden orb of Ra to a dusty metallic ball of orange. Ol' Joe left the rudder, running to his sons, talking and wildly pointing to the south as the darkness grew on the horizon. Speaking his broken English, he ran to us. "Effendi, a storm approaches, a terrible storm, the dread *khamsin*, a hot wind that blows in from the desert, a wind from the very belly of hell. We must make shore before it strikes! Aieeeee."

The storm blotted out the sun. Sharp, stinging grains of sand began pelting our faces and hands. The boat moved downstream, forced in this direction by the wind and the current. Then, in a grinding, shattering crunch, it stopped and began listing to port, as if it were about to blow over and sink. Alex and I were knocked to the deck and nearly thrown into the water. Ol' Joe came running back up to the deck, grabbing our legs. "Oh, effendi, Allah has gone against us! The boat is stuck on a sandbar. If we are not able to pull ourselves off it will go under. You help, please?"

"Yes, yes, of course." Dragging ourselves up, we crossed the deck, holding onto the railing and going down the stairs, half-blinded by the blowing sand. Dimly we could see the four men, oars in their hands as they pushed with all their strength against the sand which lay just below the surface of the churning waters. Ripping our shirts off, we wrapped them around our faces in a vain attempt to keep the biting sand our of our nostrils and mouths. Grabbing the upright oars, their broad ends lost to sight, we pushed, seven men together gripping the oar-handles, our muscles straining to free the *Star* from the imprisoning sand. Blindly (for our shirts had blown away) savagely, we pushed as the windy fury lashed out of the desert. From the ever-growing tilt of the boat, it became apparent that it would be blown over and sink.

How long we pushed against the oars I do not know, but our strength was almost gone. We lurched forwards a little, running along the edge of the deck, plunging the oars into the water. The boat lurched suddenly upwards, sending us sprawling, holding onto anything we could, as it slid into deep waters. "We must make for shore before the full force of the storm hits. Aieeee, it is a demon wind, sent by the very devil himself."

Stumbling and dragging ourselves to the oar-pits, we dug the oars into the seething waters, making for a shoreline we could not see. Ol' Joe manned the rudder, and we rowed with a fury matching the storm, our nostrils and lips caked with the stifling sand. Then, with a muffled crash, the boat hit shore. Swinging around from the bow, the aft hit hard ground with a shattering clomp that quivered throughout the boat and the wooden framework. Buffeted by the howling wind and barely able to stand, Ol' Joe and the crew tried to gain the shoreline in order to drive stakes into the ground and to tie up the boat. Their robes whipping around them, they tumbled into the water; crawling on shore they pounded the stakes and tied the holding-ropes. Afterwards, almost drowned they regained the boat. Ol' Joe pointed to the dry cabin, and we crawled towards it and, gaining our legs, rushed in. We were worn out, breathing heavily, wiping the sand from our faces and clothes. The boat groaned, heaving itself against the shore, but for the moment we were safe. "I . . . I have never seen such a wind," Ol' Joe managed to gasp. Sometimes it blows, but not this strong. It is a great *khamsin*, a wind of fifty days. It is the will of Allah."

"Fifty days!"

"Yes, effendi, sometimes longer, sometimes shorter. It is best you stay inside. If it is necessary we will go to a village and seek help."

"If the boat stays in one piece long enough."

"It is built good. Do not worry, Englishman, all will be well, if not . . ."

"I feel . . . ill. My stomach is churning." Alex leaned against the cabin wall, his hand folded across his sandy middle.

"Do you have a fever?"

"Yes, I'm burning up."

"It is a sickness that is brought by the wind. It is best the young effendi go to bed."

"No, no, I'll be all right. Nothing to worry . . ." He stopped talking as a dim light caught his face which had broken out in profuse sweating; his skin had whitened; he faltered, "Ohhhh . . ." With this Alex crumpled to the floor.

"God in heaven! Why did we come to this dreadful place?" I shouted out, but my agonized words were lost as the terrible wind shook the small boat and ground it into the shore. Rocking and heaving as it was, surely it would split apart. Outside the blowing sand pelted it, roaring against the wood. I sank to my knees, taking Alex into my arms. "God in heaven, help us."

6.

Alex lay quietly. The storm in all its fury continued unabated into the next day. Howling winds, mixed with sand, buffeted the little boat, which groaned and creaked under the lashing it received. Several times the crew had gone on shore to find help, but had been driven back by the demonic winds. Alex lay quietly.

I had drawn his blanket up around him and, sleepless, watched him throughout the day and night. Repeatedly, I wiped his brow, hoping the fever would break. The flickering candlelight danced across his pale and drawn face. His eyes were sunken. At times he would murmur something, but I could not catch his meaning.

Now, sitting on the edge of the bed, I tried to stop myself from dozing, watching the sleeping boy, who tossed about groaning. Suddenly, I started up anxiously. He was speaking in a low, distant voice. "Hephaistios?"

"Yes," I answered, my mind very tired and fogged.

"Hephaistios? Where are you?"

"Here."

"I thought you had gone . . . that you were angry with me."

"No, I'm not angry with you."

"You're always angry with me when I've had too much to drink."

"It's this place."

"Babylon. What went wrong, dear friend? Remember how it was with us so long ago? We would sit in the cool pine groves in the hills near Pella, sharing a honeycake, listening to our teachers, the philosopher, old Aristoteles, and the others. What dreams they conjured up—dreams of a single world unified by the ideals of Hellas. A world of peace and freedom. Serious thoughts for ones so young as we, eh, Hephaistios?"

"Yes, very serious."

"Certainly no man was more equipped than I to forge a new world for mankind. And you, dear friend, always at my side, sharing my dreams, training, studying, and working. Learning the art of the javelin, the shield, the mounted horse, each of these preparing us for combat. Remember how we wrestled in the sandpit at the palaestra? Our bodies, our reflexes, our strength were at their peak. Like young stallions, we were ready to go out into the world and win our race. Our walks in the forests, ha, just like schoolboys, skipping, jumping, enjoying the warm sun, falling in a pile of leaves, pressing together in love. What days they were. Where did they go, sweet Hephaistios?"

"I don't know."

"It all started out so fine. No warriors were filled with so much bravura and camaraderie as were the Macedonians when they crossed into Asia, ho, standing together in battle fray, with slashing swords, raised pikes, ready shields. Great Zeus, were there ever such men?"

"No."

"There was no stopping us. We took them all: Phrygia, Syria, Egypt, Media, Parthia, Bactria, India, the cities of Sardis, Tyre, Memphis, Babylon, Susa, Persepolis. They were all ours."

"Yes, they were ours, Alexandros."

"I drove my warriors to the ends of the world; with me they endured heat, cold, feast, and famine. No man ever asked more from his men."

"You were driven."

"Yes, driven by raw energy, ambition, and a philosopher's dream of a united world. You shared my life to the fullest, always at my side. It was all so fine, and then it fell apart."

"I know."

"Remember Hephaistios, how at Troy we stood before the altars of the deified heros, Achilles and Patroklos, those ancient Homeric warriors?"

"You slept with a copy of the *Iliad* beneath your pillow and a dagger at your side."

"They were like us, those ancients: warriors of fine blood, who fought the noble battle and who died like heros. First, Patroklos. Remember how the dead Patroklos appeared, ghostlike before Achilles, himself lying stricken with the news of the death of his lover? The ghostly figure implored his friend to let one urn contain the bones of both of them when it was Achilles' turn to die. Upon hearing these words Achilles stretched out his arms to his beloved, trying to hold him for one last time, but his love was gone like smoke into the earth. Homer told of these events, and I felt the spirit of those two immortal warriors in us as we knelt, offering sacrifice, there in ancient Illyia."

"Their love was good and true, immortal, like ours, dear Alexandros."

"We too were warriors . . . once. We did not die like warriors, our armor flashing in the dusty sunlight, swords held high, a lusty, mighty stallion carrying us to a noble and brave warrior's death."

"No."

"What happened?"

"Our souls grew tired; our bodies were consumed by fever."

"Gold and luxury corrupted and devoured us there in the sands of Persia."

"We grew apart, you and I. You ceased to love me, Alexandros."

"No, no, I did not cease loving you, it was . . . that I ceased loving myself. Ambition beyond the horizon and the scope of any man seized me. My mind was fooled by delusion, a mirage of the kind seen in the burning desert, shimmering just out of reach. My arrogance destroyed me. Ha, was I not the king of kings, the lord of lords? Had not the priests at Siwa made me a god and immortal? What use were men except to serve me?"

"You loved me still?"

"Yes, sweet Hephaistios, though I had forgotten. We were celebrating the games at Ecbatana when word came of your illness. By the time I reached you, the sleep of death had taken you. Remembering your love, I was possessed by grief. For days I would neither eat nor sleep, but lay stretched out across that body I had loved so much, touching that beautiful face I had so often kissed. Was Achilles' grief more than mine? I think not. I knew that, unable to go on without you, I wanted to die also. I sent word to the Temple of Zeus-Ammon at Siwa, and they made you a god like myself. As gods we would be together throughout time, untouched by corruption or decay, sharing the same urn, our bones mixed. We were gods!"

"Gods."

"Gods who had almost forgotten we were mortal men: men struck down with fever and earthly sickness. I died, not like a warrior, but swathed in sheets of silk in the 114th Olympiad, at thirty-two years and eight months. An ignoble death. Hephaistios, hold me; a fever has me and I need warmth. Hephaistios!"

"Alexandros . . . Alexander . . . Alex!" What was happening to Alex and me? We were caught up in a dream, drifting through time. My eyes fluttered as I regained my waking state. Alex still tossed in fitful sleep. It was like the time the Egyptian had summoned him to go back in time . . . he had fallen into a trance, imagining himself to be the Macedonian. Seemingly, the golden drachma was still working its spell. I took Alex's hand, which was cold as death. Confused and mentally exhausted I called out for the Egyptian to return my friend to the world of the living. There was no answer, except for the howling wind. What could I do? I had neither the mysterious powers nor the gifts that the Egyptian seemed to have. Alex's hand remained cold. He lay still. Was he breathing? Had the ghost of a man who lived so many ages ago taken possession of my friend, trying to lure him back in time? He would be lost forever, caught somewhere between then and now. I had to pull him back before all was lost.

Where was the drachma—the coin under whose spell Alex had fallen? He had put it in a drawer next to the chest holding his jewelry. I searched for it frantically, pawing through the neatly folded shirts, till, finally, I held the box in my hands. Lifting the heavy lid, I saw the coin, the gold of it glinting and shining on its velvet bed.

I stood looking down at it, not knowing quite what to do. My mind went blank. The gold seemed to leave the black velvet, swirling up around me, engulfing the cabin in brilliant, iridescent color similar to that of starlike clusters in a galaxy. The boat had vanished, leaving only darkness. Great columns of stone rose. A curtain of shimmering golden lace parted, and I saw behind it a great, looming figure, surrounded by mist, seated on an immense throne of gold. The glowing skin was softly creamy, perhaps ivory colored; the mighty, majestic head towered into the mist; the hair was golden as was the vast robe covering the ivory flesh. Gradually, the mist parted; the titanic figure was caught in a shaft of radiant light. Falling back in awe, I raised my arm to protect my eyes from the shining brilliance. What was this strange apparition that my befuddled mind had conjured up?

The chamber trembled, the columns shook, and the statue spoke: "Was Achilles' love for Patroklos greater than that of my son, Alexandros, for Hephaistios, or greater than Hadrian's for Antinoos, or my love for Ganymede? Did I not make them gods so that they could share everlasting life and my glory on Olympos? These men each knew a love above other loves. Be not afraid, mortal, am I not Father Zeus? Fear not, but stand before my throne brave and tall, filled with courage. Fear nothing; it is not yet time for you and your young friend to join me on Mount Olympos. You shall both know the full span of life on earth. Do you love Alexander?"

"With all my heart."

"Call him to your side."

"Alexander."

"Yes, beloved, I am here."

"Alexander, do you love Edward?"

"With all my heart."

"Then you are worthy to serve me here in my earthly temple. It is good between you; I can see your love is true. And thus immortal, as was that of Achilles for Patroklos, Alexandros for Hephaistios, Hadrian for Antinoos, as, indeed, was that of all the men who have ever loved other men in friendship and compassion. It is the kind of love that transcends the common, the earthly, reaching, in its beauty, to the very stars. My faith in your love has been confirmed; it is good and true, befitting the highest ideals of bravery and courage. Return to the ancient river that holds you fast; the storm has ceased. Remember always that there is no greater love than that which exists between a man and a man. . . ."

The golden image faded as the mists of time swirled down past the ages in a dim flickering light. What was once beautiful became a ruin. The great cities of gleaming marble—Rome, Athens, and Alexandria, became nothing. The books of wisdom and learning were piled on great fires. Wantonly, nearly everything of the past was destroyed. Afterwards, human beings groveled in the dust of ignorance, blind to beauty and learning. Only after centuries had passed did they begin to rediscover bits and pieces of the glorious past to preserve and to treasure the precious heritage that had been lost. During these dark times one man's love for another was thought to be shameful, and it was hidden, a thing shared only by those who had rediscovered its powerful force.

My mind still swirled as my eyes focused again on the gleaming coin. Alex's bunk swam before my weary eyes. Fearing the worst, I raised myself up. A beam of sunlight coming in from the cabin's windows gently stroked his pale face. His breathing was now regular, and after a time his face became once again flushed with life. He opened his eyes. Death had passed him by. "Edward?"

"Dear, sweet Alex. How do you feel?"

"The fever has passed. I am very tired. You have the drachma. I was dreaming about it. You were in my dream, too. We stood before a great image; I think it was a god, a golden god. We said we loved one another. I cannot think. My thoughts are tired."

"Sleep, dear Alex. Be at peace. I also remember the dream. Oh, Alex, I do love you so. And I want you to love me." But my words were lost to him as he had already closed his eyes. I knew the golden drachma had no magic power; my tired mind had conjured up the strange visions. I looked down at the glowing image of Alexandros, wondering what he may have looked like on that day ages ago when he met death in Babylon. He may have looked like Alex, eyes closed, tousled hair against a silken pillow, face drawn, brow perspiring, as his warriors circled his bed, grieving for their fallen hero. I knew it was Father Zeus who had spoken to us from the mists of time, and I whispered a little prayer of thanks to him for the gift of Alex's life.

The storm had passed, but not without having left our boat in shambles in its violent wake. Books, trunks, and boxes bearing the crest of the house of Capricorn littered the floor of our cabin. The fire in the stove had gone out, and the livestock had scattered. It was to take until late the next day before things were again made ship-shape. Ol' Joe rekindled the fire in our little stove; the goats, the cats, and the dogs were rounded up, and the irate baboon resumed his post high in the riggings. After a restful night we set sail early in the morning for Abdyos. Landing at Abdyos, we were greeted by peddlers, vendors, and beggars, crying for baksheesh. With a stern face Ol' Joe crossed the gangplank, Alex and I following. We would have to rent donkeys for the six- or seven-mile trip inland to the great temple that stood in the sands that skirted the edge of cultivatible land. In order for the tourists to make their selections, the creatures, some stubborn and others anxious to travel, were trotted out of their flimsy pens of reeds. They were not very big, and a rider could easily drag his boots in the earth. A thin padding covered their backsides. We would be very sore at the end of the trip, but it would be fun. Mounting the beasts, and with a flick of the willow-whip, we were off . . . almost. Alex's donkey suddenly stopped—sending him to the ground—and then sat down, refusing to go on. His dignity somewhat ruffled, Alex got up and selected another. Finally we were off down the road.

Slowly we slogged along, batting at black flies, enduring bruised derrières, surly drivers, and the dust kicked up by our animals. The grandeur of the temple, however, made the trip worthwhile. We walked into broad courtyards, through columned hallways that led to arched shrines attributed to King Sethos, a pharaoh whose reign occurred around the time of Moses. The scholarly world had never definitely decided who was king of Egypt during the Exodus, some claiming the honor not for Sethos, but for Rameses II, son of Sethos. The issue will probably remain unresolved, as the holy writ fails to mention which pharaoh let the Hebrews go up out of the land of

Goshen. For myself, I try and keep an open mind about such burning issues.

Though a ruin, the temple was elegant and beautiful; its carvings in low-relief, some dappled with faded blues, reds, yellows, browns and black, were executed with immense care and delicacy. In one panel King Sethos offers gold collars to his gods; in another the holy barque is carried aloft by a corps of priests. Here one can see the strange gods of the ancient Egyptians so derided by the Greeks: cobras, vultures, cows, and jackals—some in their purely animal forms, others with the bodies of men. Strange gods, indeed. Not animal, not human, but something other, a blend of forms difficult to understand but somehow beautiful. Perhaps the Egyptians had seen their world as embodying the spirit of the divine: in humans, in animals, in plants—the sum total of each of the parts expressing the joy of creation and, indeed, of all life. Most likely I was wrong, but it made sense to me.

Unable to share the exact feelings and emotions that caused the ancient artist to so finely execute the strange forms, Alex had trouble copying them. Finally, he closed his sketchbook and simply gazed. Toward the end of the day we mounted our donkeys for the slow, plodding trip back to the boat.

Luxor and Thebes. Both Alex and I greatly anticipated seeing them from the descriptions in the guidebooks we read while taking tea on the cabin's open-deck. If the writers had described rather sedately the other monuments along the Nile, they had summoned up their most glowing prose for the temples of Luxor, Thebes, and Karnak. "Massive, built to the scale of giants, the Great Hypostyle Hall at Karnak rivals the cathedrals of Europe in majesty. Certainly, it is one of the highest, and most colossal monuments to man's vanity ever erected. The tombs hidden in the Valley of the Kings are testimonies to man's belief in life everlasting; the fact that all were robbed is a testimony to man's foolishness." So went a typical passage. Apparently, the writers were unable to determine if the crumbling ruins were a tribute to man's greatness or an expression of his stupidity. We would have to see for ourselves.

To winter in Luxor was the thing to do in 1831. Only the wealthy European could afford such a trip. A veritable flotilla, a fleet of house-boats—some large, some small—lined up along the riverfront, the national flags flying proudly from their masts. It seemed that all of Europe had moved in for the winter.

Berthing was to be a problem; either it was a sign of social rank, or a question of how much one was willing to hand out to the locals for a select spot. The wealthy were able to easily pay fifty pounds a day for the privilege of receiving a berth near the center of town; for lesser sums one was berthed at the end of the line. It would have been a loss of rank for Reis Hassam to have taken a lesser berthing, so I paid the sum, and we were shoved into a very good place near both the town and the quay. Fore and aft were two larger *dahabiyehs*. The one forward was named the *Seven Hathors* and flew the French flag; I could not read the name of the aft boat. Ol' Joe heaved the gangplank down; we had arrived at Luxor.

The Nile valley widened here in its long journey to the sea. Lying on the western shore was the ancient land of the dead. Mighty sandstone cliffs marked the places where the pharaohs of Egypt had carved their tombs and built their memorial temples. The eastern bank was shared by the living and the gods; it had served as the capital during the so-called New Kingdom, when Egypt was at the height of her power. It must have been a sight to see then—the many temples, all brightly painted, their gateways marked with towering flagpoles, the stately white-robed priests carrying the sacred barque through the streets. And the pharaoh, in high crowns of gold, riding through the same streets in his colorful war-chariot, bringing with him captives and tribute from conquered nations. But all that splendor had passed. The Luxor we saw was a small, sleepy town; its temples half-covered with debris and sand. In fact, entire villages of dung-colored mudbrick were built right on top of some of the ancient structures. In the forecourt of one great temple, lying just on the other side of the road above the Nile embankment, an entire mosque had even been constructed.

The visiting Europeans lacked no comfort. Carriages were hired to take them for a day of sightseeing among the "quaint and picturesque" ruins, where they might buy an "antika." If they were especially energetic they might board a ferry for the short trip across the Nile to visit those well-known statues, the "colossi of Memnon," or the great ruined mortuary temples, chief of which was the Ramesseum; or if really adventurous, they might take a carriage and explore the rock-cut tombs in the Valley of the Kings. Most of them, however, did none of these things, but remained aboard their *dahabiyehs* doing whatever they did in London, Paris, or Vienna.

For Reis Hassam and his four sons Luxor was home port, so to speak, and his very large family greeted the *Star* a little after it swung into its berthing. They were *fellahin*, Egyptian peasants and workers, and were a cheerful lot, simple and good, if perhaps a bit rustic. In no time at all, Reis Hassam's entire family had descended onto the boat, carrying bundles of flowers and claypots filled with *booza*, a powerfully heavy local beer. At the end of the day, a little drunk, they left with the dogs, the goats, the cats, and the baboon, the last being a gift to one of their children. Since they spoke only Arabic it was impossible to say what their conversation consisted of unless Ol' Joe translated. But whatever it was about, clearly the occasion was happy.

The next day, with Ol' Joe as guide, we rambled through the ruins of Karnak. Even as I write this it is difficult to describe the stupendous splendor of this huge temple, spreading for acres around us. It was an enormous brown, dingy pile of broken stones, fallen columns, toppled obelisks, with long avenues of ram-headed sphinxes, the symbol of Ammon, the god once worshipped here. We ate lunch in the Great Hypostyle Hall which is large enough with its 134 columns, to contain either St. Peter's or Notre Dame. Deciding to be daring, we rambled up a sandbank, and perching ourselves on top of an enormous seventy-foot column, we ate and looked.

Several days later we crossed the Nile to the western bank and by carriage saw the huge mortuary temples built to preserve for all time the spirit of the dead pharaoh. Some distance beyond lay their tombs. Our carriage traveled along a dusty road into a narrow valley. No hint remained of the treasures that were once buried here; only an occasional black hole, nearly covered by falling rocks and debris, was visible. Except for the noisy carriages and the chatter of the tourists, the hot isolated place looked much like the rest of the neighboring sandstone cliffs and valleys, but at one time the Valley of the Kings must have known the greatest accumulation of wealth in the entire history of man. In a futile effort to achieve immortality, the pharaohs had taken the wealth of their world with them to the grave. Where was it now? Vanished, for not one single tomb had escaped being robbed; now only the black holes punctured the sides of the towering cliffs.

The name of Giovanni Belzoni, that circus strongman, came to mind as we descended into the 328-foot-long tomb of King Sethos, for it was the Italian who had first entered the tomb in 1817. This was the same Sethos who had built the temple at Abdyos. By the time of Belzoni's arrival, the tomb had long been empty except for a beautiful alabaster sarcophagus, which the Italian removed, shipped to England, and sold to Sir John Soane in 1824 for 2,000 pounds. What of King Sethos? His body was never found and most likely never will be; it was probably destroyed when the vast treasures were robbed.

Ol' Joe and his family lived on the other side of the Valley of the Kings in Qurna, a village stacked against the western hillside of Thebes. At one time the face of the hill was covered with the tombs of the nobles who had served the pharaohs, but now the Egyptians, finding them empty, had built their houses around them as had the ancestors of Ol' Joe. His house looked like the others, a whitewashed and mudbrick construction, built into the rocky hillside.

After securing the carriage, we followed along behind Ol' Joe, going up the rough pathway to his house, where we greeted his very large family comprised of many children as well as several wives, the custom here. The interior of the house was cool in contrast to the outside heat. We sipped coffee as Ol' Joe paraded his children, boys and girls of every age, before us. "My family has lived here, oh, very long time now," he said, in broken English. "We live good. My sons help me run the boat; oh, it is good to have many sons. I am old, and they will, how you say, hold me up, support me in old age, is this not so? Ah, yes, it is. We have the boat, the goats, and the cows, and a field for growing. We live good. Yes. I show you." He guided us through the rest of the house, until we came upon a gate, which he opened; lifting up a wooden beam. Through the dim light I could see that the gate opened onto a lofty room that had once served as a tomb. Now it was home to Ol' Joe's goats and cows. Still, while the lower portions of the walls had been scraped away by generations of livestock, high above, softly glowing paintings depicting scenes of daily life in ancient Egypt, remained intact, though somewhat covered by the soot of many torches. I doubt if the original owner could have imagined what would be the dreary fate of his once beautifully painted resting-place.

"Come," Ol' Joe said, closing the gate and lowering the holding-beam. "I have something to show you, something you will like, much." Back in his front room he opened a wicker basket and removed a statue from it; it was a brilliant turquoise blue faience, about a foot high. The figure was that of a mummified man, his arms crossed over the chest. The face seemed well done; the head bore a tall crown, and running in a row down the figure were ancient hieroglyphs that I was unable to read. I recognised a rounded oval, called a cartouche, which I had learned always contained the name of a king. "It is for you, effendi."

"How much?"

"For my good English friends, only . . . ten pounds. Very good, very old. My son found it. You like . . . yes?"

"What do you think, Alex?"

"It's very pretty."

I remember the tales told around Arundale's table the night before he had shot himself and knew I was buying a fake. Ol' Joe and his sons had been very kind and helpful; so I bought the statue anyway. The color was wonderful, and I wished I could read the inscriptions. What was the statue's purpose? Later, with it wrapped in a basket,

Alex and I rambled back down the hillside. Ol' Joe gave the horses a firm swat with his whip, and we were on our way along the dusty road. Little did we know the dangers that lay just ahead of us.

While once the Ramesseum had been surrounded by high brick walls, now these had crumbled into a pile of rubble. Built by Rameses II to preserve his memory forever, only a cluster of columns marked the place where a great temple had stood. Here must have been Shelley's inspiration for his poem about Ozymandius and the "shattered visage," for, lying in a monumental heap, was a statue of Rameses. It was estimated, that when complete and standing, it weighed a thousand tons, but now only huge fragments of red granite remained. Wandering around the papyrus-shaped columns, we almost bumped into a wooden scaffolding constructed along a wall deeply carved with scenes and glyphs. Looking up we saw a man perched on the runways, carefully tracing the inscriptions; around his feet were piles of books, stacked papers, and drawing instruments. He looked down for a moment and I recognised his bookish face. It was the young scholar from the British Museum that we had so briefly spoken with in Alexandria. "I say, haven't we met before?" he called down from his high perch.

"Yes, in Alexandria. As I remember, you were just on your way."

"I thought we had met. What do you think of Egypt? I've forgotten your names." Saying that, he jumped on a ladder and climbed down. "Time for tea and a break. Charles H. Rhind, here."

After reintroducing ourselves the three of us sat down on a broken column. "It must be tedious copying all those glyphs," Alex said.

"Yes, but someone must do it. Important work."

"What are the inscriptions about?" Alex looked around at the expanse of wall covered from the top to the bottom with hieroglyphics.

"Mostly about Rameses II. The old boys thought nothing of ordering stonecarvers to cut stories about how great they were into the walls of their temples. The pharaohs had colossal egos, as big as the temples they built to tell stories about their battles and exploits, but most of what's here is rather boring stuff: long lists of objects, gifts to the temples, lists of family, and list of conquests. This wall tells about Rameses' battle with a vanished race of men known as the Hittites who lived in Asia Minor. Rameses made war on the Hittites at a place called Kadesh, and from what I can make out so far, good old Rameses retreated with little more than his loincloth, as it were."

"Poor Rameses."

"Did you give up on your search for the Tomb of Alexandros?"

"For the while, we have some business at Philae . . . ah."

"Beautiful little island, quite enchanting."

"I say, Rhind, since you can read the glyphs, ah, Alex and I just bought a little statue that has some writing on it, and I was wondering if . . ."

"The fate of an Egyptologist is to translate the words written on some fake that tourists have picked up. Yes, I'll have a look at it; it's probably meaningless."

Sending Ol' Joe back to the carriage, we waited for his return. Soon he returned with my statue and I showed it to Rhind. "What is it?" I asked.

"A *shawabty*, or "answerer," a magical figure put into the tombs to serve the deceased in the underworld. See here, running down the center of the statue is the incantation that would bring the statue to life. The kings were no fools. Why work, when with a few words, you could command an army of magical slaves to do whatever you wished. The tombs and the markets are filled with them. Clever fakes."

"No fake . . . real . . . good, very old," Ol' Joe protested. "My son found it several days ago."

"Oh, where?" Rhind asked.

"Biban el-Moluk."

"In the Valley of the Kings. Where?"

' "I do not know, effendi. He is always bringing something home; I sell them."

"The statue is very nice," Rhind said politely, "It is very well made, of good color, and quality. I'm glad the craft of making "antika" is improving."

"Not fake, real thing . . . good."

"You say it is a fake?" I asked.

"A good copy. The name in the oval is well-known and easy to imitate."

"It is a royal name. Whose is it?"

"Amenophis III, a well-known chap, the fellow who raised those two giant statues down the road, misnamed the colossi of Memnon. All that's left of his temple, I'm afraid."

"Was he a great king? Has his tomb been found?" Alex asked, excited.

"Yes, Amenophis III was one of the best; he ruled Egypt at the height of her glory, and his tomb has never been found. Still in the hills someplace. All you would have to do is to copy his name, mold the clay, fire the thing, and, for your troubles, have a very good fake."

"No, no, real . . . my son found it in the Valley."

"Sorry to disappoint the old man, for he has a good story. How much did you pay for it?" Rhind turned to me.

"Ten pounds."

"Not a bad price; it has good color. I'll give you fifteen."

"You'd buy a fake?"

"It's a very good one and worth the price."

"No, I think we'll keep it as a memento of Luxor."

The young scholar frowned as he gave the figure back. "Well, I'd better return to old Rameses and the battle of Kadesh." Bidding us farewell, he reclimbed the ladder.

"Nice man," Alex was saying as we returned to the carriage. "To really be able to read that stuff, holy Rameses. When I get back I'm going to study and learn to read them as well as he can."

"A good project, Alex. We'll learn them together." Returning to the Nile we saw the big statues of Amenophis III looming up over the cultivated fields, and stopping, we checked the royal oval. There, engraved in the granite, was the same name that was on my statue. It would be easy for someone looking for an ancient name to copy this one. I was a little disappointed with Ol' Joe for selling us a fake, but I guess he had to make a living with so many mouths to feed.

Returning to the *Star* rather late in the afternoon, we found the *dahabiyeh* the *Seven Hathors* had gone, her place being taken by an even grander boat, one almost as large as that belonging to Lady Grenfell-Smyth. The vessel had been only recently built as the wood was new, and the sail had not yet been patched in long wear.

While we watched the clean, white-robed crew scurried around, making it fast. As the aft part of the boat swung around, we could see the British flag and the boat's name, H.M.S. Beveridge, which was boldly emblazoned across the wood, along with an elaborate coat-of-arms. A tall man stood barking orders to his crew. He was elaborately dressed in admiral's attire, a deep blue wool jacket and trousers trimmed with gold striping, gold buttons, and gold braid. An admiral's hat was firmly planted on his head. He might have been Lord Nelson commanding the English fleet, so gorgeous was his fanciful uniform. Staring more closely, I recognised a well-known face; it belonged to Lord William Beveridge, earl of Wessex, a distant cousin of the Duke of Wellington. English *royalty* had come to the Nile, and I wondered what so famous a man was doing here.

Lord Beveridge, "Bevvie," to his friends, had endeared himself to the public. An adventurer and soldier of fortune, his exploits, opinions, and affairs filled the papers. The books he wrote describing his adventures were widely read. Posing as a devout Moslem he had been the first white man to enter the forbidden city of Mecca, where, if he had been discovered, he would have been killed immediately. He had fought in the English-American wars, strangely enough, on the side of the Americans, and as many favored the underdog he was admired for supporting the colonies in their wars of independence from George III. After that he had lived in Virginia and ran slaves from Africa to work the plantations. What a life! But now Lord Beveridge seemed to be having the ordinary trouble one can have with a native crew. "Damn, get those lines over, you scum!" he shouted out to his men, who probably had no idea what he was talking about.

After checking the lines, he returned to the deck, and looking over, saw us standing there watching him. "Englishmen? Good, had enough of these scum." We introduced ourselves. "Hell and damnation, Lord

Caerleon, I should have known you. Met, I think, at the funeral last spring. Read about your trip in the paper. Had no idea we'd find each other in this Godforsaken place." He spoke in a clipped military manner, his language salted with swearwords of doubtful origin. Lord Beveridge, he was sixty if a day, sported a clipped mustache and trimmed "mutton chops." Though his chestnut hair was thinning, he was handsome in a rugged, out-of-doors sort of a way, and his flamboyant figure was slender and trim. Smiling graciously, he asked us over for drinks.

Lord Beveridge's saloon was spacious, if rather dirty, filled as it was with the smell of stale cigar smoke. Our host puffed at one cigar after another as we drank brandy. "Had the whole thing built from the keel up," he said, "Brought my own yacht; had to leave the damn thing in Alexandria; the river is too shallow. Did you boys run into the big wind? Blew like hell. Natives wanted to run away, damnit, but a few well-placed pistol shots put a stop to that idea. Got to keep the scum in line. So what are you boys doing out here? There was something in the papers about an old rock that you were taking back . . ."

"An obelisk."

"One of those big needlelike things? Saw two in Alexandria. Somebody will cart them away someday. Good luck. I came for gold; it's easy to melt down and more portable than a big old rock. Did some prospecting in America, but the Spanish got it all. Damnit! The tombs around here are stuffed with gold, if you can find it. My agents got noses like bloodhounds. If there's any to be found they'll scent it out, especially if they get a big commission; money talks. Ever hear of a big dealer . . . Arundale? Was going to hire him, but heard he got sick. He had a friend, an old Egyptian chap, whom I'd like to get my hands on, has access to the Cairo library. There's an old book I want. Alexandros? Ever hear of him? Has a big tomb around somewhere, maybe in Alexandria. The book is said to show the present location of the tomb. Got to get that book, one way or the other."

"Alexandros?"

"Yes, the big Macedonian general; says he's buried in a big funeral cart . . . all of gold, a real prize." Lord Beveridge signalled for more brandy, snapping out orders to his servant who made the rounds with the decanter.

"Ah, Lord Beveridge, we are also . . ."

" . . . also hoping that you will dine with us soon. Reis Hassam is a good cook." I said, nudging Alex.

"Mighty glad to, if you'll sup with me tonight. Damnit, it took a heap of training, but I finally got a fair kidney pie out of my cook and English dumplings too."

"We had better be on our way, Alex; we need to prepare ourselves properly for that kidney pie."

"Almost told him everything," Alex apologized as we left the boat.

"Best not to let anyone know of our search. We know where the tomb might be if it is still there. "Bevvie" is out for loot, and we had better keep our secret to ourselves."

"Bevvie" served a very good table, and we hungrily devoured the first English food we had in many days. Our host kept the conversation going with his tales of life in the Americas. Life there sounded rather barbaric and rough; the white men kept pushing back the frontier into lands belonging to the half-naked savages. The United States had elected their seventh president, Andrew Jackson. He sounded as rough-hewn as the rest of the rugged men and women, who had against all odds farmed the land and built cities, where before there had been only great forests. It had always been my thinking that, if George III had not been so severe with the colonies, the English would have held them to this day. Certainly, they boasted among their populace Royalists who had supported England and the Crown. The heavy hand of the King had, however, fallen hard, and the red-coats managed to raise the hatred of nearly all the colonists and were booted out. Now the former colonies were on their own and making quite a good show of things.

While England had abolished the evils of slavery in 1813, it was still the mode in the New World. Beveridge told stories of entire African tribes being kidnapped, chained to slaveships—stinking hulks—and taken to ports where they were sold to work the great cotton, sugar, and tobacco plantations lying in the southern part of the United States. In contrast, the north, dependent on industry, employed its workers from freemen. As a result the young nation seemed to have split in two parts, the free and the unfree, and Beveridge thought the situation might eventually bring conflict to the United States, though he said he supported slavery as it was a very good business.

It was a late hour before we left. "Bevvie" had drunk himself into a stupor and had to be carried to his cabin. One really had to acknowledge that this Englishman was not the best sort. Alex and I stumbled up our own gangplank. Ol' Joe would be onboard sleeping in the oarpits next to the stove. Oil-burning lanterns flickered dimly on either side of the doorway leading to our cabin. It was a moonless night, but the sky was alive with a panoply of stars. Fearing to wake the sleeping captain we walked softly across the deck, opened the door to the diningcabin, and stepped inside. Alex entered first, but quickly retreated with a yell. "There's somebody dead on the floor!"

"What?" I rushed inside. The dim light revealed the crumpled figure of Ol' Joe lying on the floor next to the dining table. "He's breathing. Get some water." I ordered, lifting him up in my arms. "He must have hit his head on the doorway." By splashing some Nile water on his face, we were able to bring the old man to his senses; his opened eyes stared at us wildly.

"Effendi! Most terrible. I was sleeping and I think I hear sounds in the cabin; you gone and I get up to see. I look in, and there was a man going through the drawers in the sleeping cabin. I rushed at him, and I could see he had the little statue . . . he was very crazy, pushing me back. He hit me and I fell. He must have run off the boat. Very sorry, effendi."

"Who was it? Did you see his face?"

"Oh, yes, effendi. It was the young scholar who translated the words on the statue."

"Rhind?"

"Yes, yes, the Englishman."

"What would he want a fake statue for?"

"Effendi, I say the statue not fake. Real. I would not cheat most honored guests who hired my boat. My son found it in the Valley."

"Remember Rhind wanted to buy it," Alex exclaimed. "Maybe he knew the thing was no fake."

"You may be right, Alex."

"Many such things are found in the Valley. Still many tombs hidden there, perhaps my little boy stumbled across one while playing. It would be like home to him since he too lives in a tomb."

"You think your son may have found a lost tomb?"

"It possible. He bring several objects home bearing the same name as that on the statue. Scarabs, jars, little statues. I sold them."

"Rhind knew the statue was real and came here tonight to steal it. Why?" asked Alex.

"It could only mean one thing," I answered. "He knows the tomb of that pharaoh has never been discovered, and he knows that your son found a statue which belongs in that tomb. He thinks your son knows where the pharaoh's tomb is located. Rhind is out of his mind; his coming here tonight, taking the statue, and hitting Ol' Joe were the acts of a desperately crazed man. Reis Hassam, I think your son is in great danger."

"Effendi?"

"Only he knows where to find the tomb. Rhind will show him the statue and use force if necessary in order to find it. We had better get across the river and see if we can find Rhind before it is too late. Hurry."

The night folded in around us as we ran from the boat, racing up the embankment; taking the roadway along the Nile, we came to the steps leading down to the quay and the ferry. Seeing no one we jumped into a raft, hurriedly pushed it away from shore, and paddled across the broad river. Reaching the other side we leaped onto solid ground. Luxor was asleep. The usual flock of merchants, carriages, donkey-drivers was gone, and it was a good eight miles to the village of Qurna. There were farms along the road, and we walked for a short distance until we saw a corral with two sleepy nags in the yard.

With some commotion we mounted up, and soon gained the road, leaving behind the owner shouting obscenities at us. We galloped past the colossi of Memnon toward the western hills of Thebes.

After what seemed like forever we arrived at our destination, and throwing ourselves off the stolen horses we ran up the hillside, past a group of barking dogs, until the whitewashed walls of Ol' Joe's house appeared against the dark cliffs. Flinging open the wooden door, he called into the dark house. At first there was no response, but then came muffled crys from the rear. We ran in that direction, calling out, the sounds of our boots making a fearful clatter. Reaching the tomb Ol' Joe flung aside the wooden bar and swung the gates open. Shouting and waving their arms, his entire family tumbled out. After a tumultous few moments he quieted them down long enough to find out what had happened. Rhind had arrived with the statue in one hand and a pistol in the other, demanding to speak to the boy who had found the stone in order to discover where he had come upon it. The boy pointed to the Valley, and waving his pistol, Rhind herded the family into the tomb. Then, the boy as his hostage, he had disappeared into the night.

"Aieee!" Ol' Joe screamed. "They will be killed, my little boy captured by a madman. Allah has turned against me. The cliffs are hundreds of feet high. One false step . . ."

"Come on," I said urgently. We had better follow . . ."

"Aieee. It is too late." The family began to moan and cry out in their grief, falling on the floor, calling to Allah to save their son.

"We had better follow Rhind," I repeated. "Find a torch, Alex." Leaving the grieving family, Alex and I ran out into the darkness, our torches held high. We stumbled up the hill, our boots slipping on the loose stones and pebbles. Climbing higher we reached a pathway running along the cliffs. Standing still for a moment we looked about; somewhere in the empty darkness lay the Valley of the Kings. Just then our light caught two blood red eyes staring up at us; with a yelp a jackel, freshly killed prey hanging from his mouth, ran into the night.

For the next few minutes it was slow going as we gingerly made our way, our boots scraping loose a number of stones which, tumbling into the valley, echoed around the sandstone cliffs. Far into the eastern horizon the first light of dawn broke, permitting us to see a little more clearly. We picked out a descending path, narrow and pebble-strewn, and started down; slipping and sliding, almost falling on our backsides, we hit the bottom of the Valley in a shower of rocks.

Gaining our feet, we paused for a moment. On the far side dawn bathed the sandstone in a pinkish glow; the bottom of the Valley, however, remained in darkness. We were on the same tourist's path that we had traveled yesterday. Without the noisy and elegantly dressed Europeans, the Valley seemed another place: isolated, foreign, raw, and primitive. Where had Rhind taken the boy? The Valley could go on for miles, an endless maze of rocky, hidden ravines.

I had forgotten the boy's name, and so we called out Rhind's name. Nothing; just the sound of our voices echoing, resounding around the cliffs. Only silence. Had Rhind fallen? Were he and the boy lying dead in a ravine? Alex and I split up. He would take the upper path, and I would take the lower, the one leading to the entrance of the tombs some miles away. As I walked, crunching the loose gravel, I could make out the black holes marking the entrance, telling by their very presence a silent tale of robbery and pillage. "I thought I heard something; somebody yelled." Alex shouted from some distance. Quickly, I scrambled to his side. "I thought it came from over there." Alex pointed to a loose pile of rocks and stones that had tumbled from the cliffside. We listened. There was a low crying sound, and we ran toward it, the light from our torches catching the boy standing in front of a hole. He was crying, wiping away his tears with the edge of his nightshirt. We knelt down, telling the frightened child that every thing would be all right, and he seemed to grasp the meaning of our words. I asked him where the man was, and he pointed to the hole. We gave him a pat on the rump and told him to go home, that he would be safe from now on. He seemed to understand our English and started down the path.

With torches held high we entered the blackness of the gaping hole. At first the passageway was very low, and we bent over, our backs scraping the stone ceiling. Torches held out before us, we descended into the tomb, finding ourselves almost immediately in a large chamber supported by four square columns. Our torches caught the painted walls, causing the mysterious figures on them to loom up at us out of the darkness. They were creatures from the ancient Egyptian underworld—rearing snakes, scorpions, jackals, strange, nightmarish monsters. At the far end of the chamber there was a doorway; the bricks used to seal it lay in a rubble heap around the portals; behind it was another descending passageway. Here human figures, in bright, glowing colors, replaced those hideous creatures we had just seen. Pharaoh sat enthroned, holding in each hand the symbols of his power; lined up before him in long neat rows were his subjects, painted one on top of the other in strange perspective. The name of the king was inscribed in the royal cartouche: Amenophis. The same as on my little statue. My heart skipped a beat. Had the boy come upon an intact tomb? Did this pharaoh lie nearby, just as he had been buried, surrounded by his worldly goods, rich treasures of gold? I could understand Rhind's dreadfully rash actions. Rhind? Where was he?

Descending ever deeper into the rock-cut tomb, laboriously carved out by workers so many centuries ago to guard the pharaoh's treasures, we called out to Rhind. No answer. After passing through several more painted rooms, we stopped. From a short distance away came the sound of pounding, a low echoing thud, thud, thud. Moving toward the sound we came upon a great chamber. Rhind was banging a rock against a far wall. At the sound of our footsteps he whirled about. "Don't come any nearer or I'll shoot!" he shouted, holding the rock in one hand and waving a pistol in the other. A nearby torch lit his contorted face. "It's mine. I found the tomb, it's mine. Stand away!"

"Rhind, you are in serious trouble; because you kidnapped the boy, the police will have to be called in."

Rhind looked wildly at us. The gentle scholar had vanished, the bookish look replaced by the fierce grimace of a maddened treasure-seeker. "Stand aside, or I'll shoot. The burial chamber should be behind this wall. I'll be the first person ever to find an undisturbed tomb . . . the gold and the jewels. I'll be famous." Waving his gun at us, he half-turned, and began pounding again on the wall; little by little the hardened clay bricks gave way before the rock.

I could understand Rhind's madness. No pharaoh had ever been found in the Valley of the Kings with his tomb intact, and if Rhind were to discover the king still encased in his golden coffin, exactly as he had been buried centuries ago by holy priests, it would cause a sensation. Rhind was gambling his name and reputation on the word of a boy and, apparently, was about to strike it rich. "I've broken through!" Rhind shouted as the bricks fell away, revealing a painted door. Forgetting us he rushed into the entrance, his figure lost in the blackness that closed in around him. Moments passed. Alex and I expected him to reemerge from the tomb his arms laden with ancient gold. Certainly, his rash acts would be forgiven if the pharoah was found. We waited breathlessly. Suddenly, a scream shattered the silence, a scream of absolute terror. Rhind staggered out of the doorway, but he held no gold. Instead, his head and face were covered by a mass of crawling and seething amber things. In the faint light the horror became ever more apparent. It was no golden treasure he had found, but a nest of stinging, venomous scorpions that clung to his flesh, injecting their poison into his writhing and agonized body.

We stood by helplessly, listening to his terrible screams of pain and watching him die. After what seemed like an eternity, he fell to his knees and toppled over. Then silence, the proverbial silence of a tomb, closed in around us.

7.

"Watch out, Alex! The ceiling is falling in." I pushed Alex out of the way as a pile of rock, rubble, and dust poured through the doorway, covering Rhind's body and with it the deadly scorpions. The flickering remains of the torch were snuffed out, and the blackness of Amenophis' tomb encircled us. Stumbling, we retraced our steps until we found ourselves at the entrance to the tomb. Outside we were greeted by Ol' Joe, his sons, and some of the villagers. Holding torches, they had been about to descend when our appearance stopped them. We told of the young Egyptologist's tragic death, and once again we entered the tomb, although, thank God, this time we were not alone.

Except for a few broken jars, bits of gilded wood, beads of turquoise, and statues similar to the one Ol' Joe had sold us, there was nothing in the way of treasure. It was clear if the beastly scorpions hadn't killed the unfortunate Rhind, the trap we now discovered lying behind the painted door would have. Still, this same trap set by the ancients had failed to protect the remains of Amenophis. As for Rhind, he had gambled and lost. The world would have to wait until some lucky searcher found a pharoah buried as he was when his priests had laid him in his resting place; that is, if such a tomb still remained untouched in the Valley of the Kings. And I doubted if there were such a tomb.

The villagers took with them the horribly scarred corpse, and the next day a group of saddened fellow Egyptologists buried Rhind in a local Christian cemetery. Alex and I attended the funeral.

Several days later *Star* got underway for the last stage of our long journey. Ol' Joe and his sons cast off the lines. Dressed to the nines, "Bevvie" waved at us as we swung out into the river, our destination Philae, the "pearl of the Nile."

Alex stood watching the temples of Luxor fade behind the horizon. He looked despondent and I asked why. "I don't know, really; I guess I'll be glad to get back home." Smiling, he threw his arm around my shoulder and gave me a firm hug. Somehow this spontaneous gesture of affection reaffirmed our friendship . . . a friendship that had grown to love. Strangely, Rhind's words spoken in the cafe at Alexandria came to mind . . . "everyone comes to Egypt to find something: a tomb, a belief, or even themselves. All things are possible here." What had I been seeking? At first it was an obelisk, then, the Tomb of Alexandros, but really, down deep, I knew I had come here seeking love . . . love from Alex, a love that my heart cried out for, a love that had held back from expressing itself, until the night in Memphis when he had come to me. Now we were friends . . . more than friends, but not lovers. In my heart of hearts the fear of completely revealing myself still remained. I dared not go further with my desires and needs.

Three days and several temples later the *Star* pulled alongside the embankment at the small outpost town of Assuan. It was here that the famous cataracts began, those barriers of rocks and whitewater, which denied access to the lower regions of the great Nile. Around us now rose sandstone cliffs. Gone were the cultivated farmlands and the peaceful river; here was the desert. The harsh, brutal, landscape of barren wastes gripped the river in desolation. Ahead of us was a wilderness that few had penetrated. Beyond were the wild unknown regions of Nubia and the Sudan. Only the rare European had gone there to map the terrain and whatever lay past the places reached by such efforts was a huge blank on the maps of the world.

Assuan was a small, dirty, sunbaked smudge on the edge of nothingness, a depot for strange and exotic goods coming in from the dim regions of central Africa. Stacks of elephant tusks, skins of lions, leopards, and cheetah, skins of great snakes, sacks of aromatic spices, pepper, frankincense, incense and myrrh, and black logs of ebony, filled the shops. Small and dirty as it was, Assuan was, nevertheless, a treasure-house of raw materials that would eventually find its way to Europe. And there was the slavemarket. Half-naked slaves of both sexes, their bodies running with open sores from repeated lashings and swarming with black flys, were chained together in long rows. They had been brought in from the desert to be sold to the highest bidder. We turned away from the horrible sight. There was nothing we could do.

The main task was to find labor to pull and to guide the houseboat through the dangerous rapids that blocked our way. Soon Ol' Joe came trotting along with a very tall, broad-shouldered Nubian; he was to be our *Shellalee*, the Cataract-Arab, who, with his crew was to take us through the channels of rock and boiling foam. It was very expensive, but the *Shellalee* worked only during low-Nile. During the winter the high-Nile would cover the rocks and he would be out of a job. No doubt he would have saved up enough to get him through the off-season.

Early the next morning he and his crew were ready to pull us through the first Cataract. Stout ropes were made fast, and first lowering our sail, a line of some twenty-five Nubians and Egyptians then pulled the ropes taut. Slowly, a foot at a time, we moved against the rapids and past the wild, strange scenery. Grotesque, misshapen forms of granite rock rose up out of the turbulent water; boulders as large as the boat blocked our way. Some of these we missed only by inches; at times the fragile hull would scrape a rock and the boat would shudder from bow to rudder. It was to take the entire morning before the cataract was left behind, and we could make it into smooth waters. Here the Nile broadened into a lake; its surface broken by hundreds of islands. Some were only huge boulders; others were real islands, crowned by clumps of dom palms. Ol' Joe and his crew let go of the wet ropes; the *Shellalee* and his men dragged these ashore as the *Star* sailed into the placid lake. There was a strangeness about the quiet, glassy Nile and the weirdly formed rocks. It was as though we had come to the ends of the earth, and if, suspended between sky and water, we were to sail on we would reach the end and fall off.

Miragelike, Philae came into view, looking as if it were some lost island unknown to man with its surface purple and mauve, and its skyline punctuated by lofty palms. As we drew nearer high gateways, rows of columns, and stately temples—reflections of ancient splendor—rose dreamlike out of the unruffled Nile. Had centuries really passed? It did not seem so. We might have sailed back into the time of the fabled Cleopatra, or of the Caesars, so perfectly preserved were the temples of Philae.

All was hushed as we glided into shore: even the usually noisy crew was silent. The nesting birds took flight when we touched land inside a shallow bay. The hull scraped bottom and we were secured. Through the palms we could see the temples. Wasting no time Alex and I immediately jumped overboard into the soft sand, and running hand in hand we scurried up the embankment. The lonely, isolated temples dedicated to Isis, the goddess of love, rose up around us in noble splendor. Before us were gateways, called pylons, girdle-walls enclosing courtyards, and holy shrines. Yet, what at first sight had seemed perfect, was not; every carved figure had been destroyed: the faces and the figures brutally carved upon and smashed by fanatics who had certainly tried and almost succeeded in wiping away the ancient faith that had raised these temples so long ago.

Though only some 400 yards long from tip to tip, the island was a maze of *colonnades* and graceful flower-topped pillars. The Ptolemaic temple of Isis was the largest structure, while to our left was a singularly odd building. It was a kiosk built by the Roman emperor Trajan and was popularly known as "Pharaoh's Bed."

Crossing the broad stone courtyard Alex and I went over to the first great pylon towering some sixty feet above us. The sloping sides, each resembling a truncated pyramid, and topped by an overhanging cornice, were filled with figures of gods and kings. We thought we had this lovely island to ourselves. The smiling faces of several Europeans, however, soon appeared, looking down over the top of the pylon and urging us to come on up. Though they were so high above us, their voices were clear and we asked them how they reached the top. They said there was an entrance in the side of the great porticos. Passing under the carved sandstone winged sun-disc and into the gateway, we saw the doorway leading inside. Taking two steps at a time, Alex was the first to make the flat roof, and he stood waiting for me, as breathlessly I climbed the steep staircase until I finally caught up with him.

There were four English visitors on the roof, and we shook hands as we introduced ourselves. Mister Robert Hayes was tall, rather stooped-shouldered, balding, with a keen, bright face and sparkling black eyes. Pamela, his wife, was shorter, her graying hair pulled back from her brow. While she was demure of character, I sensed an inner strength, necessary to brave this isolated and lonely island. The other two were introduced as Mister Carter and Mister Osgood; they were both young, perhaps in their twenties. The clothes they had on were worn and patched, dusty and sandy from their work on the pylon. The four were friendly and affable, with easy smiles and a certain nonchalance of person.

We seemed to hit it off right away. Hayes explained that he and his group were artists. They had arrived on the island last December and would stay until April. We could see the tall mast of their houseboat on the other side of the island. It was their plan to plot and diagram every building and inscription. On the stone ledge sat a device, a "camera lucida," that enabled the viewer looking through a prism to make an accurate drawing of any object reflected on a concave table by merely tracing the image on a piece of paper. I quickly formed the impression that Carter and Osgood were skilled artists, as they showed us watercolor studies of Philae, taking them from stuffed portfolios of paintings and drawings they had brought with them to the roof. Alex, having sketched himself the Nilotic scenery, was much taken by the artists and their very fine paintings. Together we stood for awhile talking and looking at the beautiful scenery.

The conversation was so interesting and the view from the pylon so enchanting that both Alex and I had momentarily forgotten why we had come to this faraway place. Suddenly remembering, I asked them if they had noticed a smallish obelisk lying somewhere on the island. Yes, they said, there was one at the northern tip of Philae near the temple of Augustus Caesar. We told them that we had come to take it back to England. Our words were followed by a stunned silence. Then Hayes cleared his throat. "We do not agree that such a valuable object should be removed. It should remain here where it belongs."

"Dear Hayes, I have given the Egyptian government 20,000 pounds for that piece of stone, and I mean to have it. And there will be additional costs of removing the obelisk, transporting it to Alexandria, and from there to England," I said, mildly irritated at my countrymen. "How much better it will be in England where it will be safe and secure. I have heard that the usual fate of such objects is to be cut up; their inscriptions sold to tourists. Is that not true?"

"Yes, unfortunately so," replied Hayes. "The entire ceiling of the temple of Dendera was cut out and shipped to Paris. It's such a pity. Perhaps you are correct, Lord Caerleon, to remove it. Come along and we'll take you to your obelisk." Descending the staircase, we went around the great temple of Isis, through the ruins and fallen rubble, until we came upon our prize, lying on one of its four sides, covered with sand. Only the pyramidion tip of red granite poked out of the rubble. At one time it must have stood upright, like its companion, the obelisk that William John Bankes removed in 1822, and which now stands in his garden at Kingston Lacy at Dorset.

Our stone must be of the same size: twenty-two feet in length and weighing six tons. Walking down the length of the fallen monolith I winced, for the task of loading the thing seemed at the moment more formidable than I had imagined. But it was mine, and I was going to take it back to Caerleon Castle at all costs. "Well, Alex, there it is, all six tons of it."

"It's bigger than I thought it would be."

"A midget in comparison to the giant the French hauled away from Luxor last year. Arundale told us to get a work crew from a local village. He also said that he had buttered up the local bigwig, the skeikh, "We'll take Ol' Joe along to translate, and before long we'll have the thing loaded and be on our way back to Alexandria."

"I'll have to see it to believe that we can," Alex said, grinning.

There was much to do for the next several days, as we prepared ourselves for the short trip to the nearby island of El Hasa where we would confer with the sheikh about manpower. It was also pleasant to have a few days to rest while Ol' Joe cleaned the boat and did the laundry, and it gave Alex and myself a chance to explore the island, which, as Hayes and his party were absorbed in mapping the temples, we had to ourselves.

We spent a morning studying the engraved inscriptions which covered the walls of some of the temples. Since our hieroglyphic lessons had not progressed very far, we wondered what they said. Soon the afternoon heat was upon us, and we prepared to return to the boat, deciding to take the cooler pathway beside the river. Feeling spirited, Alex broke into a run and I was hard pressed to keep up with him. He finally tired, and sat down beneath a clump of palms and reeds. The little bay was very lovely: a growth of blue and white lotus sprouted from the water. The drifting clouds were reflected in the glassy Nile. Alex took off his boots and socks, rubbing his feet, and I sat down beside him. He seemed to have grown older, more lean and rugged looking. The sun had lightened his hair several shades and tanned his face to a golden glow. He had not had his hair cut since we arrived, and long curls hung down around his face and neck in bright tawny strands. His grey eyes were darker, hidden beneath long lashes. The dappled light caught the straight nose, the dimpled mouth, and the angular jawline. How much he had come to resemble the face on the coin, a godlike Alexandros, fit to conquer the world.

He stood up, and smiling, asked if I wanted to take a swim. Doffing his shirt and trousers he ran to the warm water, diving into the lotus blossoms and a moment later shooting out of the water like some river god, a triton, a son of Poseidon. Covered with dark green leaves and blue and white lotus blossoms, his wet hair and chest gleamed in the sun, what a glorious blend of golden skin and muscularity. Gleefully, he dived in again and again, till, finally I took off my clothes and jumped in also, making a rather big splash.

After we had played for a while, pretending to be dolphins, Alex ran out of the water, wiping the droplets and the blossoms away and stretched out to dry in the warm sun. Lying down beside him, I propped myself up on one elbow and I looked at him. His eyes were closed, and he was breathing heavily because of his exertions. He took my hand in his. "It is good between us, Edward?"

"Yes, Alex it is good."

"I love you." He gave my hand a tight squeeze.

"I love you," I said, squeezing back. "You're so beautiful."

"You're beautiful too, Edward."

"I want to make love to you," I managed to get out. "The very sight of you inflames my soul . . . feel my heart; it's pounding."

"Yes, it's pounding, I can feel it. I . . . have never made love to a man. I . . . I've never made love to anyone. I want to. Oh, Edward, your body is so warm . . . I . . ."

"Let it happen. It is good for a man to make love with a man. Relax, let it happen. I love you so." My hand lightly caressed his chest, my fingers touching his nipples, and I saw he was aroused, his manhood lying stiff against his belly in a cluster of golden hair. Our love would be fulfilled at last. Suddenly, he opened his eyes, blushed, and sitting up saw that I was hard. At the sight of me he turned away, jumped up, and put on his trousers. Looking down he brushed the hair from his eyes, which filled with tears.

"I want to . . . but I'm afraid. I've never. Oh, I do love you so. Forgive me." Grabbing his shirt he ran down the beach. I sat for a long while feeling forlorn and miserable. I had acted unforgivably in forcing myself on him. In deep despair I dressed and returned slowly to the boat. Only loneliness awaited me there. Because of my impulsiveness I had ruined my only chance for a life shared with the one person I loved before all others, the one person I had loved and lost.

For the next several days Alex seemed distant, barely able to speak and somewhere far away in his thoughts. I knew I had lost him and felt confirmed in this belief when he asked to stay onboard while Ol' Joe and I set out in a small *felucca* for the island of El Hasa.

El Hasa was covered with neat, whitewashed, mudbrick houses; the largest belonged to the local sheikh, a certain Ahmed el Gebel, or,

as Ol' Joe translated, Ahmed the Mountain. When we were led into
his throneroom, I could understand why. Cushioned against a great
pile of pillows, smoking a hooka, surrounded by his officials, Ahmed
el Gebel looked at us with sharp black eyes. His enormous form was
dressed in a gown of silk. This ebony Nubian was the biggest man I
had ever seen, his body a mass of blubbery fat that even his loose
robe could not hide. With chubby fingers he raised a pipe to his
broad pink lips and flashed a wide smile, showing a mouthful of
glistening teeth. Next, he glanced over to his vizier, who first explained our presence, and they turned to Ol' Joe, who translated:
"Ahmed would be glad to provide men to remove the stone and to
provide a boat on which to load it, but he had understood the French
had prior claims." I produced the *firman* and the other documents to
prove my claim, mentioning as I did so, Arundale. The name seemed
to catch the Nubian's attention. He remembered the dealer; he was a
good man, but, unfortunately, his baksheesh had not been enough to
cover the removal of the stone. More would be needed to hire the
men, build the boat, and lift the stone. As it turned out we were to
spend the morning haggling over the price, but, finally, it was agreed
upon. During the negotiations we learned that approval had already
been given to the French consul in Asswan.

I told the sheikh that the French had relinquished all claims, and
my *firman*, signed by the Pasha, gave me complete rights. Ahmed el
Gebel studied the documents and finally agreed to my claims. Hand-
ing over the pound notes and thinking the affair was finished, Ol' Joe
and I returned to the *Star* to wait for the crew which was to be sent
to Philae in a week's time.

Alex seemed glad to see us return, and I told him about our
negotiations at El Hasa. He said he spent the day with Hayes, his
wife, and the two younger artists and showed me the sketches and
watercolors he had done in their presence. They had helped him with
his work; as a result a marked improvement was noticeable, and I
said as much. He was delighted by my good words, but protested
that his drawings were not as good as those executed by his profes-
sional companions. Hayes had invited us over to his *dahabiyeh* that
evening for supper.

It was pleasant to be with English people again, after having endured the slow business of hearing words translated back and forth in the inscrutable Oriental court of Ahmed el Gebel. Hayes and his charming wife, Pamela, were delightful hosts. Her slender figure wrapped in a long, homey apron, Mrs. Hayes said that she had cooked the meal herself. Indeed, her roast lamb was delicious. After supper, brandy, and cigars, we examined the pencil drawings and watercolors of Philae. They were marvelously accurate records. Hayes said he planned to publish them on his return to England, but he could not have done anything without the help of Mister Carter and Mister Osgood, who stood smiling at his gracious words. Carter then said that young Alex had much talent and he had been glad to help him. Carter was a good-looking man of about twenty-five, with bright blue eyes and long chestnut colored hair that clustered around his fine head. He and Alex seemed to have hit it off nicely as, together, they studied the drawings.

"First set foot in Egypt in 1824," Hayes said, "and have been here every season since, gathering data, making records. Things are changing so fast. The Egyptians don't care and someone must . . ."

"I hope you don't blame me for taking the obelisk," I remarked. "Perhaps it's wrong . . ."

"No, no, don't blame yourself. Maybe it is better to have it in England; there it can be studied and preserved. Many cannot afford the trip to see the marvels of Egypt, and as long as the Pasha is generous, why not? Who is to say what is right or wrong?"

"A ranking official in Cairo told me that there is a plan to build a museum to house the antiques, and the Pasha has stopped issuing *firmans* to anyone who asks for one."

"Perhaps there's hope at last. I see a new age dawning for Egyptology: an era of serious study and concentration. We simply do not know very much about these ancient peoples—how they lived, what they thought, or the way they administered their society. The Nile valley must have been inhabited for thousands of years, and the records are all here waiting to be studied. The days of mindless treasure-hunting are fast coming to a close, Lord Caerleon."

"Oh, how my husband loves to pontificate. You would think that he had discovered ancient Egypt all by himself." Pamela smiled, holding her husand's hand.

"Your husband's interests must make it rather difficult for you. Here you are so far from home."

"It's not been easy with the heat, the flys, and the horrid living conditions. Heaven knows, when I met him in Linplum, that's in Northumberland, I had no idea he would drag me out here, but we get along quite nicely. Once in a while I have to pull his ear to get him away from the "camera lucida" and to eat something, but it's been worth it."

"Alex has the makings of a fine artist. He's showed me the drawings he made on the trip, and they are very good." Carter turned to my young friend. "Do you want to be an artist, Alex?" he asked.

"I'm just a beginner, a dilettante."

"You should study in Paris; the French have a flair for art. The paintings of Ingres and David are the most brilliant done in our time. Both belong to the neo-Classical school, meaning that their paintings are inspired by the antique world of the Greeks and the Romans. There is something of the Greek about Alex's head, don't you think, Lord Caerleon?"

"Yes. We first met while viewing the Elgin marbles, and I thought at the time how much he resembled the carvings."

"Would you permit me to make a drawing of you, Alex?"

"Yes, of course, if it is all right with Edward."

"We would be very honored, Carter."

"The Elgin marbles," Alex mused aloud. "Our first meeting over two years ago. Little did I know the circumstances that would bring us together. Remember, Edward, how I bumped into you and father introduced us? Here we are thousands of miles from the Elgin marbles and together. That was a happy moment for both of us, eh, Edward?"

"I . . . hope it was."

"It was, and I'm beginning to realize how happy it was." Alex's smile was dazzling. He seemed friendly again and I was pleased.

"I think you two get along very well." Carter gave me a sharp look and then glanced at Alex. "Very well, indeed."

"Yes, Carter, we do."

Carter looked over to the others who were chatting with Pamela and sipping coffee. Alex had opened another portfolio and was going through the drawings inside it. Carter asked if I would like more brandy, and we walked over to a side-table. Holding the decanter, he poured the amber liquid into my glass. "You know, Lord Caerleon, I envy you and Alex. A person gets lonely out here so far from home . . . you know. One reaches out in friendship to another person, a person you admire . . . to be friends with . . . only to find that person does not feel the same about you, if you know what I mean."

"Yes, Carter, I think I do. Friendships have boundaries beyond which the other person is unwilling to go, and it is sometimes best . . . to stay inside those limits. Half a loaf is better than none, they say."

"I thought you and Alex. . . ."

"No, we've those boundaries, and I've settled for half a loaf."

"Alex is so handsome, it must be easy to be his friend."

"His friendship is very dear to me . . ."

"One has desires . . ."

"Desires that go beyond friendship?"

"Yes. A person could want that, couldn't he?"

"Yes, he could. Sometimes it is best to leave well enough alone."

"What if one cannot?"

"I do not know, Carter. I've learned to live with the situation."

"It is difficult to live within such bounds, Lord Caerleon. At night one's heart is aching . . . being so close on a boat . . . a few steps might be as faraway as the other side of the moon."

"Does this person know the way you feel?" I asked.

"Yes, I've told the person . . . poured out my heart for nothing."

"I'm sorry, Carter, I wish I knew something I could tell you . . . you see . . . Alex and I are only friends and nothing more. I too have reached out with an aching heart . . ."

"I say, Lord Caerleon, when are the men coming to load your prized obelisk?" Hayes broke in. "If you had a hundred men, you could lift the thing like a feather."

"Don't worry, Carter," I said in a low voice. "Sometimes things work themselves out for the best." Then, speaking more loudly I responded to Hayes' comment. "Oh, that pompous Nubian said in about a week or so. I don't think anyone hurries down here, at least when you are as fat as Admed el Gebel."

"He's a legend around here. It's said that it takes as many men to hoist him into bed as it takes to hoist your obelisk. Maybe more." Hayes laughed.

"Well, you may be right. But I see the hour is getting on. Ready Alex?"

"Yes, Edward."

"Perhaps you can sit for Mister Carter tomorrow. All right, Carter?"

"Yes, I'd like to sketch Alex; something besides the old temples."

"You are all invited over to the *Star*. Ol' Joe is a fair cook, though he has not your skill, Mrs. Hayes." Having said our farewells Alex and I walked down the gangplank. It had been a pleasant evening, and we talked of it loudly, climbing the embankment, until we came to the temple courtyard, where we stopped. A full moon, a luminous ball of silver, hung a little over the horizon, bathing the temples in soft pearly light. The pylon towered into the night sky; the *colonnades* etched themselves against the darkness. The sandstone, catching the moonlight, sparkled like a field of diamonds. Was there a sound of chanting priests coming from the holy sanctuary, or was it only the wind whispering through the palms? Was the sacred barque bearing the image of the goddess about to be carried out, born on the shoulders of her priests, or was it only the night birds? We were intruders, strangers from a different age, alien observers to the ancient mysteries that defied modern attempts at unravelment. Alex took my hand as our footsteps echoed around the ancient temples.

Crossing the deck of the *Star*, we were careful not to wake the crew when we went to our cabin. Bright moonlight streamed in through the windows. After we had undressed, we lay down in our beds. I could hear Alex breathing, tossing, waiting for sleep. Moments later, dozing off, I heard my name. Alex stood beside my bunk. "It's such a beautiful night, let's take the bedding up on deck and sleep there." Snatching up the bedding, we left the cabin and climbed the stairs. We placed the bedding on the open deck beneath the stars and moon and crawled under our covers. "What were you and Mister Carter talking about?"

"Nothing, really. I think he was a little lonely and wanted somebody to whom he could talk. He liked your drawings very much."

"I can't wait to see what my portrait will look like."

"I'm sure he'll do a good job." I lay, my arms folded behind my head, staring up into the night sky. Carter. It was strange that he would reveal his innermost thoughts to me. Though his language was guarded, it was plain that he wanted his young friend the way I wanted Alex. Perhaps he thought Alex and I were lovers . . the other side of the moon, how aptly he had put it. So near and yet so far. Had he fallen in love with the charming Mister Osgood only to have his advances rejected?

"Edward . . . Edward. I'm sorry about the other day at the beach; it was my fault. I should have been more sensitive, had more feeling."

"Don't worry about it. I did the wrong thing; that's all."

"No, it was my fault. Please forgive me. Take my hand . . . please."

I reached out, taking his hand into mine. "It's over, I know. Are we still friends?"

"Oh, yes, Edward. I wasn't thinking about . . . deep in my heart I knew about . . . love, but the feelings, the emotions were not what I expected or knew anything about. It has no reason, no logic, only you know that you cannot face another day without the person you love. I didn't know how to handle the emotion. When did you first love me?"

"When you were attacked in Alexandria. My heart bled; you were so weak and in such pain. I longed to take you in my arms; my feelings were laid bare, stripped of logic and reason once I saw your torment. I knew then that I could not live without you."

"I felt it just that night in Memphis. It was all so new to me; I could not fully acknowledge even to myself that I loved you. Now, here, holding hands in the moonlight, it is as though we have always been in love. Perhaps, defying logic and reason, the souls of Alexandros and Hephaistios are reunited in love on this ancient river."

"It's possible. On a night like this anything is possible."

"Oh, Edward, love me. I've been yours throughout all of time, eternity upon eternity, eon upon eon. Our love is immortal."

"Oh, beloved Alex, I want you so much." Alex leaned over and our lips touched. Throwing off the covers, we came together in a tight, fierce embrace, almost frantic in its passion. Our arms held each other, our naked bodies quivered in expectance of our first embrace, our first kiss. It was as if we were drawn into the iridescent, shimmering silver moonlight itself, while a soft wind whispered unknown love songs through the palms of Philae.

Our bodies became absorbed into the eternal cosmos, as swirling in a starry firmament of consumed emotion, we crossed the barrier of time. We had become moonlight, starlight, sparkling dust – dissolved into the radiant mist, that was set against the stygian blackness of the night sky. The tiny boat becoming a barque of the ancient gods ascending to the sky; the Nile, a star-spangled Milky Way, as we sailed with unknown winds toward some unknown starport where we would meet our unknown destiny.

Fragile and tentative, wanting to give pleasure but uncertain how to in this first embrace of love, Alex explored me with tender fingers. I knew in my heart of hearts that my feelings must rise to a splendid intensity, that this must be a moment above all others. Alex would know how much I loved him by my passion that, surging deep within my soul, would now be expressed by a touch, a kiss, and an embrace. Our voyage would begin on our imaginary barque. We would cast off the restricting lines, set sail into the moon-mists, and ride the currents of love.

Dawn. Alex had fallen asleep in my arms. In the morning light dew drops sparkled on the deck; each held a rainbow caught from the golden reflections of his body. Careful not to wake him I laid him back, lightly brushing the dew drops away from the fine hairs of his chest and stomach. How sweet had been the moment of love; our bodies tense, strong, each against the other, our fingertips alive to every sense of touch, our minds intent only on giving and receiving pleasure.

Cast adrift in our moon-barque, we were brushed by the stars. Stiff, erect, our manhood surged with power, sailing on into the cosmic infinity of overwhelming desire, charged with burning passion that sought relief. The voyage was a tempestuous storm of ecstasy. My lips caught the fine hairs, now damp with sweat, touched the carved muscles, nibbled playfully until they found the cluster of hairs around his rearing manhood. Alex had groaned softly as I plunged fully down, my lips caressing his throbbing shaft. His body tensed, arched up into the moonlight, as he shot his pulsing fluid into my eager mouth. It was an infinite moment of perfect love, the climax of joy, as I took his explosion of passion. Excited beyond anything my heart had ever known and unable to contain my tumultuous emotions I emptied myself. Afterwards we lay in each other's arms in our moon-barque, watching the distant light of the many stars.

Was there ever such a night? Our passions seemed boundless as we embraced again and again. Alex grew more passionate each time his lips sought my manhood. Only as the golden dawn turned our silver barque into shining solar orange, did he finally drift into a peaceful sleep.

Lightly touching my love, I brushed the dew drops from his body. He woke, dreamily looking up at me; his fingertips caressed my nose, my lips, my hair, and falling on top of me he made love again. When we had finished we looked into each other's eyes. There were no words to express our elation, the joy and ecstasy we felt. We knew we had found each other. Our love was a love above all loves, timeless and eternal. There was no past, no future; the only time was now and we would share it together.

Little by little the templed isle of Philae came into focus. Nesting birds cried out from the verdant rushes and waving palms. There was the smell of coffee in the warm air. "Effendis, you were not in your cabin . . . ohoooo." Ol' Joe's head appeared up on the deck, instantly popping out of sight. "Effendi will want morning coffee?"

"Yes, we'll be down in a moment." I shouted out, giving Alex one last, very deep kiss. "It's time to get up sleepyhead." Gathering our bedclothes around us we went down the stairs. Ol 'Joe and his sons stared at us with knowing, smirking smiles. "Well, we certainly gave them something to talk about."

"Oh, don't concern yourself with them. I've heard some very

strange noises coming from around the fire very late at night. Now I know what they were doing." Alex laughed. We dressed and sat down for coffee. While we were breakfasting Carter ambled across the gangplank, his sketchbook under his arm, obviously prepared to do his portrait of Alex. He looked happy, whistling a merry tune, as he turned the pages, sharpening his pencils, while Alex got ready to pose. "You know, Lord Caerleon, what I said about the other side of the moon, so near yet so far? Osgood and I . . . well, he and I . . . it was such a beautiful night. I don't think I'll ever be lonely again."

"Neither will I, Carter, neither will I."

"Effendi, some men from El Hasa to see you." Ol' Joe announced, as several huge, burly Nubians crossed the gangplank. "They come to clear sand from the stone and to see what way is best to move it to river." Leaving Alex and Carter we crossed the gangplank, heading for the northern end of the island and the fallen obelisk of Ptolemy Euegenes II.

The sounds of picks and shovels broke the serene morning quiet, as the Nubians worked to clear the obelisk. By teatime the three sides lay bare. The other side remained hidden in the sand. From what we could see the red granite was smoothly polished; the glyphs, running the length of the needle, were carefully cut and neatly incised into the hard stone. What did they say? If this were the twin to the Bankes's stone in England — whose inscription had been deciphered — it was an authorization by Ptolemy Euergetes II and his two queens, each named Cleopatra, allowing priests of Isis freedom from taxation. It would seem that old Euergetes had been most generous with his priests.

I made a survey of the area, measuring the stone, and making tracings of the glyphs; it was important to make a complete record, so if the stone were to be lost, say, at sea — which could happen — there would be a record for scholars to read. Meanwhile, one of the Nubians made an estimate of how many men it would take to move it to the water. As we worked the stone seemed to get bigger and bigger, and the task of moving it seemed also to increase in difficulty. I wondered how in the world such a primitive people as the ancient

Egyptians, without iron or steel, could ever have transported something so massive as, for example, the thousand ton statue of Rameses II at Luxor. Faced with a lesser problem of moving the obelisk, I gained a new appreciation for those ancient people and their way with very hard and very heavy stone.

Grunting and groaning the sweaty Nubinas, their fine muscles covered with dust, finally announced to Ol' Joe, who translated their message, that fifty men could move it down to the river in one morning, and during the afternoon of the same day hoist it aboard the special barge they were building. The Nubians would make their report to Ahmed el Gebel and return in two days. Smiling broadly, they gained their *felucca* and set sail for their island.

Ol' Joe and I sauntered back to the *Star*, enjoying the early evening that came so softly to Philae. The days were warm, but not unbearably so. During our absence several other *dahabiyehs* had braved the cataracts and tied up around the island. I could smell cooking odors, and the sound of voices drifted through the clumps of palms. High overhead nightbirds and bats had emerged from their hiding places to feast on clouds of buzzing insects. Philae had become almost home; one could feel almost cosy in the presence of its ponderous temples. I was supremely happy in the peace surrounding me. Alex. The thought of him had never left my thoughts throughout the long day, and I was anxious to see him again.

The houseboat sat in a mist rising from the river. The four sons called out to us as we went aboard, holding up a Nile perch; another fish dinner seemed to be our destiny. At first Alex was nowhere in sight, but there he was inside our cabin looking at some sketches — presumably the ones Carter had made of him. At my entry he ran over, giving me a big hug. "Look, aren't they beautiful?" he said, holding up the sheets of paper.

"Yes, very fine."

"Golly, I didn't think I looked like that."

"They are beautiful, but not as beautiful as the real thing." I said, drawing him to me, our lips meeting in a long kiss.

"Oh, Edward. . . ."

"Do you still love me?"

"Yes, of course, you goose, though I think I've caught the eye of Mister Carter."

"Oh . . ."

"He is quite taken by me . . . wants me to pose in the nude."

"Oh."

"He just couldn't keep his hands off me."

"Ohoooo?"

"Oh, Edward, I was just fooling."

"I knew you were."

"I could not have eyes for anyone but you."

"You had better not."

"But, look, it's the first time I've had my portrait done."

"Yes, very fine . . . I see he got you to take your shirt off."

"Wellll. . . ."

"Hummmm. . . ." Carter was of the French school and his drawings resembled the few I had seen in the British Museum by Jacques Louis David and others of the neo-Classical school that had recently emerged in Paris. Carter's line was crisp and clean, his anatomy fully understood. In his hands Alex had taken on a very Greek look; his nose was straighter, his mouth fuller, his chin more rounded. In fact, the artist had made him look like an ancient Greek statue, rather cold and lifeless. "Yes, Carter is a very fine artist, really more of a draftsman."

"He did ask me to pose in the nude . . . you know, like the Greek statues of athletes, the wrestlers and the discus thrower, though they always have fig leaves covering that part. He said it was a shame that natural man could not stand free and naked."

"A silly custom, but propriety should be maintained, I guess. Certainly the ancients had no fig leaves. I suppose it would be all right for you to pose without clothes, but remember you belong to me."

"I'm your devoted slave. Oh, I nearly forgot. We're invited to a picnic. Mister Carter and Mister Osgood, or Lawrence Carter and Samuel Osgood want us to join them at the kiosk this evening, before dark. They say Pamela will furnish the meal."

"Tell them we'll be there. I would never turn down English cooking."

"Neither would I, and I already told them we'd be there." Alex grinned.

The sun was still warm when we ambled down the gangplank, heading toward Trajan's temple. The two young men waved to us, as we walked across the sandy courtyard of the Isis temple. They greeted us warmly. The two had an easy familiarity; soon it was just Edward, Alex, Lawrence, and Sam. "I thought we'd have a picnic at 'Pharaoh's Bed.' You'll be leaving soon, returning to Cairo and civilization. God knows when we'll see another Englishman. We'll be stuck here until spring," Lawrence said. He had draped his arm around Sam's shoulder. Lawrence was about twenty-five. He was tall and rather thin. His long chestnut hair fell down over his ears, framing a pleasant face with a willing smile and sparkling blue eyes. Sam was shorter, with reddish auburn hair, his ruddy complexion heavily sprinkled with freckles. I assumed him to be about Alex's age. Our friends' long stay on the island was beginning to show; their loose open shirts were almost threadbare, and their trousers were patched, no doubt, by Pamela's able hands.

"Here's where we'll have the picnic, away from prying eyes. We've carried some rugs inside and have lit a fire. It'll be fine." Sam gave Larry a little hug, and we followed the two men inside the temple.

The sky was darkening, and already, Trajan's roofless temple was turning from a tawny yellow to soft shades of purple and pink, as dusk settled down on Philae. While the lower part of the temple, except for the entrance, was screened by stone walls, fourteen beautifully carved floral columns supported the wall where the roof might have been in ancient times.

The two artists had set down carpets on the sandy earth in the center, placing on them rather chipped dishes and tarnished silver. Wonderful aromas rose from several wicker baskets. They had built a fire nearby and its flames flickered across the darkening stone walls. Alex and I sat down on a carpet, as Lawrence and Sam poured a cup of Egyptian beer out of a heavy clay pot into pottery cups. The thick "booza" was cool, the pot containing it having been hung in the Nile during the day. The beer was reputed to be quite potent. The floral columns were now silhouetted against a rosy sky, streaked with violet and mauve. Bats and night birds darted about quickly, seeking their evening meal from the insects that swarmed around the island.

Lawrence gave Sam a little kiss. The two held hands, sipping their beer. Larry must have noticed my sharp glance, as Alex and I had not yet touched. "Relax, Edward. Who's to notice? I think Hayes and Pamela know anyway. They don't seem to care. I think they're glad we found each other."

Except for a handshake or a friendly pat on the back, I had never openly shown affection for another man, at least in polite society. I took Alex's hand in mine and gave it a little squeeze. He grinned and squeezed back. "It's good to be in love and to have someone." I said.

"Yes, it's wonderful. Isn't it Sam? Say you love me." Lawrence's words were playful.

"Yes, I love you, Lawrence. I guess I've loved you since we joined the Hayes's expedition a year ago. I simply didn't realize it then."

"A year ago. It seems like a million years, God, we were innocent. But I'm glad we came. If it wasn't for Hayes and his efforts to preserve Egyptian relics, we might not have ever found each other," Lawrence said, looking fondly into Sam's eyes.

"I was happy to get the job. After graduation from the London Academy of Fine Arts I thought I would conquer the world. Tried to get an exhibition, but got turned down." Sam spoke bitterly.

"Should go to France like I did. England is no place for artists. Had a year at the Sorbonne and studied with Ingres. Your problem, dear Sam, is that the neo-classical style is out. People are tired of draped Romans and undraped Grecian girls, though it is a good way to get a little flesh and sex into a painting. It's archeology, not art. Ah, Paris. Perhaps we can go there when we return."

"I would like that, Lawrence. I've heard it's quite wild."

"I would say. Nearly starved and froze to death, but hell, it was worth it. The male models can be very accommodating on a cold night."

"I thought I was your first. I know you were mine."

"Afraid not, dear Samuel. I rather thought you were a virgin, but I took care of that, didn't I?"

"Yes," Sam blushed. "I was glad to lose it to you. Damn glad. I was lonely, very lonely and scared, I guess. When you first approached me I had no idea what you were talking about, but the other night when you took me into your arms, it was wonderful."

"It was wonderful for us, also. Edward and I . . . and everything. What a strange place to find love. Four lonely men on a faraway rocky island in the middle of nowhere," Alex said softly.

"Love is a powerful god, Alex. Even in a stilted and rigid society such as ours the god wins out, as he always does. Men will find men to love, as will women find women. It's natural," I said, before giving Alex a big kiss.

"So what will you two do when you return to England? It's going to be hard getting that obelisk back and expensive, dear Edward." Lawrence remarked.

"Go back to live at Caerleon. God, how people will talk. But to hell with their small minds. We'll find a way. Love conquers all, they say."

"Perhaps, we'll return, someday," Alex said excitedly. "I've got a crazy idea about searching for the source of the Nile. Now that would be something. The discoverer would be famous. Who knows what lies at the other end of the Nile?"

"You haven't told me about that idea, Alex."

"It comes into my head now and then, Edward. At least we could be alone without the world to bother us with its bigotry."

"Well, each of us will have to face difficult problems. Let's eat." Carter said, reaching for a basket.

Alex and I ate with relish, knowing this would be our last bit of English cooking for a long time. Pamela had prepared boiled chicken, roast lamb, baked Nile perch, and fresh bread. We washed down the entire meal with some local date wine. It was dark when we all finished. The stars hung in bright clusters, and the nearby fire dimly lit the ancient building that rose up around us. It was a languid and mellow time. Alex had stretched out, his tousled mop of tawny hair lay in my lap, as I leaned back, munching on a chicken bone. Lawrence and Sam looked up at the stars, occasionally kissing and hugging, running their hands down inside each other's open shirt. Alex looked into my eyes while I wiped my hands with a linen napkin. "I want us to remember this moment, Edward, and to think about it when we're old and gray."

"It is a precious time, beloved. A time to remember. I want to be with you always, but I'll not hold you, Alex. You're a young man with your entire life before you. You're alive and vital, and I'm afraid I'm a bit settled down at Caerleon. It's a dull place, as you know; however, I like it. It's home. When you come of age you'll be a very wealthy man and can do anything you want with your life. I'll not hold you, beloved. That would be wrong."

"I want to be with you always. I want what we've found here on Philae to last forever."

"I want that too, sweet Alex. More than anything. But there'll be problems, people will whisper about us. There will be problems that will, perhaps . . . destroy our love. You don't know but I've seen it happen. Two men living together. The world doesn't think kindly about our kind of love, Alex. I've considered it and I know our life won't be easy."

"Our love will be tested. We must be strong, Edward, and preserve what we have against all odds. We will endure, because our love is eternal and will not be destroyed by others." Alex reached up and took my hand.

"Brave words, Alex." Lawrence rose up on his elbows, looking over at us. "Edward speaks the truth. You're wealthy aristocrats, members of the ruling class. Scandal could ruin your lives. Nobody cares what artists do; we're all supposed to be a little crazy anyway. You have talent, Alex; go to Paris with Edward, rent a garret, and love and live as you want. Study art. You won't make much money, unless you get an important commission, preferably a royal commission, and then you're set for life. But I don't suppose you two have to worry about money. . . ."

"No, we don't. I've an idea. Come to Caerleon after you've returned to England, and we'll give you a commission to do our portraits. I can guarantee that they will find a place in the national gallery. That should set you up. And it'll be good to see you again."

"Edward, what a marvelous idea! We'll turn Caerleon Castle into an artist's colony, and then everyone will most certainly talk." Alex giggled, a little tipsy from the beer.

"Is that a promise, Edward? Can I bring Sam?"

"It is a promise, and by all means bring your lover. We'll have a great old time. Caerleon is a rather picturesque place, near to the sea . . ." I stopped, remembering another time and place. "I think you'll like it."

"Yes, I would like it very much. Would you like to go to Caerleon, dear Sam?" Lawrence asked. "We could live off of the nobility for a while."

"I'll go anywhere you want me to go, Lawrence." Sam spoke softly, giving his lover a kiss.

"You'll find it to be a generous commission, Lawrence . . . Sam. Now if we can get that damn obelisk loaded up, it should be back in England by the time you get there."

"Damn nice of you, Edward. You're right in taking the stone. The locals don't care anything about it."

"I'll be sorry to leave, dear Edward," Alex said, with a hint of nostalgia already in his voice. "Philae is truly the land of love. Perhaps the goddess brought us all together."

"Yes," I took up Alex's thought. "In this place, though it is abandoned and in ruin, the ancient gods of Egypt still have power. Why not? I think I'd rather fall on my knees to the ancient gods than worship in Westminster Abbey. I've always thought myself a pagan."

"What a romantic idea," Carter exclaimed. "Let's all be pagans and call on the ancient gods to bless us. I don't think we'll get such a blessing from the clergy at the abbey. Who wants to call on the gods? Why not you, Edward? You're the oldest. . . ."

"Don't remind me. All right, I will. Stand up. We can't greet the gods looking like a group of drunken fops." I was amused, watching the four of us, outcast lovers of men, wobble to our feet to greet some vanished deity. The flickering fire cast strange shadows on the carved walls of Trajan's empty temple. From their great height the chiseled gods of old Egypt looked down at us.

"Say something, Edward," Alex implored, smiling.

"I'm thinking. Raise your hands and try to look serious. We call upon you, gods of Egypt, to bless our love and to look after us. Let us never forget this wonderful time and place—this holy island where Alex and I, and Lawrence and Samuel found love. Bless us with the strength and courage to face the future and whatever it may bring. And if we should part let it be without harsh words. Above all, let us keep this sacred moment of true love in our hearts forever, lover and beloved." After the greeting we lowered our arms and clasped each other's hands to make a circle of friendship and love. While we stood thus in the center of that ancient temple, a full moon rose in the sky, and a soft fragrant breeze ruffled our loose clothing. It was a warm and magical moment as each of us felt the strong pressure of other hands, held onto for a precious instant. Had the gods of Egypt heard our prayer? They seemed to smile, as they looked down at us from the walls of Trajan's temple.

There appeared to be nothing more to say, so we broke the circle. Lawrence and Sam fell into each other's arms, clearly, they wanted to be alone to make love. Hand in hand, Alex and I wandered, back to our boat and did the same.

Two days later the Nubian crew arrived on the northern end of the island in a flotilla of graceful *feluccas*, bearing heavy ropes, hefty stakes of palmwood to be used as levers, and heavy palmlogs on which to roll the stone. Floating behind one *felucca* was the barge on which the stone would be loaded. The burly Nubians, all tall and strong, some fifty of them, would pry the stone loose until the logs could be rolled underneath it. Apparently, methods of moving large stone had not improved much since the days of the ancients. With men on either side of the stone, the stakes were driven into the soft sand; at first the stone did not move. The men began to chant: "Bismi llaahi r-rahmaani r-rahiim." Ol' Joe translated, "In the name of Allah, the compassionate, the merciful." I wondered what worksong the ancients had used.

The six tons of granite were mired in the sand. Though the granite looked solid it might have unseen flaws which would cause it to crack and to break into pieces. It was a tense moment, but slowly, inch by inch, the fallen obelisk began to move upwards. The end of the tapered stone would have to be lifted enough so that the palmlog could be pushed beneath. Then ropes would have to be secured around the granite, so it could be pulled upon the logs and rolled to the quay of stones built out into the shallow water. By later afternoon the logs had been placed in position, and the stone was high and dry, poised to begin its journey to the water. An exhausted crew prepared the evening meal, boiled coffee, and bedded down on the beach. Shortly thereafter most of the Europeans on the island who had gathered around the temple of Augustus Caesar to watch the operations, also left for the night.

Early the next morning we all assembled to watch the final stage: rolling the stone down to the quay and loading it aboard the barge. Holding the heavy ropes that secured the stone, the crew lined up, waiting for the signal to begin. With a shout the men tightened the slack ropes until they were taut. Straining now, their black bodies running with sweat, the chanting Nubians pulled the stone along its bed of logs. As soon as it had rolled over the last one, it was brought forward and placed upon the pyramidion tip. Slowly, grumbling, the obelisk moved over the sand. By teatime it was ready to be rolled out onto the quay, a rough structure of rocks and pebbles, built alongside the barge. This would serve as a bracing so the stone could be dragged onboard.

Standing waist deep in the now muddy Nile the Nubian crew tugged and pulled: ponderous, rumbling, the stone inched its way onto the quay. There was a loud cheer from the gathered crowd; the obelisk was ready to be moved onto the barge. The loosely piled rocks groaned beneath the six tons; little by little the quay began to fall apart as though made of sand. We watched helplessly as the proud obelisk of Ptolemy Euergetes II sank into the muddy waters, only the pyramidal tip remaining in sight. With the dust of the ages washed away, the highly polished red granite caught the sunlight, glinting like polished steel.

A loud groan was heard as it sank, but another sound accompanied its unfortunate end, a loud popping noise as if guns were being fired. There, under full sail, making for Philae, was a tall masted *felucca*. Standing on its bow a neatly dressed European waved a pistol, while an armed crew shot into the air, causing little puffs of smoke to rise above the boat. It was only a matter of minutes before the bow of the *felucca* ground into the soft sand, and the European jumped out. He was small and sported a waxed goatee. It was the Frenchman. "Ah, Monsieur Caerleon, you may remember me, Dominique Jomard, the French consul-general. I have come to claim my obelisk." Looking around at the workmen, the ropes, the poles, the logs, and the rest of the Europeans, he waved his gun. "Where is it? What have you done with my obelisk?" Silently, I pointed to the water and to the tip of granite, now turned to a rosy, dusky red; Jomard raised his hand, no doubt shocked. "Mon Deux," he said; rushing to the gleaming pyramidion, he embraced the wet granite. "You have sunk my obelisk!"

"My obelisk, Monsieur Jomard! That is, it *was* my obelisk."

8.

What ancient sculptor, having so laborously carved and polished his creation could have foreseen such a bizarre moment? Dominque Jomard, standing boot high in the muddy waters, with an armed, threatening crew at his back, was claiming the ownership of a nearly submerged stone. And I, fifth earl of Caerleon, was also claiming the same object, having paid out a great sum for it. Who would win? I had no idea.

I drew myself up, facing the challenge. "May I remind the French consul-general that I have permission to remove the stone. Where, may I ask, is your *firman?*"

"Ah, Monsieur, my *firman* exists in the barrels of these rifles."

"What if I were to tell the pasha of your actions?"

"He couldn't care less about this or any other non-Moslem object."

"I take it you mean to remove the stone by force."

"If necessary."

"There seems no limit to your greed."

"It is not a question of greed, but of aesthetics."

"How so?"

"It will be sent to my gardens at Lyon; a very pretty addition to the other treasures I've accumulated here."

"It would look better in my gardens at Caerleon Castle."

"Enough of this useless verbiage. Ask your crew to return home; then my men can dredge up the stone, which your men have so carelessly lost, if you please, Monsieur Caerleon."

"Ol' Joe, tell the crew to go to the stone and stand around it." Reis

Hassam shouted out the orders, and the Nubians waded in, standing defiantly in the water. Jomard found himself staring into the faces of fifty huge Nubians. "Would you fire on these men?" I asked, scornfully. "Even the kindest of the Egyptians would have little mercy on the foreign white-devil who ordered them killed." Jomard turned beet red and stomped back to his boat. We had reached a stand off.

From a distance the sound of gunshots could be heard coming from a second *felucca* making for the island, as it drew near we could see that it was brightly painted, festooned with flags, and there, sitting on a pile of cushions, smoking his hooka, was the enormous pile that constituted Ahmed el Gebel, the sheikh of El Hasa. The boat bumped onto shore, the crew threw over a heavy gangplank, and the silk-robed, bejeweled, and feathered sheikh was lifted up on a carrying platform by his slaves. Like some monstrous Oriental potentate he was carried ashore and set down. His servants put up a silk tent, rather like a papal baldachin, for shade, and two servants began to fan him with ivory-handled, ostrich-plumed fans. Would a pharaoh have arrived so grandly, so ostentatiously? I think not.

Calling a translator to his side, Ahmed el Gebel spoke, "What is this? Two men of mature years fighting over an old stone for which there is no use except if it is cut up and used for doorsteps. Upon my missing testicles, I've never seen anything so silly."

"What did he say?" Ol' Joe replied that the sheikh said he was a eunuch and that we were silly men. "Remind the unfortunate man that I've a *firman* signed by the pasha and that I've given much baksheesh for his help with the silly stone, and that, moreover, the French have no claim. This is clearly a case of highhanded piracy." My temper was rising, and I could feel the blood pounding in my head. If I had not been so involved, this might have been an amusing situation. At least it was to the Europeans who had gathered to see the obelisk lifted on the barge, or to the workers who stood guard around my stone, to the sailors who made ready to fire, and the natives, who sat in their boats, watching the commotion. I, however, was not amused. "I have first claim, and I mean to have my prize, or else!"

"Or else . . . what, Monsieur Caerleon?"

"Or else there will be hell to pay."

"Ha!" Jomard sneered, making an obscene gesture.

"Alex, run back to the boat and get the *firman*. Make haste." Doing as I bade, Alex soon returned with the impressive-looking document. I held it up, asking Ol' Joe to translate and to shout out my words. "Here in my hand . . . is the *firman* signed by the pasha . . . giving me permission . . . to remove the stone . . . in question. Are there any who would doubt the signature? Here is the seal of the government of Egypt. I ask the French consul-general to produce his *firman* . . . signed by the pasha of Egypt." Sentence by sentence Ol' Joe translated what I said. The Egyptians muttered, clustering around the sheikh, who asked to examine it more closely. After pressing it to his nose, he returned the *firman*.

"I can swear the signature is true," he said reluctantly. "It is the same that was on the order that lost me my most prized possessions years ago when I guarded the women of his harem. Poor creatures who were only too willing to slip me a few coins to find a well-endowed palace guard to make them happy when the pasha was otherwise detained. Ha, how I outsmarted him, and through the years I amassed a fortune, one large enough to enable me to buy my freedom and my island. Yes, the Englishman's claim to the worthless stone is true and if he were to report to the pasha that . . . your watch, Englishman, can I see it?"

My watch. It had been my father's and a family heirloom that I always kept chained on a golden fob. I would hate to give it up but if that were the price . . . "It keeps very good time."

"I have always wanted a fine English watch. How does it run?" I went over, showing it to him, explaining how to wind and set it. Placing it to his ear he listened to the ticking, and smiling, tucked it into this robe. "The matter is settled. The useless stone will be loaded aboard the barge, floated through the cataracts, all under my direction . . . if there are any who stand in my way . . ." Giving a signal to his men, he sat back. In an impressive volley of noise and smoke, his men emptied their guns into the air. Then they lowered them pointing their barrels in the direction of the Frenchman. Jomard sputtered in anger, virtually dribbling into his finely waxed goatee, and gave instructions to his captain. Immediately, the sail was raised and the boat pushed away from shore. Seeing that I had won the battle, the Europeans cheered. The sheikh of El Hasa was lifted up, his slaves groaning beneath the terrible weight of the carrying-chair, and lifted back aboard his vessel. The setting sun caught the clouds in a dazzling array of red, purple, and pink, the light glinting off my obelisk. Tomorrow it would be raised and floated aboard the barge.

"Bismi llaahi r-rahmaani r-rahiim." The melodic chant sounded loudly and clearly the next morning, as the men prepared to raise the sunken obelisk. Stripped to the waist, the Nubians waded into the placid blue waters, which soon turned into a muddy, frothy mess, as they worked their levers and ropes. In forty-eight hours the stone again stood high and dry. The following day it would be loaded aboard the barge, a day that I looked forward to with some apprehension.

Four stout palmlogs bore the weight of the stone, as it was pushed and pulled from the bank to the barge. A padding of grass and canvas had been laid down to protect the fragile granite from chipping when the obelisk was finally moved onto the barge. There was a loud cheer as the six tons settled onto the deck of the forty-foot *felucca*, which creaked and groaned while the stone settled down into its protective bed. It was a tense moment as the Nubians secured it to the barge, but the boat seemed strong enough to hold the additional weight. My captive prize, now bound by stout ropes, lay gleaming in the afternoon sun. As Alex and I walked the length of it, I wondered aloud if it had been worth the trouble. Alex smiled and patted my back.

Hayes and Pamela, who were always nearby with gallons of tea and coffee, warmly shook our hands as the hour of our departure drew near. As usual their clothes were sandy and dusty. But it didn't matter; the two had won our admiration for braving this wild and desolate place to record its antiquities. Meanwhile, Lawrence and Sam stood close together on the beach. When the time came to shake their hands, they said they would journey to Caerleon as soon as they reached England. In my heart I was glad the two had found each other, as Alex and I had. Lawrence gave Alex a large portfolio of drawings that he had done of the lad, with or without clothes. While most of the drawings were neo-classical in style, some were not so tightly rendered. Perhaps Lawrence was searching for a new technique.

We had roped the barge to the stern, and while Alex and I watched from the deck above the cabin, Ol' Joe and his boys cast off all lines, pushing the *Star* out into the slow northerly-moving current, using stout poles. Brown hands and arms hoisted the patched lateen sail. It caught the wind, and before long the holy island had faded from sight. I took Alex's hand as we watched. Philae would remain in our memory forever as a place where, our bodies naked in the moonlight and pressed together in burning passion, we had found love one wonderful night. We were lovers now. I had wanted Alex's love with all my soul and heart, but I had wanted him to love me as I loved him. Now as the sacred temples disappeared below the horizon, and the Nile waters swirled around the *dahabiyeh*, and the sail bellowed out, I knew in my heart of hearts that he did love me as much as I loved him. We had discovered love, true love. Throughout all of time we would be lovers.

It was to be an arduous journey upriver to Cairo. The obelisk seemed to have developed a mind of its own, it was as though it hated to leave its native environs. The towing-ropes broke several times, sending us on a mad dash to retrieve the barge before it drifted to shore. Ol' Joe and his sons and Alex and I became almost a part of the Nile as we repeatedly plunged into the muddy and chaotic waters, trying to reach and hold onto the broken lines. Due to the heavy weight and the low draft of the barge, it got stuck more than once on a sandbar and only after several days could we pry it out of the muck. Natives would gather on the shore giggling and laughing as they saw the seven of us tugging, pulling, pushing, and lifting the damn barge.

There was little time for ceremoney or for observing social customs while we retraced our journey upstream. The strong current moved us along, as the Nile flowed from its unknown sources to the sea. While the trip was trying for all of us, it was, nevertheless, a happy time. At night, after dinner and a few cups of beer, Alex and I would take our bedding up to the deck and make love. Afterwards we smelled the Nile waters, felt rather scuffy with our faces unshaven, and had weary bodies. But it was a good fatigue.

The 600 mile trip from Philae to Cairo was to take over a month. We changed physically during that time, becoming leaner, our bodies hardened beneath the blazing sun, our soft English muscles strengthened in the cold water, as we wrestled with ropes, poles, and gleaming granite. Because of our sunburnt bodies, both of us might have passed for Egyptians. We had cut the legs off our trousers, and only our middles were still English pink, oddly contrasting with the rest of our brown selves. Being naturally dark I might have really been mistaken for a native; Alex, however still looked a bit English. While his fair skin had turned the color of mahogany, the sun and water had bleached his hair to a silver white. His hair had grown very long and he now boasted a beard. I would watch him as he climbed into the rigging to look out for the treacherous sandbars, the sun catching his lean, muscled body, the wind blowing through his hair. Something magnificent was taking place. Alex was no longer a boy, he had become a man, a man whom I loved and who loved me in return.

It was late April before the angled shapes of the three great Pyramids appeared over the far horizon, signalling that we were back in civilization. We changed into our wrinkled trousers and shirts, combed our long hair and beards, and after a kiss saluting our success, we went on deck. Alex raised the union jack and it whipped proudly in the stiff breeze. There was a feeling of exhausted exhilaration as the *Star* slowly moved through the flotillas of *dahabiyehs* and *feluccas*, their sails gracefully swooping over the reflective water like birds in flight. Brown hands firmly held around the steering rudders, Ol' Joe and his sons prepared to make a landing, as the domes and minarets of Cairo came into view.

It would take several hours before holding lines had secured the barge and the *Star*. Issuing forth a stream of invective Ol' Joe ordered the others to help move the barge in against the shore. When this task was accomplished and our houseboat moved alongside, the gangplank was laid down across the obelisk and the lines secured with heavy wooden stakes driven into the packed mud. The Egyptians gathered around to see our great prize, but discovering it was only an old stone of no value, they shook their heads, shrugged their shoulders, looked at us with doubtful eyes, and wandered off.

Alex and I had planned to spend several days resting and regaining our equilibrium after the arduous journey and before sailing onto Alexandria some 130 miles to the north. While tired and looking rather haggard, Alex had a new gleam in his eyes. As our trip to Philae had been completed, he realized that we could begin anew the quest for the Tomb of Alexander the Great. Hiring a carriage and leaving the *Star* in Ol' Joe's able hands, we went straight to British House to seek lodging and to pick up our mail. The clerk brought out several large bundles. Alex had turned nineteen in February, and he had received many cards from friends wishing him well, both from England and from his school. There were also in addition, a number of letters from Caerleon castle, some from my solicitor in London, stating my current account! I winced, for my fling in Egypt had been expensive. Along with the figures he had enclosed a note, saying that cousin Carlotta had begun proceedings in the courts to take custody of Alex. She would have a fight on her hands. . . . Near the bottom of the bundle there was a note from the Egyptian, Abad al-Jalil, asking that we stop by and see him, as he had important information for us.

Our reading was disturbed by the British counsel-general, Major E.P.H. Browning, whom we had first met at his reception. He now marched out of his office with a firm, military stride, giving us a firm, military shake. He looked at us rather oddly. In the two and one-half months since we had attended his glittering reception, we had changed remarkably. Our fair English complexions were burned brown, our hands calloused from hauling rope. We had both lost weight, and our clothes hung loosely, were rumpled, and were not,

I'm afraid, very neat. Also I had grown a beard too as shaving was such a chore. We might have looked like two river rats had we arrived in London and shown ourselves in polite society. But now, here in Cairo, we were seasoned travelers, men of the world, veterans of a long voyage, who had not yet quite adjusted to Major Browning and his neat, ordered world. Despite our appearance he invited us to stay at British House for our few days in Cairo, and gratefully, we agreed. Shortly thereafter a servant showed us to our rooms. He placed what little baggage we had brought on the carpeted floor and left.

"We've made it; we're back in Cairo," Alex joyously threw up his hands and grinned.

"Yes, at last. It's been rough and difficult. I wonder if getting that stone was worth the trouble," I said once again.

"Yes, it was something we accomplished together, just you and I."

"And our crew. But I know what you mean, dear Alex. Our first adventure . . . as lovers. Oh, Alex, I do love you so much." Taking Alex by the hand I drew him to me for a kiss. It was to be a light kiss, a kiss of shared joy, and we embraced as our lips touched. I felt the lean sinews of his warm body, now hard and muscular beneath his shirt. My hands pressed against his back, bringing his body close to mine. We stood for a moment locked in our embrace, our hands feeling, exploring, and touching; the kiss of joy had become a kiss of passion that swept over our tired bodies. I cupped Alex's face in my hands, looking at him with almost tearful eyes. "Oh, Alex. . . ." There were no words that I could find to express my perfect feeling of absolute happiness, as I looked deeply into his soft grey eyes and he looked into mine.

"It is good between us, beloved Edward. Do you think that two men have ever shared such a love as ours."

"Not in all of time has there been such a love," I replied firmly. Alex smiled, the gentle afternoon light catching his teeth, a dazzling white in contrast to his dark, tawny beard. His long hair clustered in heavy locks around his shoulders. The sun had bleached it and it was now silver, the silver of moonlight on restful waters. His face was dark, age gently touched his brow, as I ran my fingers over his forehead, perhaps wishing to erase those tiny lines. He had been a youth when I had fallen in love with him, but now he was becoming a man. He must have noticed some trace of fear in my glance, for he looked at me quizzically as if trying to read my thoughts. What would he be like as a grown man? Perhaps in time he would find others and look back as I had once done on the sweetness of first love, times shared, and bodies meshed in passionate embraces. No, I would not think of such a prospect. I would think of the present, not of the future.

Out of fear, love, and other confused emotions I pressed my lips to his, hoping to preserve this moment forever. While we did not speak I knew, sensed perhaps, that he may have had the same fears, for his touch was intense as his hands pressed into my back. It was as if we had mutually agreed to shut out our fears that the outside world might come between us to destroy what we had found at Philae.

The room vanished as if in a mist; the world and its cares had no meaning for us now as we stood, our bodies responding to the touch of one other and to the minute sensations that shook every nerve. We were consumed in the glowing flames that only love, deep love could quench. There was no time, no world, no one but ourselves, and the roaring sea of passion sweeping over us. It was a primordial and innocent sea that existed eons ago when our kind of love was pure and knew no taint of shame, when no harsh words of derision ground its fresh blossom under the hard heel of the hatred and the stupidity of the uncaring. We were alone in that ancient sea, two men, mindless now, our only goals to give and receive pleasure. As our muscles tensed we were aware of each subtle touch of the fingertips, of the pressure of our lips. Unaware of our surroundings, absorbed and flushed with desire, we shed our restricting clothing; shirts, trousers, and boots were thrown into a pile. In a flash we stood naked, reveling in the loving sight of each other. His manhood, excited and fully erect, jutted out of the soft cluster of still golden hairs around his loins. The hairs of his belly and chest were as silvery as that of his curls. I grinned, "Dear, dear Alex, you're as brown as a desert camel and very thin. Now that we're back in civilization you'll put the flesh back on with some good meals."

"You're very thin also, beloved Edward. The trip has been difficult, but I think we'll recover. You are very beautiful naked. I love you so much. . . ." Alex touched his manhood and came to me. Then, wrapping his arms around my shoulders, he touched his lips to mine. Again our embrace swept us into that primordial sea. All was salt and sweat as we playfully bit and nibbled each other. My lips caught the fine hairs of his chest; my tongue caressed the silver aureoles of his excited nipples. I could feel the blood pulsing beneath his brown skin as I knelt, taking his manhood in my mouth, sinking down upon it until my lips touched the golden hairs lying matted at its base. It was sweet and good, its strength filled my mouth, its hardness rode easily against my lips, my fingers caressed the full sacs, furry and rounded, shadowed between his muscular thighs.

He groaned softly as he lifted me up, leading me to the bed. Together we fell into its welcome softness, the first we had known in a long time. Alex lay on top of me, his fingers touching my lips and beard. With unexpected strength he pressed his lean, strong body against me. Our erections were hard as we pressed together even more closely. More deeply now we fell into the throbbing, pulsing, excited waves of that sea of passion. We were somewhere, a time outside of time, engulfed in the consuming, surging emotions that held us in a tight embrace. The moment was near.

Our bodies writhed with mindless, almost animal passion. Our senses were fully alive and vital. We were bathed in sweat, each fiber, each sinew, each nerve quivering, every muscle shaking with excitement. Our lips touched, briefly as we tossed about in the waves; our arms circled each other's loins. His hardness was near to my lips, and mine to his lips that in a moment plunged down, taking full the aroused manhood. Eagerly we sought to give pleasure, to share this moment of love, my lips riding against his shaft, his against mine. Our loins burned with savage desire, the sea had become a sea of flames, licking at us until we could not stand another second of its consuming fires. It was an explosion of fiery lust as we took one another, drinking full the pulsing flow of manhood. It was sweet as Alex emptied himself, groaning with ecstatic pleasure. The sea, our sea, had subsided, washing us ashore.

We lay for a long while in each other's arms as the afternoon drifted away. It was a supreme, golden moment; again and again we shared our love. Each time we made love our fingers and mouths became more aware, more sensitive. In our delicious stupor we had forgotten everything, but harsh reality soon came knocking at the door. I grabbed my pants and opened it. A beaming servant announced it would soon be time for the evening meal and that we should make ready. He said there was hot water for a bath and a shave. I turned to Alex, who had propped himself against a pillow. "A hot bath, Alex, I think I've got at least ten pounds of Nile mud in my ears, and my beard is infested with lice; it itches like hell."

"I think we share the same lice," Alex said, grinning. "God, I'd forgotten what a bed could feel like; I could stay here forever."

"So could I . . . with you in it; you'd better get up, however. We've got to get some flesh on those young bones of yours." After some fussing, Alex being unable to make up his mind as to keep his fine beard or not and finally deciding to only trim it a bit, we dressed in our cleaned and pressed clothing, arriving just in time for dinner.

It was an odd, half-forgotten experience to be sitting down on real chairs, and to have before us a table spread with fine white linen, shiny silver, painted china, and to eat once again heavy English food. Blinking several times I erased the vision of palmtrees, mudbrick villages, camels, donkeys, and temples from my mind, along with any thoughts of Ol' Joe and the stubborn obelisk. Alex dove into his food with great gusto, gulping down roast beef, boiled rice, fresh vegetables, and a glass of fresh goat's milk that the plump Mrs. Browning had ordered, saying that it would quickly fatten us both up. It was a long English evening, capped by our reading the latest newspapers from England. Still, we went to bed fairly early, having just ordered a carriage for the next morning to take us to the house of Abad al-Jalil.

9.

By mid-morning we had risen and dressed. By then our carriage had arrived and we set out. Our vehicle rumbled over the rough stones and dusty earth of the streets, passing from the bazaars of Khan el-Khalili, with their maze of twisting alleyways, old arches, wood-filigree balconies, and innumerable tiny shops, into the hidden, mysterious section called Old Cairo. Pausing by an open square the driver pointed out the mosque and university of al Azhar. The square was filled with young men carrying books and talking as do students in the public squares of Oxford or Cambridge.

With a flick of his whip the driver turned the carriage, slowly making his way up a narrow alleyway. Soon he stopped before a house, the outer walls of whose courtyard faced the street. Jumping down from his seat he pulled a bellcord and we heard a soft tinkling. A very old Egyptian woman opened the ornately carved Arabic door, and the driver gave our names in rather garbled English. The woman closed the door, and we heard the sound of voices coming from over the high wall. She returned a moment later and opened the door, bidding us to enter. Telling the driver to wait, we entered the house, crossing the tiled courtyard. Abad al-Jalil rose to greet us and smilingly shook our hands. He said something to the woman, whom I assumed up until then to be a servant as she wore no veil. Knowing very little about Egyptian customs, I now thought that she might conceivably be a secondary wife. After we had sat down on a low divan, she returned with steaming coffee.

It was good to see the old Egyptian scholar and librarian. Though he had done me out of a packet of money to build his museum, I realized it was for a noble cause. There was a certain grace and elegance about him, as he handed us small cups and saucers of thick, rich coffee. His white-bearded face was wreathed in a gentle smile, and again I was reminded of a monk just returned from his cloistered prayers.

The old Egyptian was anxious to learn about our trip, and so Alex and I narrated our adventures on the Nile to him. His eyes sparkled with delight as Alex recalled how the obelisk was almost lost in the river and told too of our encounter with the sheikh and Jomard. When this tale was finished Abad al-Jalil took a sip of his coffee. "Ah, so good, so fine. You've seen my country almost from one end to the other. It's a shame you didn't have time to journey to Abu Simbel."

"There was just not enough time. Soon it'll be summer."

"And the dreadful heat. Not a good time for the English to be in Egypt."

"After we left . . . Arundale and the terrible vision of Anubis. Did he regain his health?" I asked.

"Alas, no. His was a painful and devastating disease. He wasted away and died a senile old man. I was able to locate his family in England and to pursuade the pasha to buy his collection at a handsome price. His family came to reclaim his body and left quite wealthy. If I was a superstitious man I would say he was indeed cursed by Anubis; it may however, have been some unknown disease. His palace was closed and the servants dismissed. (I liked the man despite what he did. Alas, even without him, the plundering still continues.) There is serious news that may effect your search for the Tomb of Alexander the Great."

"Yes, yes. Now that we've returned to Cairo we can begin the quest for his tomb," Alex became so excited that he almost dropped his cup. "My father's goal can now be fulfilled."

"Yes, Alex. The moment that you've been waiting for so patiently has arrived." I said, sharing his enthusiasm.

"But, the curse!" Alex slumped back against the pillows. "Suppose we go the way of poor Arundale?"

"Ah, good lad, put your fears to rest. The agent plundered the tombs of Egypt for only the most base of reasons: to sell the remains to tourists. To speak the names of the dead is to make them live again, so goes an ancient inscription. I feel your reasons are far more noble, at least that is my hope. There is little anyone can do for you if you were to offend the ancient dead." Abad al-Jalil smiled.

"I would not offend them! The discovery of the Tomb of Alexander the Great would have great scientific value. But to really tell the truth I've no idea what I would do if it were located. Finding it has so filled my thoughts that, well, I've not gone further than that in my thinking."

"The search, the quest, the finding is sometimes more vital than the object that is found. I can see that this obsession drives you, and I pray you'll reach your goal. Once you discover what you're looking for, if you find it, ha, then there will be time to think of what to do with it."

"His remains and his treasures will be treated with the greatest respect for his noble name. You said there was news that affects our search?"

"Yes. The university library at al Azhar was broken into and several old books were taken, including the book of Jabir ibn Hayyan. Someone else knows the presumed location of the tomb!"

"G-God, when did it happen?" Alex stuttered.

"Two weeks ago. The agents seeking ancient treasures are voracious scoundrels of the lowest kind; nothing is sacred to them. Yet only scholars knew about the book. I can't understand it." Abad al-Jalil said, his voice sad.

"He knew about the book, 'Bevvie' knew about it." Alex spoke rapidly.

"Who?"

"Lord William Beveridge, earl of Wessex, an English eccentric we met in Luxor. His agents knew about the old book and may have taken it from the library. He was out for treasure, gold he could melt down. If he's found the tomb there will be very little left, only a pile of Macedonian bones!" I said, visualizing the terrible plunder.

"The book of ibn Hayyan also indicated the tomb may have been moved to the oasis of Siwa."

"Yes, yes. That's so." The old Egyptian leaned back in his chair. "Truthfully, we've really no idea where it might be. Remember the trance, 'Where you find the star of Macedonia so shall you find me.'"

"Yes, when I spoke as Alexandros. It has given me hope. The tomb is a very great prize. Beveridge did not strike me as a gentle man, and he would use every device at his command to get his hands on the gold." Alex said, his voice filled with disappointment.

"If he was anything like the Italian, Belzoni, the treasures are in the greatest danger of being lost. Belzoni battered the tombs down, destroying the ancient artifacts in his search for gold. Perhaps he also bore the curse of Anubis. He died a miserable death ten years ago in West Africa, having been stricken with severe dysentery. He plundered and destroyed everything, looting the tombs in his mad search for gold. How long are you planning to stay in Cairo, Lord Caerleon and young Alex?"

"A week or more."

"Perhaps it would be wise to go on to Alexandria if ever you are to find the tomb intact."

"Yes, Edward. Perhaps we can leave the obelisk here. Ol' Joe and the crew can watch the *Star*. After we've returned we can float the stone up the Nile and put it aboard a ship bound for England."

"Yes, Alex, a fine idea. It'll hasten the trip by weeks."

"Ah, the quest begins," Abad al-Jalil said, rising in his slippered feet, brushing the folds of his long white *galabia*. "I wish that I was younger and could join you on this noble quest, but, alas, an old man would slow you down. I've grown very fond of you both, for I believe you have good hearts and thoughts. I perceive there's a closeness between you that I didn't see before. A fine and good friendship that binds you. Such friendships are to be treasured above gold."

"Yes, we've become devoted friends . . . friends." My words stopped. Would I dare tell the old Egyptian of our love?

"There are thoughts in my mind, thoughts that you would not understand. My time on this good earth grows short. Perhaps after your return from Alexandria we could meet again. There's something I must say to you, something I must explain, paths that must be explored and revealed. Difficult things that will be beyond your comprehension now. If the location of the tomb at Alexandria proves to be a false lead . . . time grows so short."

"What are you saying?" I asked, unable to follow the old Egyptian's strange words.

"You'll forgive the muddled thoughts of a very old man. It was nothing. My mind is unclear, but everything seems so right. You will see me again when you return to Cairo. If you find the tomb there'll be so much to discuss, and then . . . perhaps I can tell you what's on my mind."

Abad al-Jalil stood there, looking at us with piercing black eyes, as though he were searching our very souls for some unknown answer to his questions. He shook his head as if dismissing his doubts. "All will be well. On to Alexandria, then. I'm with you in this quest for I also have an interest in the Macedonian, an interest that I cannot explain. *As-salaam alaykum.* Peace be upon your friendship. A safe journey to Alexandria." He bowed, touching his heart and brow, and we did the same as is the custom. In silence we left the house, wondering what he had wanted to say to us and what thoughts so puzzled him.

The next morning's light filtered in through the heavy velvet drapes of our room at British House. We lay close, snuggling beneath the quilts, for the air was rather chilly. Lazily, Alex had thrown his arm around my chest, and I felt its delicious weight against my skin. Still half-asleep and groggy, I kissed his fingertips, feeling the strength of his hand and also the hardened callouses on his fingers, caused by battle with the difficult obelisk. Alex's bearded chin rested against the nape of my neck, and his long hair tickled my ears. The moment was wonderfully sensual. His lean muscularity pressed my back more firmly into the mattress, and I could feel the hairs of his chest and belly, as he had entwined his sturdy legs around mine, bringing us even closer. I could hear his slow breathing. Now that the scent of perfume had worn off, his body had taken on a more manly smell, of sweat, faintly musky and sweet.

He stirred a bit and, fully awake, began to playfully nibble the nape of my neck, pulling the hairs gently and running his hand down over my chest. He circled his fingers around my erection, pulling back the loose skin, fingering the swollen head. I could feel his stiffened manhood hard against me, and I rolled over. Easily, but powerfully, he sank his shaft down inside me with a soft groan, his hands still circled around my erection. With the firm thrusts of a young stallion, he let his manhood surge into me with long strokes, which quickened when he neared his climax. His muscled loins were moist from sweat, as he drove his hardness deep, sending charges of lightening through my panting body.

Lustfully, with animal passion, he bit my neck, licking my salty sweat. Quivering with intense excitement, frenzied and wild, reaching heights of ecstatic pleasure, he gripped my manhood with a strong hand and I shot. Feeling my wetness in his hands he pressed his loins, gripping me with his muscular arms, and groaning as he throbbed, he emptied himself. Afterwards we lay pressed together, our arms and legs entwined, our bodies meshed against each other for a long time, rapturously enjoying the touch and the smell of an endless embrace.

There was a knock at the door and, with proper decorum we drew the covers up around us. The smiling servant brought morning coffee and a pot of hot water for shaving. After opening the drapes he left, and we sat up drinking the strong, black brew. We had decided to keep our full-beards and longish hair, though we had had them trimmed by a native barber. I looked at myself in the mirror, noting several unwelcome grey hairs, but Alex said they made me look more distinguished. Perhaps they did; I wished, however, they had sprouted on the head of some other man.

I had an idea, and it was necessary that dear Alex not know about it. Therefore, I sent him with a hired dragoman into the bazaars of Cairo on the pretense of finding some new shirts, as ours had become worn and threadbare. I told him to take his time, for I wanted to return to the houseboat to check on the crew. I said that I would return in the late afternoon. As it was our first time apart in many months I experienced a tug at my heart, but I felt fairly safe in letting

Alex go, as the burly Egyptian dragoman came highly recommended. Nevertheless, I still felt leery about the unknown dangers lurking in the busy streets of Cairo.

I watched Alex being driven away in the open carriage, the dragoman at his side. After they were out of sight, I ordered my own carriage and dragoman, and when they came, I set out for the Nile on a secret and joyous mission that was to take almost the entire day. It was late afternoon when I was driven back to British House. The carriage rumbled into the spacious courtyard, and I walked quickly into the marbled foyer, past smartly dressed, redcoated guards, who snapped to attention as I passed by. I opened the door to our room, and Alex flew into my arms, giving me a warm kiss. "Well, I'm afraid I was a failure; there's not an English shirt in the whole of Cairo. I could have had some made, but it would have taken several days."

"Don't worry about it. We'll just have to go around dressed as ragamuffins. We'd better return to the *Star* this evening if we are to arrive in Alexandria in time to save the tomb from the greedy hands of 'Bevvie,' though our fears may be unfounded. I wonder what the old Egyptian wanted to see us about when we return to fetch the obelisk?"

"He's a strange man. I feel good when I'm near him; it's an aura or something that is difficult to define."

"Yes, I know what you mean. I think he only wishes to bid us farewell. We'd better be off. We'll sail tomorrow." There was a sudden, sad look in Alex's eyes and he turned away. "What is it, beloved?"

"This is our last chance to find the tomb and to fulfill my quest. If we discover and enter the tomb it will be my father who enters; his great spirit will be with us. Oh, Edward, we'll be world famous as the discoverers of the Tomb of Alexander the Great. I think he's been with us, Edward, during the past months. I think he wants us to find it. My strange visions that occur when I look at the drachma, my time travels at Arundale's house, and the moment during the storm when we stood together before Zeus and said we'd be true and faithful. It's all been so odd. I feel as if our steps have been guided by some unknown force. I know we'll find the tomb." He turned, his face bright. "What in hell will we do with all the gold?"

"Ha, I knew it, Beneath all your noble words, there lies the heart of a treasure-seeker, like poor old Rhind, who thought he had found a pharaoh's tomb, but only found dishonor. I really have no idea. I suppose most of it would go to the British Museum and some to the Egyptians. Perhaps they'll let us keep something. It would cause a sensation. Not only might we discover the body of Alexander the Great, but perhaps that of Cleopatra VII, the most famous Egyptian queen in history, lover of Julius Caesar and Mark Antony. We sometimes forget she was pure Greek. Yes, Alex, the riches would be beyond anyone's imagination."

"It makes me shake just to think about it. Somehow I wish we would not find it."

"What do you mean? During the last year and a half that is all you could think about."

"I know. Still, what we propose to do is a form of desecration and is sacrilegious. Remember the old Egyptian's words about someone carting off Westminster Abbey? It's rather like that I suppose. Perhaps if we find it we'll not tell anyone and keep it our secret." Alex smiled at the thought.

"Now that would be a secret!"

"Well, we'll know soon enough. We'd better get packed. I hate to leave the bed, just when we've gotten used to some comfort, it's back to the wooden bunks of the *Star*. I think my backbone knows every board beneath our thin mattress there."

"I thought you liked the boat, at least a little."

"Oh, you know I do. God, it's been fun, a real adventure, quite unlike anything I had ever dreamt of. The beautiful temples, the Nile, and you, Edward. You've made it all so wonderful: finding love, and your damn obelisk too." Alex grinned.

"And your damn tomb. I've engraved every second into my memory and in addition I'll have that damn obelisk in the garden to remind me for the rest of my days."

"What about me?" Alex teased. "I wish I were carved of stone so you'd put me in your garden."

"I fell in love with a statue once, and it was no fun. I think I'll keep you in the bedroom."

"Oh, you've the heart of a debauched lecher, but I love it. I must have you in my arms, dear, sweet Edward. One more time, you pagan rascal, before the long trip, the wooden boards, and the journey back to Alexandria. When I'm in your arms nothing else seems to matter," Alex said. In response I unbuttoned his shirt, kissing his nipples. And so we made love one more time in that wonderful bed.

With regret we left British House, and it was dusk when our carriage returned to the Nile. We chatted idly, watching the passing parade of donkeys, camels, desert bedouin, mounted warriors with flashing scimitars held at the waist, veiled women, and raggedy children who ran about in the crowded streets. Carts and wagons passed by with loads of fodder, pottery, and mudbricks. The ancient horses and donkeys carrying these loads looked shaggy and miserable in part because of the swarms of flys that clustered around their sad eyes. Not even a weary flick of a tail could keep the flies away. Soaring towers and domes, crowded public squares, ramshackle houses—some with high walls hiding whatever lay within from sight—all passed before us as our carriage rattled through the streets.

While my manner was nonchalant, my heart raced with excitement as we neared the waterfront. The carriage having turned a corner, I saw ahead of us our rented *dehabiyeh*. With eager anticipation I watched Alex as his eyes quickly found the *Star*. There she sat, her starboard side to the shore, and the barge holding the confounded obelisk tied to her side. Alex's eyes widened and his mouth dropped open. "Edward, it's beautiful."

"Happy birthday, Alex." The houseboat was almost a floating palace, its masts beribboned, festooned, garlanded, and tasseled with red, white, and blue bunting. Its rails and stairways were entwined with flowers, its decks bright and clean. It glittered in the golden rays of the departing sun. Ol' Joe and his four sons had worn fresh white *galabias* and stood forward near the stove. They raised their hands in greeting and ran across the gangplank when they saw our carriage. Alex gave my hand a delightful squeeze, and there in front of everyone we kissed. "You thought I'd forgotten."

"I'd forgotten about my birthday. Oh, you shouldn't have. The houseboat is just lovely."

"I spent all day finding the decorations, sending the invitations, and buying some gifts for you. It's not every day a handsome young man turns nineteen. Ah, to be nineteen again."

"I think I'd rather be your age, settled into life and secure with myself."

"Enjoy your youth, Alex. It'll not come again. Now, get off your beautiful behind and come aboard. I want to show you your gifts before the guests and musicians arrive. I rather thought a native party would be perfect." Without a qualm we walked hand in hand to the boat, leaving Ol' Joe and his boys to bring our baggage aboard. In an instant Ol' Joe had lit the candles and had put away the baggage. The next moment he was gone to arrange the food and see to the native musicians that I had hired for the evening. I gave Alex his gifts, and he excitedly tore away the silk wrappings. Opening the first, a long box, he gasped when he saw the antique sword. Arabic in design, its scabbard was of gold bronze, its surface was set with lapis, turquoise, and carnelian, and intricate arabesques of bright cloisonne encircled the gold settings. The blade was of flexible Damascus steel, and the hilt was a cluster of stones, capped with a blood red ruby. Another box held five large cabochons of robin's-egg blue Persian turquoise, four of which could be set into gold for cufflinks and one for a watchfob when we returned to England. His other presents included several heavy chains of pure gold, some vials of heady perfume, and a set of matched caftans of gold and silver thread for us to wear that evening. "I almost bought a fine Arabic stallion for you, but didn't know how in the hell to get it back to England."

Alex gave me a big kiss. "These gifts are marvelous. How can I ever thank you?"

"Just being with you is enough."

"The sword is beautiful. It makes me feel just like a pirate on the Spanish Main or Lord Nelson at the Battle of Trafalgar." Alex swung the sword, cutting the air with a soft swoosh.

"Be careful with that thing, you can almost shave with it."

Alex smiled as he replaced the sharp double-edged sword into its colorful scabbard. "Who have you invited?"

"Some of the English people we've met; the Brownings, the Lloyds, the MacQuittys, and the Gardiners. I didn't really give them much time to respond, and I've no idea who'll arrive. I suggested native dress in my notes; I don't think, however, many will give up their proper dress."

" 'Rule Britannia.' No, I don't think so. It's my opinion that they look upon Cairo as a district of London. What time are they to arrive?"

"Around dusk, almost now. We'd better get dressed. I told Ol' Joe and his sons to help get things ready. Well, anyway, dear, dear, Alex, happy birthday. Next year I'll give you a really proper party at Caerleon Castle."

"I'll be twenty then. God, I'm getting old." Alex grinned as he stripped, pulling the heavy embroidered gown over his head, yanking the stiff silk down around his body. He giggled as he caught my eye, knowing that I was looking at him. "Later, beloved. We'll get rid of the English, and then. . . . " He gave me a big kiss and we finished dressing.

Almost glittering in our rather gaudy caftans, we left the cabin. The native orchestra had taken their places on the deck above the cabin, near to the steering rudders. Steaming brass plates held canapés of roast goose, piles of rice, and fine Egyptian bread. There was native beer and date-wine. We heard a din as the several musicians tuned up their instruments: a flute, a stringed instrument, called an *ude*, which looked rather like a lute, several pottery drums covered with goatskins, and wooden clappers. The torch and candlelight caught their wide smiles and bright eyes. "Effendis, Lord Caerleon

and the young Marquis. Please, you remember me?" The fellow with
the flute stood up and we saw it was Hamid, Arundale's houseboy.
We grinned as he came running down the stairs. He bowed, "Most
gracious Englishmen, you do remember me?"

"Of course, Hamid. We think of you often. We were sorry to hear
of your master's death."

"Oh, it was very sad. I miss him very much, but perhaps it was the
will of Allah. I worked for a while. . . . I speak English very good,
don't you think? But, I do not like my new masters. They're English,
and, well, when I would go to their rooms and offer myself the way
Arundale wanted before he got sick, they'd get angry and chase me
out of their houses. I don't understand at all the ways of crazy
Englishmen."

I laughed and Alex, having grown wiser, also laughed. What a very
funny situation. It was easy to imagine the boy asking some stuffy
lord-of-the-manor if he wanted to "bugger" the toasty behind of
Hamid. "Yes, Hamid, Englishmen are crazy. But, it looks like you've
found a job."

"Oh, yes. I now play the flute for a few coins. It's not a bad thing.
Someday maybe I'll find a master who'll do me again. Arundale was
big, like a horse, and when he got in me . . ."

"Yes, Hamid, we hope you'll find another good master like Arundale. Well, Hamid, the best of luck." We shook his hand and he
scampered off up the stairs. Later I asked Ol' Joe to give him a few extra coins.

With a flurry of prancing horses, torch-bearing runners, rumbling
carriages, and elegantly dressed English people, Alex's birthday party
began. We stood together at the top of the gangplank, receiving our
guests who had all brought small gifts. Though few of the men wore
red, tassled tarbooshes to get into the mood of the party, even they
were dressed in suits, while the women had on gowns. I think our
guests were rather shocked to see two Englishmen dressed in flowing
robes. Alex had stuck the old sword into his belt and had also worn
the gold chains, all of which gave him a decidedly Oriental flair.
Probably thinking that another of their countrymen had gone to the

dogs, they looked with some curiosity at him, but he was charming: kissing the gloved hands of the women and firmly shaking the men's hands; in short, quite laying their fears to rest. After the Brownings, the Lloyds, and the MacQuittys, the Gardiners walked up the gangplank, laughing and talking. Mrs. Gardiner, a striking woman, was escorted by a man, who held her arm, while her husband followed. The stranger spoke with an Italian accent, his long flowing ash-colored hair, brushing against the high collar of his waistcoat. His conversation was animated and punctuated with sweeping gestures. "Ah, of course, von Beethoven was the greatest composer who ever lived. The entire world went into mourning when he died in 1827. He was the consummate master. No one can approach his genius. I have memorized his complete piano sonatas, a herculean task, if I may say. But there is a new genius on the horizon, Frederick Chopin. His debut in Vienna in August of 1829 was nothing short of brilliant. I was in Warsaw in 1830 when he played his two piano concertos. He is the epitome of the romantic style. I told him in Warsaw to come to Paris, the city of life and music. It was an occasion . . . ah, our hosts." The couple stopped as Mrs. Gardiner introduced us.

"Edward, earl of Caerleon, and his ward, the Marquis Alexander Saint-Hilaire, this is my very dear friend, the eminent concert pianist, Maurice Anton Barbarossa. He's only just arrived from playing on the Continent. He's superb."

"Ah, Mrs. Gardiner is too kind. We met several years ago when I played in London, and I received an invitation from her when I finished my tour in Naples. She is so kind." With great elegance Maurice kissed her gloved hand. "Ah, Lord Caerleon and the Marquis, you both look so . . . so unusual in your Egyptian dress. I shall have to rush out and buy one of those gowns, and. . . ." Maurice's words trailed off, and he gave me an odd look as though he recognized me.

"The caftans are most comfortable. We've just returned from the island of Philae; our clothing is worn, and we've not had time to have new ones made."

"The Earl of Caerleon has returned with that stone. It's the talk of Cairo." Mrs. Gardiner added graciously.

"What stone?" Maurice asked, looking around inquiringly.

"The obelisk. You're nearly standing on it." Alex pointed down into the darkness. "Edward and I have just had a very long and difficult journey bringing it back," Alex said with a note of pride in his voice. "It's of dark red granite and very hard to see. I can get a torch."

"No, that's all right. I'm certain it's a very fine obelisk. Marquis . . . may I call you Alex? You are most stunning in your robe and your sword. A young Achilles at the walls of Troy. All you need is a helmet and a shield. You look most Greek, if I dare say."

"I am a Greek, at least half-Greek. My mother was from that country."

"You see? I knew." The pianist shook our hands, as he and the Gardiners moved off the gangplank. "Do you have a pianoforte? I feel in the mood for Chopin."

"No. We had a chance to buy one when we left for Philae; we did not have enough room, however," Alex explained, as he led the group to the food, which was being heaped on plates by Ol' Joe and his sons. Meanwhile, the native orchestra busily played the somewhat percussive music of Egypt. While the guests nibbled sweetcakes I saw Maurice glance at me sharply. Somewhere, sometime, our paths had crossed. But where?

Alex held the group's attention, as he explained how he and I had brought the obelisk from Philae. The pianist wandered over to me. "Your ward is very handsome, Eddie." His voice was low and droll.

"What?" I said, being unaccustomed to being called 'Eddie.' "

"You don't recognize me do you?"

"No, I do not."

"Certainly you remember the *Turk's Head* in Soho. It must have been almost ten years ago." Maurice smiled, brushing his long ash-colored hair out of his pale green eyes, smoothing down his pearl gray waistcoat, and touching my arm.

"Tony! God, it's been years."

"I had no idea you were a member of the aristocracy. You were always 'dear Eddie' to me. You've certainly got yourself a prize this time."

My mind shot back to those days in London. Tony Barret. I had met him during the year before the death of my father. He was so young and beautiful. Not the rugged good looks of Alex, who did look, with the candle and torchlight flickering off his bearded face, rather like a Greek warrior standing before burning Troy. The Tony Barret I had once known had resembled an angel painted on the walls of a Renaissance church. I had loved him briefly. We had met in a bistro called the *Turk's Head*, a popular meeting place for young, and not so young, men. He had a certain flair for music and had come to London to study. My father was far from generous with my allowance and Tony had little money. We had taken rooms at 18 Wipple Mews. I had never told anyone, not even Tony, about my noble lineage, choosing instead to pass myself off as a student of architecture and to use a variety of last names. My cautious behavior was the result of fear.

There was nothing in my relationship with Tony that resembled the love I sought. It was one of those ephemeral things, and once the heat of passion had gone there was only tedious boredom; because we lacked money to go our separate ways, however, we stayed together for almost a year. He had been seeing a piano teacher for some time when the letter arrived saying my father had died. Soon after, Tony had gone to live with his new friend. All of those thoughts passed through my head in an instant, as I now gazed into Tony's green eyes. "Tony. Apparently your teacher-lover taught you something."

"Dear, dear, Eddie. Of course. I wouldn't have gone to him if I had thought he would not have been helpful. If ten years ago I had known that you were a member of nobility, I would have stuck to your waistcoat like glue. I've always found friends who have furthered my career."

"You look successful."

"I am. I'm only twenty-seven and have concert tours everywhere. You must come and see me the next time I play in London."

"I suppose it helps to change your name and to acquire an Italian accent."

"Even members of the aristocracy don't tell the entire truth, Lord Caerleon. We all have secrets that best remain hidden, Eddie." Maurice wandered away, pausing to listen to Alex.

A shudder of fear passed down my backbone. Tony or Maurice, or whatever he called himself now, was not one to hold secrets. But we both had secrets that could not be exposed, and I hoped he'd keep quiet.

Throughout the evening my eyes followed the pianist. He had been with Alex much of the time, staying by his side as I talked with the other guests. More than once I saw him touching my young friend, rubbing his hand against Alex's and smiling sweetly. I wondered what they were saying. Perhaps they were talking about me. With growing agitation I saw Maurice touch Alex's beard. They were getting friendly. The pianist was still very handsome, with a debonair manner, and he was much younger than I was. Hell, it was nothing. I was working myself into a fury. The best thing to do was to not simply stand by. Excusing myself from the couple I was with, I seized a plate of food and went over to the two. "Are you having fun, Alex?" I asked.

"Yes, of course, Edward. It's a beautiful party. Too bad we didn't buy the piano. I would love to hear Maurice play."

"I'm sure he plays delightfully," I said, my voice edged with sarcasm. "Perhaps we can go to London to see him sometime or other."

"Eddie is such a sweet man. We knew each other a long time ago, a very long time. Eddie is much older now, but I think his greying hair gives him a certain flair. Don't you think, young Alex."

"Yes, it makes him look very distinguished."

"Almost fatherly, I would say. We roomed together for almost a year. Eddie gave me the tip of his boot."

"You had already moved in with the piano teacher when I left."

"Eddie has a certain flagging interest in his friends after a while. He grows tired of them, dear Alex, and tosses them out into the street without so much as a goodbye. I learned my lesson and you may learn yours, dear Alex. When he tosses you out, you can always come to my chateau near Paris."

"You bastard! You know you left me months before." I said, my voice revealing my anger.

"Temper, temper, dear Eddie. If I remember, oh, it has been a long time, Eddie was a bit stodgy, lacking passions in certain matters; in fact, he was rather dull, impotent, you might say. Not much where it counts. Come to Paris, sweet Alex. It's so exciting there, and I don't think you find me as dull and boring as you must find Eddie."

"Edward and I are . . . are." Alex stammered for words.

"Get off my boat, you conniving bastard!" I said. Pushing him away from Alex, I took the hilt of the antique sword out of its scabbard. "Alex and I have something you'll never know about." Brandishing the blade in Maurice's direction, I seethed with blood red anger. I suppose I might have run the dastard through with the sharp blade. Luckily for him, Mrs. Gardiner walked over.

"I was noticing the beautiful sword. My goodness, you could easily kill someone with it," she said sweetly.

"It would be so easy, Mrs. Gardiner, so very easy." I stood sword in hand, watching Maurice, who had backed away from me.

"Oh my word, have I said something wrong?" Maurice arched his elegant eyebrow, all the time watching the glinting point of the sword. "Ah, Edward, you're a veritable old lioness protecting her brood. I had not expected such passions. Now put that thing away before you hurt someone."

Calm reason overcame my anger, and I returned the sword to Alex who slipped it back in the scabbard. "Perhaps sometime we could visit you in Paris. I've heard it's a lovely city." Alex stammered, trying to smooth over my angry outburst. "Edward and I will return to Caerleon with the obelisk. He plans to place it in his garden."

"That'll be very sweet, I'm sure. All stiff and erect. It's said in ancient times that the obelisk had a phallic meaning." Maurice quickly glanced at Alex.

"Oh, Maurice, you can be so naughty," Mrs. Gardiner giggled.

"Perhaps Edward found two obelisks at Philae, one not made of granite," Maurice suggested slyly, with a smirk.

"What do you mean by that, dear Maurice?" Mrs. Gardiner asked.

"Nothing, dear Mrs. Gardiner, nothing. Well, we must be going before I raise Edward's ire again. I'll be giving a concert at the Gardiner's home tomorrow evening, and you're both invited. While the robes are most becoming to you, Alex, they do cover up interesting areas of the male body. Wear some nice tight English trousers, just for me."

"We'll be leaving for Alexandria early in the morning, and I don't think we can come." Alex replied.

"What a pity. Perhaps, then, we can meet in London or in Paris. I'm sure Edward would be content to stay at Caerleon. I believe it's a farming area with a multitude of pigs, cows, and wheat. A perfect setting for an old country squire, but not for a handsome young man with a brilliant future. In a few years the glow will have gone from your beautiful grey eyes if you stay in that dreadfully bucolic place, and you'll be just as dull as Edward." Maurice shot me a look filled with hate. "My Paris chateau is yours if you decide to leave." Quickly taking Mrs. Gardiner's arm, Maurice Anton Barbarossa, or Tony Barret, walked down the gangplank, followed by the elderly Mister Gardiner.

"Aren't you going with him, Alex?" I snapped. "Perhaps you'll find the Paris life more interesting than stale Caerleon."

"I could never do that, dear Edward. The man was an unspeakable cad to have talked to you in that way. I should have done something. I'm sorry if he hurt you. . . ." Alex stammered, afraid of my anger.

"I said I'd never hold you. What he told you is quite true. You're young, Alex, and should have some fun in your life."

"I'll be content to be with you, Edward. Don't you know, don't you realize, how much I love you?"

"Not until this moment. . . ."

"Oh, Edward, we're having our first quarrel." He smiled graciously. "Who knows, dear Edward, someday I might leave you, but not for some concert player with an evil tongue. He's a very small person and I dislike him. As long as you'll have me, I'm yours. Did you really give him the tip of your boot? I would've done the same. Well, we've got some guests left; we'd better join them," Alex said, giving my hand a quick, loving grasp. In a moment we had joined the others. I felt immensely sorry to have doubted Alex's sincerity. Now that I knew that he loved me as much as I loved him, my heart leapt with new joy.

After all that had happened, we were pleased to see the last of our countrymen rattle away in their coaches. Leaving Ol' Joe and his sons to clean up the boat, we returned to our cabin. Tomorrow, at first light, we would leave for Alexandria.

It seemed only a minute before the rosy dawn peeped through the cabin windows, causing me to open my eyes. Ol' Joe rushed in through the door. "Most terrible news. The boat has sprung a leak and will be unable to sail," he said anxiously. It was true. A tiny leak had allowed almost an inch of Nile water into the shallow hull of the *Star*. The boat would have to be taken onshore and the leak repaired. Ol' Joe looked at me with sorrowful eyes, but I told him that we would obtain another vessel for the trip to the coast. I said that we would return in two or three weeks. During this time he should repair the hull and guard our possessions. I could see "Bevvie" breaking down the doors of the Tomb of Alexander the Great and carting off the gold to America to buy more slaves. We had to move quickly in order to save Alex's dream.

10.

A week later our carriage pulled up before the Hotel Trafalgar, where
we were greeted by the plump Levantine proprietor, aglitter with
gold ornaments. After our rooms were secured, we asked about an
old mosque, el Qurn Mosheh, the Horns of Moses. Although he
could not understand why two Englishmen would have an interest in
an abandoned mosque, he ordered the driver to take us there. This
was the same man who had driven us to the Serapeum so long ago.
His wizened, coffee-colored face looked at us quizzically, as if he was
trying to remember something. Then a light of recognition came to
his eyes; he whipped the old nag and the carriage started up with a
jerk. Turning into a broad street, the *Viol Canopique*, going west,
toward the Serapeum, we could see in the distance the lonely granite
shaft of Pompey's Pillar. Turning to the right, heading north, toward
the sea, the carriage rumbled into a litter-filled alleyway. The dirty
mudbrick houses around us were ruined, but still lived in. Evidently,
children were playing games and we could hear their shouting voices.
Rubbish was piled against the fallen walls; the alley itself was covered
with offal and slop thrown out of the houses. In the near distance we
could see a fallen minaret; the upper portions were gone and only the
round base remained. A fine dappled Arabic stallion was tied to the
standing-wooden supports of the gateway; further on, a crumbling
wall defined the area where el Qurn Mosheh stood. The driver
jumped down, securing the carriage, its tinkling bells disturbing the
stallion who reared and snorted. Perhaps some devout Moslem had
come to pray at the mosque.

Alex and I jumped down from the festooned carriage, telling our driver to wait; passing beneath an arched portico, we entered into a courtyard. A domed kiosk stood in the center, a place for the devout to wash their hands and feet before entering the mosque to pray. But the water had been shut off ages ago, and only drifting sand covered the water troughs. Around the courtyard were the usual covered colonnades, though there was something different about the columns. They were of fine, colored marble, the ornate capitals of Greek and Roman design. Most probably they had been taken from some fallen temple and reused here by the Moslem builders. Passing under the colonnades we came to the entrace. Its wooden doors had fallen away. We then passed into the large columned prayer area where the devout had once knelt, facing toward the east and Mecca. Our boots hit the stone pavement and the sound they made echoed against the walls and the ceiling. I noticed that large chunks of it had collapsed. Bright rays of sunlight streamed through the holes. The mosque was empty.

"Damnit, man, what are you doing here?" Beveridge suddenly jumped out from behind a column, a pistol held in his hand, looking at us with fierce eyes. "I thought it was those scummy Turks."

"I might ask the same of you, Lord Beveridge."

"Exploring."

"For what?"

"If you're here you understand damn well what I'm looking for . . . the gold of Alexandros. You knew about this place; you talked to the old Egyptian."

"Your agents stole the book showing this location."

"Clever of you. I paid them well. You're wasting your time. The tomb is not here. The gold is gone, disappeared centuries ago. The only way you're going to find any is to rip the place apart, and since it is still held to be holy, the locals might take a dim view of that."

"You searched?"

"Damnit, man, every corner, and except for snakes, scorpions, and spiders the place is vacant."

"Well, Edward, we rather knew, didn't we?"

"We thought . . . hoped."

"Sorry boys, if there had been any gold to be found it would be aboard my yacht. The hell with this place and Egypt; no gold left! Going back to the Americas and run slaves and fight savages. You can have whatever you find – that is, if you like snakes, scorpions, and spiders. Ha, good luck." Beveridge looked disgusted as he stepped into the light, putting away his pistol. Then, reaching inside his shirt, he pulled out the stolen book and flung it to the floor; its ancient leaves settled into the dust. "Give this book back to the Egyptian; it ain't doing me any good." Beveridge stomped out of the mosque, and in a minute we heard his stallion thunder away.

Standing in the middle of the deserted mosque, Alex looked grim, his hopes ground into sand, his dreams unrealized. Thinking that "Bevvie" had missed something we searched. There was nothing except the fine marble columns also probably salvaged from some ancient Greek or Roman temple and the ornate prayer niche embedded into the eastern wall. It looked as though it had once been part of a Pagan temple. There were limestone borders carved with intertwined leaves and flowers, festoons of grapes and rosettes. During its long history the mosque had seemingly even served as a Christian church, for several crosses had been carved into the limestone and then nearly erased. The star of Islam was covered by a strange blend of Pagan, Christian, and Moslem carvings. Each faith had used the stone for its own purposes.

Alex and I sat down on the stone steps leading up to the prayer niche and looked out at the dusty room. We felt defeated and discouraged. "Beveridge was right! There's no treasure here."

"We had such high hopes of finding the Tomb of Alexandros."

"Yes, I know. But it's gone."

"It says in the book that the treasure was moved to Siwa." Alex thumbed through the parchment pages of the ancient book. "It could be there."

"Probably another wrong turn. Siwa must be hundreds of miles from here, across the Sahara."

"Alexandros went there to become a god," Alex said stubbornly.

"Yes, he did."

"We . . . could go there."

"What? You don't know what you're asking, dear Alex. Miles and miles of desert, with no water, just to find nothing."

"We would be following his route to the temple of the Double-Horns, the temple of Zeus-Ammon."

"It would take weeks."

"I know, but we've come this far. . . ."

"Dear Alex, you ask too much. We could die out there."

"In each other's arms."

"Food for the vultures. It's a waste of time to go tromping all over the Sahara desert looking . . . it's gone, Alex."

"Edward."

"Oh, Alex I love you so, and if you want to go . . ."

"Edward, it would mean so much to me. My dream and that of my father would be fulfilled, and we would know once and for all if the Tomb of Alexandros exists. I will be satisfied with whatever answer we find." Alex gave me a big hug; we kissed and walked out into the sunny, warm air. Tomorrow we would begin preparations for the long journey across the Sahara to the oasis of Siwa.

Alex was in heaven as we made inquiries about the trip. It presented formidable obstacles; a caravan would have to be formed with suitable guides, enough food and water for the 300 miles into the desert and for the return. The British consul-general advised against it along with the ranking officials of Alexandria. Entire caravans indeed, entire armies had vanished in the drifting sands. But we were determined by now to go.

One afternoon the Levantine called us to the lobby. A tall man stood up to greet us. It was the police chief who had warned us so sternly against our trip just after the attack by the Tuareg slavers. Now our paths crossed again. Seeing Roumer Ibrahim, with his tall, commanding figure, piercing eyes, and arched aquiline nose, I was again reminded of a bird of prey: a hawk, a falcon. Snapping his riding crop against his hand, he clicked his heels together and bowed. "Ah, we meet again Lord Caerleon and Alexander Saint-Hilaire. It is good to see you once more. You both look well, and young Alexander is as handsome as ever. We have received word of your dangerous trip to Siwa. A foolhardy journey. It is late in the season, and you will roast alive out there."

"We fully realize the dangers, sir." Alex replied, his voice low and strong. "We've taken every possible precaution against danger. Our guide is highly recommended, and the caravan is amply stocked with food and water."

"You Englishmen . . . ah, I have never understood your race. You are all quite mad, and this trip is insane."

"We know the dangers."

"But you will go anyway."

"Yes, we leave in the morning."

"What can I say, Englishmen? It is a very long trip; you will be alone, isolated from the pleasures of civilization and from protection. I wish you well. Perhaps we will see each other again . . . when and if you return." With a smart snap of the crop to his tarboosh, the policeman left, his heels clicking over the marble floors.

"He always seems to be warning us against dangers, dangers that do not exist, eh, Edward?"

"Yes, he does."

It was early morning when we left the hotel and gained the street. Our Arabic guide greeted us and showed us the camels we were to ride. To our rear a caravan of twenty-five hired camels would follow, carrying food and water; ten drivers stood by the side of the kneeling beasts of burden, waiting for the guide's signal. Throwing a long cloaklike, hooded garment, called a *burnoose*, over our western clothes, we were helped onto the dusty, dirty camels, who snarled and tried to bite us. For all the grimy conditions surrounding us it was a romantic moment, as dressed in our flowing robes, we sat at the head of a long line of camels, accompanied only by the laconic Arabs who were to take us to the ends of the world. With a snap of the whip our burly guide gave the signal, and the camels lurched forward. We rambled down the empty streets in a stately procession, passing beneath a ruined Roman archway, before we headed into the Libyan desert. I turned for a moment, watching the skyline of Alexandria disappear behind the caravan. Both Alex and I were thinking the same thing: better go back and forget our mad adventure. Ahead of us were vast reaches of sand, stretching from horizon to horizon. Giving our camels a sharp snap of the whip, we descended into the desert.

Slow days. Endlessly over the huge banks of sand. It is written that Alexandros had divine help marching over the same path two thousand years ago. Two great hissing snakes led him and his army through the wasteland; we, however, had no such help. Just how our guide kept on the path when there was no path, I did not know. Perhaps by observing the star clusters that sparkled in the night sky, or by watching the movement of the sun as it crossed the baking desert, but unerringly he knew. Slow days of endless horizons, each one looking exactly like the other.

A week, perhaps more, passed; our rations of water and dried meat and fruit was cut by half. Now and then we came to an oasis and filled out goatskins with water and rested. At night Alex and I would climb into our blankets and snuggle together as the darkened desert was cold in contrast to the blistering heat of the day. Now and then we could see other caravans passing, but they might have been only mirages, shimmering in the terrible heat. Day after day we passed through nothingness into nothingness.

Somewhere in the second week the arid and barren landscape began to change. Gradually, sandstone cliffs began to rise out of the sand, and the terrain became rocky. Now the camels' padded feet clomped on the stones, rather than on soft bumps of sand. The caravan stopped; the guide, jumping down, pointed to some rocks ahead. Making our camels kneel, we also jumped down and followed him across the gravel. We were about to enter a canyon bounded by towering sandstone walls which seemed to change in color from pale pink to russet with white banding. There was a path! A man-made path leading through the canyon, and on either side of it were carved sphinxes. The stone was worn and pitted, but the shape of a recumbent ram was clear; it was the symbol of Ammon. The horns cut around the head were the same shape as the horns seen on the golden drachma. Siwa was near.

"I wonder what Alexandros thought as he neared the oasis?"

"Besides wondering when he would find the next fresh water, I guess he was filled with apprehension, thrilled even, at being made a living god, the true son of Zeus-Ammon, or Jupiter, as the Romans called the diety."

"He seemed possessed by the idea of becoming a god."

"His mother had told him that he was sired by one or the other: perhaps he came to believe it in time. Besides, it was the thing to do in ancient times. Who would ever want to be a common mortal when one could be a god, probably with a lot of baksheesh passing hands. Amusing really, eh, Alex?"

"There's a little of god in all of us."

"And much of the devil." I smiled.

"Perhaps too much, Part man, part devil, part god . . . the moment has made me a philosopher, I'm afraid. Tomorrow we'll arrive at Siwa. I almost hate to reach there."

"Afraid we'll find nothing. Afraid of finding . . . nothing," he added.

"At least we'll know. You and your father's dream will be realized one way or the other. You'll know that you did all you could to find the lost tomb."

"Yes, Edward, I'll know that at least. Maybe we can find a priest and have him make us gods, with some baksheesh, of course."

"Much baksheesh. We'll find out tomorrow." Alex and I looked out over the pathway. The great solar orb, burning a dusty orange, hung over the horizon. "We had better get some rest. The run to Siwa will take most of the day, and who knows what we shall find there."

The final rays of the sun caught the mountains and softened the harshness of the landscape. We would make camp around a pool and some palms. Until we arrived at Siwa we would have to wait for fresh water. The pool looked inviting, but the desert creatures — snakes, mice, and scorpions — who had come to drink, lay dead around it. Evidently, the water was poisoned and saline. Our men started a fire, using dried branches and dried camel dung left by some other caravan. The guide and his ten Arabs sat around the fire, chewing brittle meat, joking and laughing at stories that Alex and I could not understand. How isolated we were. We must have been the only Europeans around for hundreds of miles. The English were truly a race of madmen and governed by insanity. I could not think of any other reason why we found ourselves in such a spot.

Taking our bedrolls down from the saddle of our tethered camels, we kicked rocks out of what would be our sleeping places. Then we put down our thin blankets. We had chosen to sleep near the fire. Our guide taught us to tie our boots together and to hang them on a branch out of the reach of scorpions, whose bite could be fatal. We had also to beware of the dangerous snakes that might crawl beneath our blankets, seeking warmth from the cold night. The Arabs stood watch to scare away or kill any such intruders into our camp. Still, that night I could not at first sleep, and rose several times to remove offending pebbles that pinched me here and there. But, gradually, I drifted into unconsciousness. Groggily looking over at Alex I could see that he was snuggled up in his blankets, wearing his burnoose for more warmth.

Suddenly, the stillness was shattered, "Aieeeee!" There was a cry of terror and a shot sounded, reverberating in our ears. The early light of dawn caused my eyes to blink as I awoke, sitting up in my blankets and shivering from the very cold morning. A figure lunged at me, stumbling away from the low fire, his face torn by pain as he fell at my feet with a thud. Confused, I turned. Alex was still sleeping and snoring. Peering across the campfire, I could make out figures dismounting from camels and horses, the long ends of rifles sticking out of their robes. The guide was on his feet, as were his men, their hands probing for their rifles, as the strangers started firing. What was happening? Were we about to be robbed of our precious water? Or were they about to steal our camels, leaving us stranded in the desert to die a lingering death. Before I knew it our guide and some of his men were cut down by the intruders. The rest of our men surrendered, raising their hands in the air. Who were these marauders who had come into our camp killing everyone who stood in their way? The sun eased over the horizon, and I recognized them. Heavily robed in black, daggers glinting from their belts, dark, obsidion eyes stared at us through veils of blue cloth, were the Tuaregs.

Alex sat up, rubbing his head, stretching out his arms, scratching his hair, yawning, and asking about the loud noise that had awakened him. He stopped when he saw the Tuaregs. "It's them; the Arabs who tried to rob us." He reached for his rifle, which he always kept beside his blanket. I had already gripped mine, and gaining our feet, we waited for the desert-warriors. Ten or more stood near the fire, their weapons leveled at us, while a tall blue-veiled man walked over to us.

"Ah, my dear Lord Caerleon and young Alex. We meet again." The man reached up, removing the blue cloth from his face. It was Roumer Ibrahim, the police chief of Alexandria. His lips parted a little and his black eyes glittered like a snake. "We have caught up with you at last. How do you like our little desert? But no matter . . . dear, dear Alex. Both of you put your guns down, you are surrounded."

"It's you! What do you want?"

"You, dear Alex."

"What do you mean by that?"

"I was taken by your manly beauty when I saw you wounded. My men were rash and should have waited until a more opportune time. I hope there is no scar."

"They wanted me?"

"Yes, of course. Did not Lord Caerleon tell you? His Christian senses were shocked, and he thought us barbaric, perhaps. I . . . I tried to warn you to leave Egypt, as I said, I was much taken by your beauty. My heart softened when I saw you . . . but it is not soft now. Take them!" Ibrahim's men rushed at us. We fought for a moment but there was just too many of them, and after a brief scuffle, Alex and I were held, our arms pinioned behind our backs, our guns knocked from our hands. Ibrahim watched Alex carefully, and seeing that he was defenseless, walked over to him, running a finger over his chin.

"Take your filthy hands off me!"

"Ah, the lad has spirit; that is good."

"Leave him alone, Arab!" I spit out my words. In response to this outburst, my arms were cruelly yanked upwards; I yelped with pain, and the round, cold end of a rifle was stuck into my face. Seething with pain and anger I twisted this way and that, but I was held. "Leave him alone!"

"Take your hands off Edward!" Alex screamed, seeing my pain, but he was also tightly held, as the Arab continued to caress his face.

"We will treat Alex very well. Ah, so handsome and a prize worth the wait." Ibrahim touched Alex's nose and eyes, and ran his hands through the flaxen curls that the light of dawn had turned a golden yellow. Suddenly, he seized the burnoose that Alex had slept in, ripping it away, and opened Alex's shirt. "The English have such fair skin. We greatly admire it; a few weeks of confinement out of the sun and you will loose your dark tan." The Arab ran his hand over Alex's muscular chest, caressed his nipples, and moved down to the line of fine hair on his stomach, but stopped at the beltline. He pulled a little at the hairs growing around the navel. Starting to unbuckle the leather belt, he paused. "We will do that later."

"Damn you, you Arab pig!"

"Such hard words from one so young. I have come to save you from a dreary English life. Only the very, very wealthy will be able to pay the price that I will ask for you. Your life will be one of ease, surrounded by jewels, silks, and palaces. There is nothing your owner will not give you."

"My owner?"

"Oh, I promise that he, or perhaps she, will be of the best breeding, an aristocrat who can afford my price."

"You would sell me into a life of slavery?"

"I know . . . unchristian and barbaric, but it is our custom and for you the very best . . . all for a few favors. Be careful not to give in too quickly, be a man, and stand up to your master. They all like that, show some manliness, but do not wait too long. . . . Even the most lusty will play for only so long. Are you a virgin? I suppose not. Boys are not like girls who give their innocence only once. I will say you are a virgin; no one will know the difference."

"How can you be so cruel?" I shouted, before my mouth was covered by a brutal hand.

"I am not cruel. As I say, dear Alex will have a very fine life behind the walls of a palace, pampered by every worldly luxury that he can imagine." His hand still played with the fine golden hairs, and he smiled with satisfaction. Alex was trembling, his eyes wide in sheer terror, and he strained against the hard hands that held him. "Be careful, you fools. Do not hurt him or bruise his skin. He must be perfect for the slave-block. We would not get top price here in Egypt. We will take him to rich Bagdad or Damascus. The Mediterranean is not far . . . your skin is so warm and smooth, your hair so golden, beautiful one . . . I should keep you for myself, but a policeman must make a living." Fingering Alex's belt, with a hard yank he tore it away. Without a belt the trousers dropped and Alex stood naked. The parts untouched by the sun were pale, the skin a creamy gold. The Arabs, excited by such fair skin, ran their hands around his naked loins. Ibrahim, a crazed look in his hawklike eyes, fondled Alex's penis and testicles, pulling them up, feeling the soft skin, exposing the glans. Eagerly, the men touched him while he twisted, trying to escape. It looked for a moment as if they would throw him down on the blanket in order to commit further atrocities, when Ibrahim knocked them away. "Enough! Pull his trousers up and tie him. Pay those men who are still alive; they will have no objections to some coins. Tell them to be on their way. Bind Lord Caerleon. We will leave him to whatever fate Allah has in store for him. In a short time the sun will bake him dry. Allow his legs to be free, perhaps he can run for Siwa. Ha . . ." Strong ropes bound my hands. Tied up, screaming, and struggling against the harsh Tuaregs, Alex was carefully placed by them on a saddle, while Ibrahim mounted the stallion behind him. "Do not worry, Lord Caerleon, sweet Alex will have the best of care. I fear your fate will not be so good." Frantically, I ran over to the stallion, but the hard butt of a rifle slammed into my face, and I fell backwards into the sand and gravel, landing hard, with a painful thud. I must have passed out from the blow.

How long I lay in a crumpled heap I do not know. The sun seemed high, the stones and rocks were burning, and my mouth was very dry and parched. I could taste blood. Far overhead I could see hungry vultures circling patiently, awaiting my death. I must have gotten up, for I remember running and stumbling, trying to go toward Siwa and toward the ones who had taken Alex. The last thing I remember was that my face hit the hard ground. Pebbles bit into my skin. I knew that I was finished. The end. My weak eyes stared out over the desert; I saw a strange vision: a big brown toe sticking out of a sandal. Darkness closed in around me for the final time.

11.

White. My senses read white. I was surrounded by white. I was in a white box. Had they put me here before shipping me off to heaven, or to that other place? No, it was not a white box; it was a white room. A small white room. But where? I was lying on a narrow bed; I could feel the warmth of blankets covering my body. I was still dressed in my shirt and trousers, but my heavy boots had been removed. On the opposite side of the small white room there was a wooden table and a chair. I was in a doctor's office in London. I had been found, but in a coma, and they had taken me to London. I tried to clear my head of these confused thoughts.

Alex! The horror of his capture by the vicious slavers broke through my confusion. Had he been found? Had he been lost forever? I groaned in terrible despair. Was he now enduring some obscene slavery in the harem of a wealthy Arab in Baghad? I would go back and find him, even if I had to break into every palace in the mid-East.

I was aware of a small window set in the wall high above my head. It was daytime and a bright beam of light fell on a wooden door. The door opened; it was the London doctor; he would clear things up. The man was clearly not a London doctor. He was dark-skinned, bearded, and an Arab. He smiled as he silently placed a plate of roast meat, rice, and some fruit on the table. I sat up and asked him where I was. He put his finger to his lips, and set a clay water jar on the table. Taking a knife and a fork from the pocket of his long, cowled white robe, he turned, bowed, and left the room. I watched, too weak to speak, as he closed the door. Damn him! I wanted to know where I was. I had forgotten that I had been injured and winced when I swung my legs over the edge of the bed. I stumbled to the door and opened it. There was no one in the long corridor. Defeated and breathless, I closed the door. I was not in London. Where in the hell was I? I did not know. Exhausted, I softly touched my face as I sat back down on the edge of the bed, trying to think. It hurt terribly. Hungry and thirsty I bolted down the food and water. I felt rather better and lay back on the bed, looking up at the window. I must have fallen asleep.

My rest was disturbed when the bearded white-robed man again entered the room. Though my jaw was aching from the blow I had received, I opened my mouth painfully and demanded to know where I was. He picked up the plate and the silver, again placing his finger to his lips, and indicated that I was to follow him. My senses were now alive; the grogginess in my head cleared. I would get to the bottom of this business, or else. I slowly followed the bearded man down the corridor. The place was cool; light came from high windows, and the walls were carved out of rock which had been whitewashed. I was not in London. Where was I?

The long corridor widened out, and we came to a ornately carved door of Arabic design. The man opened it and led me into a large whitewashed room, its walls covered with tapestries of European make, its floors spread with thick carpets. There was a desk at the far end; piled on it were many books and papers. There were several chairs in front of the desk, and the Arab indicated that I was to sit on one of them. I crossed the room and sat down, waiting.

Another man entered from a door near the desk. For a moment I thought it was Abad al-Jalil. This man, however, was younger, his close-cropped hair and beard peppered with gray. He too wore a cowled white robe and sandals. His dark eyes were luminous and friendly. He smiled, "Ah, Lord Caerleon, you're up and looking much better. You gave us some anxious moments. You were delirious when we found you. The men who ran the caravans are sometimes unfeeling and abandon sick animals to die. The vultures gather, circling high over their prey. One of the brothers saw their vigil of death and went to find their prey. We try and save the unfortunate camels and donkeys if we can. This time we found you sprawled half-alive in the sands. We carried you back here and gave you some laudanum. Your jaw is not broken and should heal without any problems. The scrapes on you face will also heal."

I was in no mood to put up with his pleasant words. "Where in the hell am I, and who in the hell are you?"

"I can understand your anger, Lord Caerleon. You've had a dreadful experience. Be at ease and I will explain."

"My friend, Alex, has been taken by slavers. God in heaven, it was terrible. I must find him!" My nerves were shattered and I broke down. Tears swelled up in my eyes. Weakly I wiped them away. "I must find him at all costs."

"Your name is not unknown to us, or that of your friend, Alexander Saint-Hilaire. You were unconcious for nearly two days. You spoke in your sleep and cried out his name."

"I've lost him. He's gone forever. I'll never find him."

"I can understand your grief. The young man was more to you than a friend . . . you rambled in your fitful sleep."

"Yes, he was more than a friend. We were lovers. He means the world to me. I cannot live without him at my side." The Arab handed me a handkerchief and I wiped my nose. It suddenly occurred to me that I had said the wrong thing. Perhaps my frank confession would offend. But to hell with the Arab. I glared at him from across the desk and repeated my words, "We were and are lovers."

The Arab smiled. "Yes, I can understand. It is a beaufiul love, such as was the love between Alexander the Great and the young Hephaistios. It is a beautiful love. We have taken steps to free the young man from the slavers."

My mind jumped. "Where is he? Is he safe?"

"He is near; he is safe and he is being watched. No harm will come to him. Be at ease."

"How do you know that?"

"There are ways."

"Damn it, man! Where am I? And who are you?" My words were harsh, because I was confused, though I was relieved to learn of Alex's safety.

"You are not very far from the place where you and Alexander Saint-Hilaire were so brutally attacked by the slavers."

"Near Siwa?"

"Yes. Please let me explain. I am Brother Khalid, and the men here are members of a small monastic order. The monk who served you was still under a vow of silence; I, however, have been here long enough to have passed my vows. I now serve as a host to those who come our way in times of distress."

"A monastery in the middle of the desert? Quite unbelievable!"

"Nonetheless, we are here and have been here for a very long time."

"Yes, I know who you are. Coptic Christians. . . . Coptic Christians are known for their love of solitude. Saint Antony and the temptations of the flesh. You are Coptic Christians who have come here to escape the sins and evils of the world."

"Alas, no, we are not Christians, and we have not come to this isolated place in the desert to escape the world. We have come here to guard the world."

"I do not understand."

"There is no need for you to do so, Lord Caerleon. We know of you and your friend, Alex. You have friends in Egypt who have helped you on your various quests. Your journey to Siwa was unexpected, as was the raid on your caravan. It is destiny. The circumstances that brought you here are above the ordinary."

"What are you saying?"

"You and the young Alex have a destiny to fulfill, a special destiny, one beyond your immediate comprehension."

"I don't know what you're talking about."

"God moves in mysterious ways, Lord Caerleon. At the present time things must remain unexplained. And while God moves in mysterious ways, we must move less mysteriously and rescue Alex from a different fate, a terrible fate. Are you sufficiently rested, Lord Caerleon?"

"Yes, I feel well."

"You've undergone a painful ordeal. We are men of peace and the slavers are not. We must move quickly if we are to save Alex. Tonight under the cover of darkness is the best time. They will not expect us, I think. Return to your room and rest, for we have dangerous work before us. Be of good spirits. You will have your lover by your side before morning." Brother Khalid smiled.

I returned to my small whitewashed room and sat down on the edge of the bed. My tired mind was filled with confused thoughts. Indeed, I found myself in the companay of strange men in a strange place that I did not understand. But they were going to help me rescue my beloved Alex from the grasping and cruel hands of the slavers who had taken him. That would be enough for now. Exhausted, I fell back in my bed and rested.

There was a knock at the door and I got up and opened it. It was Brother Khalid and several of his fellow monks dressed in hooded black robes. He gave me one and I slipped it over my head. The corridors of the monastery were dimly lit with an roseate light that came from an unknown source. Quickly we moved along, the sound of our boots echoing off the stone walls, as we passed through hallways of the vast, hidden monastery. It had taken the hard labor of many men to carve these halls, chambers, and stairways out of the living rock. Who had done it and when? There were no answers to these questions as we moved silently down a long flight of stairs into the open desert.

The night sky was alive with stars, and I heard the sound of movement. Shadowy black-robed men stood waiting beside kneeling camels, or were already mounted on horses. Brother Khalid helped me mount a camel and with a lurch it rose as I awkwardly clung to the reins. "We must ride silently and take the slavers while they sleep. Their hiding place is near the holy oasis of Zeus-Ammon. They tread on sacred ground. They are evil men but we are not. We can only meet violence with violence if that is what is necessary to save the young man." Brother Khalid flourished an out-of-date flintlock and pointed to my saddle. I took the ancient gun and waved it in the cold night air. With a cry of desert vengeance we turned the horses and camels into the crisp night and galloped off through the canyons and into the sands of the desert to rescue Alex.

It was an eerie feeling riding out to some unknown place with these robed and silent men. What had called them to this desolate spot? I did not know; all I knew or cared about was that I would soon have Alex in my arms again.

At a quick pace the swift beasts crossed the endless sands that shimmered with the reflected light of many bright stars. We slowed. There was a faint light out toward the horizon. The light came from a window! A hooded man came running across the sands; the lead camel stopped, as I saw the man whisper some words to the driver. We went on and I could see the high wall of a house. Beyond I could see palm trees silhouetted against the sky. We must be near the oasis and village of Siwa. This must be the place where the slavers kept their captives before selling them in the market.

Carefully, silently, the monks dismounted from their kneeling camels and from their horses. Brother Khalid took my hand and with rifles held at the ready all of us crept toward the whitewashed wall. Hoisting ourselves over it like acrobats in a circus, we jumped or fell into a garden. There was a thump and I heard someone fall, no doubt the watchman. Beneath the light coming from the high window of the house, the monks bunched together. "Alex is up there. My man kept watch. It'll be necessary to break in and grab the slavers while they sleep. We are not violent men, but we are dealing with men who are. Do not fire unless absolutely necessary. Are you ready, Lord Caerleon?" I nodded and we moved against the wall, coming to a closed door. Several monks heaved themselves against it, and it gave way, falling with a loud crash. We rushed in. A flickering oil lamp lit the barren room. For an instant there was nothing. I could see the dark-skinned slavers, the dim light glinting off their naked bodies as their muscular forms shook off their sleep.

Their growls and snorts were almost bestial as they roused themselves. They looked at us with wide, frightened eyes when we jabbed our rifles at them. Several monks took the weapons while the others held them at bay.

"Alex is upstairs." Brother Khalid pointed to the dimly lit staircase leading to the upper stories of the house.

"God in heaven, I hope he's all right." Anxiously, I leapt for the stairway, with Brother Khalid and some of the other monks following. A light came from beneath the wooden door. My shoulder against it, I broke it down and rushed in.

No doubt aroused by the noise Roumer Ibrahim stood next to a low bed, his rifle in his hands. The light glanced off of his powerful naked body. His hawk-eyes glared out at us with grim ferocity. "It's you! The Englishman. We left you in the desert, food for the vultures. How?"

"Sorry to disappoint you, Ibrahim. We've come for Alex."

"He's my merchandise and you'll die if you try and take him!" The slaver waved his rifle and quickly glanced at Alex. My dear, sweet Alex. They had taken off his clothes. He was bound, his arms cruelly behind him. His fine body was bathed in sweat, his mouth gagged to prevent his screams of terror. His eyes were icy with fear, but widened into a glimmer of hope as he saw me. Though his legs were spread-eagled, he tried to get up.

"If I were you, slaver, I would put your gun down." Brother Khalid said, pointing his rifle. "Your crime is an abomination to us. The greatest evil one man can inflict on another is that of slavery. Men were made for freedom, not to be bought and sold like cattle in the market."

"You'll never take him, he's mine! He'll bring much gold. He's a prize. . . ." The slaver's black eyes glittered. Suddenly, he reached down, grabbing Alex by the shoulder and yanking him to his feet. "The ropes that bind him are of silk to prevent chafing. My men were attracted by his English beauty, and had I not protected him from their carnal desires. . . ." Ibrahim jerked Alex before him, keeping with one hand the glinting barrel of his rifle trained on us, and with the other holding Alex close.

"Take your filthy hands off of him!" I cried out, seething with anger.

"Ah, do I perceive something? You have made love to the handsome boy. I desired him and watched him; he was so frightened and so at my mercy." The slaver's hand moved across Alex's chest, his brown fingers touching his nipples. Playfully, he ran his hand down over Alex's taut belly. With his hairy, swarthy muscularity the Arab seemed like some demon ready to pounce.

"Take your hands off of him!" I shouted.

"One move and you're a dead man, Lord Caerleon. I could easily train the gun on your beloved Alex." The slaver moved his hand down into Alex's groin, caressing his white flanks, and then taking the limp shaft into his hands. Pressing his body against Alex, he moaned with sexual pleasure. "Ah, such delights." Ibrahim moved slightly away and the light caught his hairy groin. His member stood erect. Stiff and massive, it jutted out of his shadowed crotch. Alex struggled, his eyes tearful, as the Arab's hand closed around his manhood, clenching the soft flesh with a greedy, hairy paw.

There was a sudden noise, and the sound of shots being fired. "The slavers have broken loose!" someone shouted. A moment later several hard, brutal men ran into the room, followed by the cowled monks. The slavers held rifles and fired them at the monks who fell back. The naked Arabs gathered around Ibrahim, their weapons carefully trained on us.

The hawk-eyed Arab smiled evilly, when he saw his men force their way into the room, their smoking weapons grimly announcing the bloody carnage below as did the several wounded monks who staggered into the room. It was a hellish scene, one of evil incarnate, and my mind reeled in frustrated anger as silence fell. The slavers had taken charge, while the monks and I stood helplessly by.

The Arab laughed seeing his victory. "The men who have come with you to save dear Alex are no match for the hardened men of the desert." Ibrahim gave his weapon to one of his men and watched us with hard eyes as he held Alex. "How delightful it is to touch your young friend. How delightful it will be when we take our pleasure. He will be slightly blemished when he is sold. . . ." The Arab's face became savage as a beast, as he held Alex's body to him, jerking the boy's head down and brutally yanking his bound arms up out of the way. Firmly holding Alex, the Arab straddled the boy's buttocks, his massive shaft seeking the warm entrance. "When I finish, the rest of my men can take their needed pleasure."

"You can't. You'll kill him. I'd rather die than see this terrible atrocity!" I swung my gun, expecting death. What was it? Dawn? The tiny room was filled with a brilliant, glowing light that came from somewhere and nowhere. The naked slavers, the monks, and I became bathed in a golden radiance. The dreadful scene was frozen. From somewhere, from nowhere, we heard a hissing, slithering something that sounded like speech. What was the language? I could not tell, but I understood the words.

Loftily and from a distance, hollow and echoing, it spoke: "Who is it that disturbs my long sleep? Who screams the screams of pain and agony? Is it the famed Alexandros who makes holy pilgrimage to the sacred oracle of Zeus-Ammon? Did not the god send me to protect the young hero? Lo, with flames at night and speech at day, I guided him hence where he became a living god. What are these screams of terror that have broken my ancient sleep?"

"Look!" Brother Khalid and the monks raised their arms as a vision took form. Curling sensuously above our heads a great serpent coiled and reared. The scaly plates of its huge body sparkled with the iridescence of jewels. The mighty head was of softly glowing gold. Its awesome fangs were gleaming ivory. "It is a manifestation of Zeus!" The monks fell to their knees, as the glittering eyes of the serpent watched.

"It is indeed Alexandros who silently screams with fear." The creature's shimmering, powerful tail wrapped itself around the clustered slavers. Tightening its grip, it lifted them upward. The serpent watched as its tail crushed the life from their mangled bodies. As if mesmerized by the serpent's terrible glance, the slavers seemed paralyzed, unable to fight against their terrible fate. I ran to Alex. Having suffered the most horrible of experiences, his pale face was briefly flushed with joy before he collapsed into my arms. I caught him and held his limp form. Tearing off his bindings and clutching his nearly lifeless body against me, I must have broken out with cries of joy; tears came to my eyes. I held my beloved once again.

The apparition, its serpentine form coiling around the bodies of the slavers, had done its work. The slavers lay in bloody heaps of crushed flesh and bones. Slithering and hissing, the ancient thing, sent to protect Alexander the Great on his desert trek so long ago, vanished as full light of dawn filled the room. Now the monks had regained their feet and looked over at Alexander Saint-Hilaire. Brother Khalid and the other monks knelt.

"It's him. Alexandros. He's returned to us. We've waited such a long time. Our prayers have been answered." Reverently, they stood up. "We must return to the monastery at once if we are to save the life of the young man."

"I think he is . . . dead!" I cried out. The body I held now seemed drained of life.

"No! That cannot be. God will save him. His fine heart still beats, though faintly. Quickly, find a robe to cover him with. We must return at once." Brother Khalid looked around at the carnage. "Some of the brothers have died, but they have been avenged."

"What was it?"

"The will of Zeus. The gods still protect their sons." Brother Khalid looked down with sorrowful dark eyes. Gently he brushed the dried tears away from Alex's closed eyes. "We must return to the monastery at once. The boy's fate is now in the hands of God."

One of the monks found a clean robe and pulled it up around Alex's body. Still holding him close to me, I regained my camel. Dawn bathed the oasis and the surrounding desert in a bloodlike glow. Then, swirling like some monstrous tornado, the glow caught the house containing the dead slavers. Before I knew it there were flames. As I watched they licked at the walls, climbing higher and higher until the infernal house was no more. The sacred oasis was cleansed of the evil that had invaded it. Holding the reins in one hand and firmly grasping the form of my beloved with the other, I let myself be led across the sands by my new friends.

Somehow, without my knowing it, we had neared the hidden monastery. Curiously, my eyes searched the honey-combed rocks for some sign of a structure, but only barren rocks seemed to surround us. Soon, however, the camels and horses entered a cave, which I assumed lay beneath the monastery. Without losing a precious second I carried Alex up the stairs to where the monks had prepared his room.

Here I stayed with my beloved, only taking enough rest to enable me to watch him more carefully. Alex was very sick, passing from a semi-conscious state to a fitful sleep. Sometimes he cried out, screaming in terror, as nightmares passed through his feverish mind. He was unable to throw off the thoughts of his terrible ordeal. The days passed with tortuous slowness. The gracious monks also hovered by his side, wringing their hands and silently praying. Time after time I wiped the perspiration from his troubled brow. He shivered with cold, so more blankets were brought. When he awoke, as he sometimes did, he refused food. He was growing weaker and weaker, and there appeared to be nothing we could do to prevent his life from draining away before our eyes.

I had just returned from my room after a quick nap to once again watch life leave the body of my beloved. Entering the small whitewashed stone chamber, I saw a black form leaning over Alex. A dim oil lamp flickered off the newcomer's dark robes. My heart jumped and I seized the shape by the shoulder. The form turned; it was Abad al-Jalil. His usual bright eyes were tired, his mouth was turned down at the corners, and his white beard was dirty and ragged. "Lord Caerleon, we meet again in terrible circumstances. An unexpected tragedy."

"You! What are you doing here?"

"The reasons are not important now, but saving Alex's life is. The demons inside his mind writhe like snakes; he cannot forget the terror caused by the slavers. His mind is destroying itself, trying to erase the dreadful experience."

"How can we save him?" I asked, pale with anxiety.

"The memory of the raid must be removed from his thoughts or he will die. Leave me now. I must concentrate if we are to save his life." Trusting the old Egyptian, I left the room. Alex's life was in his hands.

"Our master has great powers," Brother Khalid said, standing outside the door. "There is no one else who can save the boy from his agony. Come, we'll take coffee in the library." Following along after him, I entered a large room. The bookshelves that covered the walls from floor to ceiling were filled with books. Tables held scientific equipment of all kinds. It was a scholar's room, a room devoted to study. I was curious.

"The monks must spend their time in study. So many books."

"Yes, Lord Caerleon. The order is devoted to learning and knowledge. Mankind is beginning to stir in the Christian year of 1831. It has been a long sleep. Man is again curious about his world, investigating and researching, perhaps once again ready for the knowledge we have to help him move into a greater world than he can ever expect to know, a new world."

"You call yourselves Guardians. What do you guard?"

"I cannot tell you, unless the master says so."

"You bowed before Alex, calling him Alexandros, his name in Greek. Do you worship the Macedonian or something?"

"Hmm, not quite. We keep his legacy alive; we guard his legacy of learning and knowledge. I cannot say more. I must leave for a time. There are some cakes and coffee and many books that will interest you. Be at ease." The monk left the room. Sipping the strong coffee, I selected a book and settled down for what could be a long wait. A wait that would determine Alex's fate.

I thought I heard a door opening, and I shook off the drowsiness that had overcome me. Alex stood at the door dressed in a white robe. He was dead and had become an angel; his ghost had come to bid me farewell. But no, he was alive! Though he looked weak, his eyes danced and a broad grin covered his face. Startled, I got up, the book in my lap falling to the floor. He ran to me, and we embraced, holding each other tightly. Tearfully, we kissed. So great was my joy that I was hardly able to speak. "You are alive and well."

"Yes, dear heart, I feel wonderful, if a bit tired. I woke up, and there of all people, was the old Egyptian. Did I have a dream? Are we back in Cairo?"

"No. We are in the desert among friends who have helped us."

"Is this Siwa?"

"No, but we are close."

"Are we going there?"

"I do not know."

"Is the Tomb of Alexandros here?"

"I do not know. These men belong to a religious order of some kind . . . that I really do not understand."

There was the sound of shuffling sandals as the Egyptian entered the room. He looked happy, and the signs of his former weariness were gone. "You see, Lord Caerleon, young Alex is well again."

"Was I sick? I feel wonderful."

"It was only a touch of the fever."

"I cannot thank you enough."

"I have done only what was necessary to clear the cobwebs."

"He. . . .?"

"No cobwebs, sir. I hope your stay at the monastery has not been too unhappy. We are simple, plain men and lack the social amenities."

"We have been treated very well . . . I do not understand this place, so isolated, hidden away in the mountains, the rooms carved out of solid rock . . . Brother Khalid spoke in mysterious terms about guarding something . . . knowledge and learning."

"He is not permitted to tell more. Yes, we are guardians of a great treasure. A treasure beyond mere gold. Knowledge and learning are treasures beyond price. I have grown fond of you both, for you are good and not evil. It was not my thinking that you would find your way to Siwa; instead, I hoped you would return to Cairo. There is an Arabic word, *qismah*, which means a man's lot, portion or fate in life. It is fate that has brought you here. If I had told you about this place in Cairo, you would not have believed me. Now, however, my words bear the weight of proof."

"The monks call you 'master.' Do you run the monastery?"

"I function within it. From time to time in the course of history there are those who are given special gifts. They are seekers after higher knowledge, individuals who are not stifled by the superstitions of their time. I am growing . . . old. The work of the monastery must go on."

"What work?"

"Working for the betterment of mankind. Work begun by Alexandros when he founded his city so long ago."

"What are you saying?"

"You had the book of ibn Hayyan in your saddlebag when we found you."

"Yes. Lord Beveridge's agents had taken it from the university library in Cairo, and I brought it with me."

"Lord Beveridge was a fortune hunter of the worst kind. I am glad he has returned to England. You remember the scenes of destruction that ibn Hayyan described?"

"Yes, of course."

"It was the end of a world, the end of ancient knowledge and learning that had been carefully accumulated through the ages. All destroyed by aimless fanatics who cared nothing for what the books contained. It was terrible. But there were men at the time who, on seeing their world shaken to its very foundations, tried to preserve what they could. A very small fraction of the ancient world was saved by these wise men."

"What are you saying?"

"In the vaults and the crypts of this monastery lie the treasures of ancient Alexandria as well as other treasures that were also rescued. The knowledge of the ages!"

"I cannot believe that."

"Nonetheless, it is true. The lost knowledge of mankind is here, guarded, preserved, waiting."

"I do not believe you."

"There is no reason to believe me, but this storehouse exists . . . I must . . . find another. Are the signs correct? Have I read them correctly? Is there another? Come, I will erase your doubts. I will show you. Follow me."

Abad al-Jalil rose from his chair, and we followed him out of the library into the corridor and down a long hallway. The walls of the hallway were of stone, the entire passage lit with a glow of roseate light that seemed to have no origin. Going deeper into the mountain we came to a solid stone wall. We stopped as our leader raised his arm; a great stone slid upwards, thundering into its place in the ceiling. We passed beneath its enormous weight into another passageway. Going even deeper down, we saw other stone doors raised by unknown means. "These passages were built at the same time as the Great Pyramids to hide Cheop's body after it was robbed. His architects had to find a safer resting place. Cheops and other pharaohs are still here, undisturbed." Finally, we came to a stone wall, which when raised up, led to a great room. I could not determine its size. "It is here," said the old Egyptian.

Caught in the mysterious light, Alex and I looked about us. We were surrounded by row upon row of scrolls, each bearing a label. Here were ancient books of science and knowledge, literature, plays, poems, histories that had been thought lost or destroyed. But this was only the beginning. There were other rooms stacked with golden treasures, articles of unimaginable wealth. Breathlessly, we went from room to room, each containing objects that anyone would kill to possess, for we had come to know the extent of man's greed. During our passage the roseate light grew brighter, until at last we came to another great room. We seemed to be looking at a wall of gold that shimmered before our eyes. In fact, it was a curtain of gold that we saw, and beyond it was something . . . straining our eyes we could see a great figure, grand and majestic. "If I were permitted to part the curtain you would see one of the wonders of the ancient world, the Olympian Zeus, carved by Phidias" said our guide. "Its flesh is of ivory, the vestments of solid gold. Yes, it was saved, brought here piece by piece and reassembled. Other things, however, were lost like the ivory and gold statue of the goddess Athena housed in the Parthenon, which the Christians stripped and then burnt. You see, Lord Caerleon and young Alex, why we are Guardians. Things lost through the ages, objects thought destroyed, are stored here, waiting for a more enlightened world, a world that will be tolerant, under-

standing, and loving of things they do not understand. Destruction is
a terrible thing. Man is blinded by his passions and his intolerances
which drive him into the slime of madness. Here, then, is our mission: to guard and to preserve this knowledge, these treasures until
man is ready to receive them. Someday when man is ready. . . ."

"The time is not now?"

"No, not now. Who knows how many ages will pass before it is
time. The last oracle passed from this earth, and Zeus no longer
speaks to mankind, telling us of the future. But when the time is
ready there will be signs: omens that will tell us."

"What signs?"

"We will know them when they come, and we will be ready to
leave our hidden monastery and step out into the world and say to
man what is here; boundless knowledge and unimaginable wealth
that will lead to a future beyond anything ever conceived by man. I
know this to be true. I have seen it, and it will come . . . someday."

"It will be the greatest gift mankind has ever received."

"Yes. Man will put aside his wars, his hatreds, his prejudices, and
rise to greater glory freed from his madness. Sometime . . . it is here
waiting. Come now, we will return." Alex and I stood for a moment
before the shimmering curtain of gold. Once before we had stood
before such a statue, and it had spoken to us declaring that our love
for each other was good and true, predicting that we would spend the
rest of our days together. Was this the same Zeus that had spoken to
us? I did not know. What is a dream, an illusion? I do not know.
Were we dreaming now? Were we transfixed by an illusion, standing
as we now did before the golden curtain? I did not know. We turned
our eyes from the awful presence of the Olympian Zeus, retracing our
steps through the passageways, the rooms of gold, and rooms containing the great stacks of books. We took our last look at the
treasures so carefully guarded, treasures which would someday
benefit all of mankind . . . when the time was ripe.

Back in the room where he had come to us, the Egyptian sat down
and ordered some fresh black coffee. He smiled. "You see now the
vital importance of our mission here in the desert, and why it must

continue until the signs are given. My time on earth is drawing to a close, and I must seek a successor who will take my place. He must be a person who will be trained in certain crafts; he must study for many years in order to know the powers of his mind."

I sat there looking at the old Egyptian, and it suddenly became apparent that he was thinking of Alex. I looked him straight in the eye and he nodded. "Yes, Lord Caerleon, what you are now thinking is true. The moment I saw him I knew."

"Saw whom?" Alex seemed startled, his eyes still dazzled by the piles of gold.

"You, Alex. My time is nearing its end, and a successor must be trained. The moment I saw you . . . your mind is still fresh, eager to learn."

"What are you saying?"

"I have chosen you, Alexander Saint-Hilaire, as my successor."

"I . . . do not know what to say. I could never learn your powers. I could never stay in this desert. Edward and I are. . . ."

". . . lovers and are devoted to each other. . . . I know. All the brothers here share the same love and are bound together by holy vows. Ours is a community of men who love men; a love which is good and true. I knew when we first met that you loved each other, but the love was not yet expressed . . . but perhaps, now. . . ."

"Yes, we have declared our love."

"Ah, yes, I can see it, and it is beautiful for me to see. Alexandros and Hephaistios. . . ."

"Alexandros . . . his tomb. It's here! Edward. . . ."

"I know it was your dream to find it, but it is not here or at the oasis of Siwa. We have searched for centuries. Perhaps the words of ibn Hayyan were not read correctly. Perhaps it was moved here at one time before the murder of the oracle of Zeus-Ammon. The Christians broke into the temple. It is a mystery that will never be solved. I am sorry, Alex; I knew how much finding the tomb meant to you. A dream unfulfilled."

Alex stood up, running his hands through his golden curls, looking up at the collection of books, breathing heavily, as if he were trying to make a decision, a very difficult decision, one that could change his entire life. The Egyptian had summoned him to an enormous task that few men would ever be asked to assume. I knew what was going on in his confused and muddled head. He would be guardian of a vast treasure, the recipient of knowledge beyond that of other men, and he would wait for a sign that mankind was ready for his wisdom and knowledge, but for how long? Perhaps for the rest of his life, and in his time he would select another to carry on the mission. Lifetime upon lifetime, until mankind had grown more tolerant, more understanding, and more loving, until men found peace and brotherhood and were ready to seek new horizons somewhere in a glorious future. A dream once realized by a Macedonian boy who had the known world at his feet. His world, to change and mold into a universal state where all men were brothers. His dream had ended in failure, blown away in the corrupting sands of Persia. His city of Alexandria had become his legacy of learning and knowledge, and now some of it was here, hidden deep in this mountain . . . waiting. Would such a man come again? Strong, heroic, a man fit to set others again on the correct path to a glorious future. Perhaps Alexander would be that man. I did not know.

It was a long time before Alex turned, his gray eyes somehow sad, his handsome figure drooped, as though the weight of the world had fallen on his broad shoulders. "You have chosen me to carry on your great task, Abad al-Jalil. I do not think I am worthy. I know very little, and my grades at school were not very good. I must have time to think. My mind is running in circles and I cannot think clearly. It all has been so fast, so sudden. To spend years of my life here, away from the busy world; perhaps my world is empty, vain, and frivolous, but it is a world I like."

"Yes, I can understand how you feel. The passions of youth. It has been a long time. In truth I've returned to the monastery to live my final days. I've had a long and good life since my birth in 1701. . . ."

"What! I thought you to be around fifty, not more than sixty. Men do not live to be 130 years of age."

"The secrets of longevity were known in ancient times. If I remember the Old Testament correctly, Moses lived to be 120 and

Methuselah to the very ripe age of 969 years, or so it is recorded. Certain secret herbs can prolong life, but not forever. It was a century ago, when, like yourself, I became lost in the desert and was taken in by the monks then living here. I fell deeply in love with one of them, and we were to share our lives for many years. It broke my heart when he passed on and I was alone. My brothers, however, gave me solace. I'm tired now. My mind is strong but my bones are brittle. I will die here with my brothers."

"That makes us both very sad," I said with a heavy heart, for I had grown to love the old man and his wisdom.

"Do not grieve. Perhaps in the other world I will find my lover again, and our love will be reaffirmed. Recently, I knew my time on earth was drawing to an end so I set out to find you, Alex, and your lover, Edward, two men brought together by love, each for the other. Both of you are welcome to remain here together sharing your life, learning, and studying. We will teach you things beyond your scope of understanding, wonderful things. Oh, it is true we do not live in luxury and ease. Our table is not that of the British House. Our fare is the simple food of the sand-dwellers, I'm afraid. You would not be asked to leave the world forever, and there are no bonds to hold you here. You would be free to come and go after a novitiate of a year. I know your estate at Caerleon Castle means a great deal to you, and you could spend much of the year there. All we ask is that you never reveal this place, and I know that you would never . . . I trust you both, or I would not have shown you. . . ."

"No, we will never tell your secret. We understand the gravity of being a Guardian."

"The hour grows late and it is time for supper. Food will be brought to your rooms. Think deeply about what I have said. Our future and that of the very world itself is in your hands. Farewell, Alex and Lord Caerleon." The Egyptian left the room.

Silently, we walked back to our rooms to eat our simple dinner. Alex sat looking down at his food, but soon stood up, turning his face to the stone wall. "This is all mad. Here we are two perfectly normal Englishmen about to say we'll spend the rest of our lives in this dried up place in the middle of the desert."

"The mission, the guardianship, the powers."

"The old Egyptian was enjoying himself at our expense. We don't belong here; we belong with the living, dear Edward, not with the dead past. We belong where there are parties, laughter, and fun, not stuck away in some desert hole, waiting for a sign that may never come."

"He said that we could return to England."

"I want to return now, or at least as soon as we can return to Cairo and float the obelisk to Alexandria."

"The old Egyptian is dying and you'll become his successor. Together with the monks we'll guard the lost treasures of mankind. There'll be a better future for mankind."

"Peace and love, not likely in our time. And even if we were to live as long as he says he's lived, no one can see what the future will bring. Oh, dear, sweet, Edward, I want to leave. It's spring in England and everything is green and fresh, not barren with endless sands. I'll go crazy if I stay here. I'm not Alexander the Great. It's all a pretty story. The monks will get along, God knows they've survived two thousand years without us. We can get the obelisk and go back to England." Alex's eyes showed a fearful desperation. "God, I want to leave this dreadful place. It's all been horrible. Why did we come here?"

"We'll leave, if that's really what you want." I took him into my arms. I could feel his body quivering beneath my touch, and saw tears come into his beautiful eyes. "Yes, beloved, we'll leave. It's all been a strange dream."

"A dream, sweet Edward, and nothing more. I want to see green trees and walk in fresh, green grass and smell the fragrance of an English spring. Alexander the Great is not here and my quest has ended. But I have found something: your love, Edward. Let's go."

"If that's really what you want." A monk came for the dishes, and we asked for a guide and camels to return us to Alexandria. The next morning we mounted the tawny beasts, and the caravan headed into the endless wastes of the Libyan desert. I glanced back at the hidden monastery, and I thought I saw a robed man looking down at us from the top of a cliff, but perhaps it was only a mirage.

12.

Ol' Joe and his sons beamed as we crossed the gangplank. The *Star* looked the same. "Ah, effendi, you've been gone long time. My boys and I almost give up hope. Everything is just as you left it."

"Well, Alex, the old boat looks good. I think I grew very fond of the *Star*."

"Yes, it has meant a great deal to us here in Egypt." Alex looked around, running his hands over the somewhat battered and worn wood. "It looks so small now. How we ever got along . . ."

"It was fun, but at the time . . . the obelisk, that damn obelisk is still here. I was hoping . . . oh, not really, that some brave soul had stolen the six tons of it."

"All we have to do is to get it to Alexandria, load it aboard a ship, and sail it off to England. Shouldn't be much trouble . . . if we're lucky. Everything that could go wrong, did go wrong on our trip up here."

"Another two weeks and that will be that."

"Have you decided where you're going to put it?"

"I thought in the garden, near the graveyard, near father and mother, alongside the rest of my noble ancestors."

"Not a bad place, but no one will see it. If you put it in the middle of that circular garden in front of the castle, then everybody will see it. You'll be the rage of Caerleon, and everybody will want one."

"If they want one, let them come to Egypt and get it. Yes, we'll put it in front of the house."

"Egypt . . . Egypt." Alex spoke quietly. In his words were a bit of awe, of wonder, and of love . . . the feelings of remorse and sadness that seemed to summarize our trip. Awesome monuments symbolizing an ancient culture in many ways superior to our own; temples to forgotten gods, tombs built for powerful men, memorials that would stand after both of us had turned to dust. Love for a simple race of men, good, hard-working men who tilled the land, observing the endless cycles of nature and the everlasting cycles of the Nile, the great river that imposed its will on all those who lived on its banks. We felt remorse and sadness because we would have to leave this timeless place. However there was something else in Alex's voice that I did not understand. "Egypt."

"We should shove off at first light, get an early start." Alex and I went to our cabin to get some fresh clothes, for we wanted to go to British House and settle our affairs. I would need to cash some cheques to pay Ol' Joe and his crew. The cabin was musty, filled now not only with our baggage, but with the mementos of our journey: portfolios of drawings and artifacts collected along the way — the head of Antinoos, the figure of Amenophis, the statues, some scarabs, bronzes, both fake and real. It did not matter; they were the sum of the memories that we would take back to England and were precious to us. We would have to pack them for the voyage home.

British House gave us a little party, and before sunset we rode back to our boat. Already the days were getting hotter, and soon the tourists would leave behind the dreadful heat of summer, returning to their castles, villas, and manorhouses. No doubt most of the wealthy Europeans would think of the entire trip as a lark, a jaunt, something to tell stories about for the rest of their lives. In winter they would come again, batting the flys and the bugs, coming down with "Cheop's revenge," exploring the ruins, buying fakes, cursing the slow natives, playing cards, and drinking. All jolly good fun.

The *Star* pulled away from the shoreline. The fabulous domes and minarets of Cairo faded away, and far to the western horizon the Great Pyramids dissolved in a dusty veil of purple and gold. The boat caught the north-moving current. We had set sail for Alexandria. Two weeks later we arrived after a smooth trip. The obelisk was

hauled on shore. From there it would be hoisted aboard the next sailing vessel headed for England. We said our final farewells to Ol' Joe
and his sons, giving them their pay and a letter of recommendation
for their good services. They would sail back to Cairo, wait out the
hot summer, and be ready for the next influx of tourists in the
winter. We returned to our hotel.

"Here we are again; the same rooms we had when we started out."
I said.

"Tomorrow they'll load the obelisk, and we'll be off."

"Back to England. They should have started spring plowing at
Caerleon by now. I'll be glad to get back. You know what the poets
say about the English spring, the daffodils and all."

"I was wondering . . ."

"What, Alex?"

"If we might drive around this morning for old times sake."

"Where? We've seen just about all there is to see."

"To the old mosque."

"Still haven't given up hope of finding the tomb, eh?"

"It has been on my mind, along with many other things."

"But we searched. There was nothing, but if you think you want to
go there."

"I have a feeling . . ."

"I'll have the Levantine call a carriage."

"Just one more search."

Once again the festooned and tasseled carriage made its way
through the streets of Alexandria. The mobs of people and the city
did not seem as exotic as they had when first we arrived. We had
become part of the landscape, almost natives. The droopy nag
clopped through the streets until we reached our destination. Going
down the alleyway we saw again the tumbled walls and the founda-
tion of the once tall minaret. The same dirty children ran through the
rubbish and the offal, but the dreadful odor no longer bothered us
when the carriage came to a stop. Telling the driver to wait, we
crossed through the dusty courtyard and into the dingy mosque. It
was dark and cool; again the stone pavement was dappled by sunlight

streaming through the broken ceiling. Alex walked slowly, running his hands over the marble columns, looking at the finely carved capitals. He seemed lost in thought as he looked at the prayer niche set into the eastern wall. He suddenly looked up. "This is really a mosque?"

"Yes, of course, deserted now."

"The prayer niche? I can't remember what it was called."

"A . . . a *mihrab*, or something like that, Arundale . . ."

"Arundale had converted the mosque of his Moorish house into a showroom for his antiques. And there was another room where he kept his finest treasures . . . the golden drachma. I was thinking of it today as I packed it away with the rest of the things. The treasure room ·behind the secret door, and I thought . . ."

"Yes, the secret room, the . . . *maqsura*, where the Moslem officials prayed in privacy."

"If this is a mosque it should have . . . whatever you said it was . . . a secret prayer room behind the *mihrab*. I don't see one."

"Arundale had a secret door that opened."

"Yes, I remember . . . he pushed something. Let's look." Alex and I climbed the several steps up to the prayer niche with its carved limestone surface of flowers, intertwining grape leaves, rosettes, and Islamic stars. "If this thing has a secret door it's been a long time since anyone has opened it." We ran our fingertips over the surface of the dusty limestone, but there was nothing unusual. "Well, it's not along the sides, maybe overhead." I looked up at the carved architrave some feet above our heads.

"Hoist me up." Alex put his boot in my hand and I lifted him up. He ran his hands over the carvings. The dust fell into my eyes and face, and I wobbled."

"Steady, dear Edward, or I'll fall and break my leg."

"See anything?"

"Just a big stone with the star of Islam carved on it. Looks solid."

"Press on it anyway; you're strong enough."

"I'll try and reach it." With a grunt and leaning forward with both hands out, I shifted my position, almost collapsing, as Alex swayed this way and that. "The damn thing is solid . . . no . . . wait, it's moving . . . the stone is moving." Something deep in the old mosque rumbled. Scared by the strange sound and movement, Alex leaned backward, sending us both into a spin, and in a clumsy heap we fell to the floor, dust and debris flying up around us. "Look! The wall has lifted." The dust had settled, and we could see the solid-looking wall had lifted up, and a stream of sunlight struck another wall in a blinding flash of gold. Emblazoned into the wall was the sixteen-pointed starburst, the symbol of the royal Macedonian dynasty of King Philip and his son. "Great Zeus, we've found the tomb." Alex stood up, wiping the dust away.

"Yes, it must be. Remember, 'Find the royal star and you will find me.' I wonder who ever put it here?"

"Perhaps the Guardians moved it here for some reason. Perhaps they did not think it was safe at the monastery. It was a time of great turmoil and grief."

"This could be it."

"Come on, Edward, let's see where it leads."

"Be careful, Alex, remember how the ancients set traps for unwary tomb-robbers. Careful." Climbing back up the stairs we entered into a small passageway, passing the emblazoned star, and saw a flight of stairs leading downwards. It was dark. "Better get some torches. I'll go back to the driver and have him rummage up a couple."

"Don't tell him, or he'll have every Arab in the place in here."

"I won't." Quickly I ran out to the carriage, explaining to the driver that we had found an old column that we wanted to examine more closely. He grumbled, but ran off after I gave him a few coins. Returning with two torches he lit them with his tinder-box, and I fairly ran back to the mosque. I found Alex looking down into the very black passageway. "Let's go."

Down we went into the darkness. There were steps; the walls of the passageway were narrow on either side, and the ceiling was low. Stopping long enough to adjust our torches, we bent over, almost crawling along. The walls felt slimy, the floor slippery. Further along, the passageway broadened, and we could stand upright. Our torches caught the arched ceiling. It reminded me of the crypts we had seen beneath the Serapeum. The ceiling was dripping salt-water! We must be beneath the bay of Alexandria. The air was bad and we had difficulty breathing. Our torches flickered in the poor air and sizzled when drops of water hit their flames. Ahead there was only darkness, and we went forward, slipping on the wet floor. Suddenly, the torches caught a flicker of gold ahead, and we seemed to have reached the end of our journey, as we came to another star-burst design. Alex ran his fingers over the bright gold. In the center of the star-cluster was a medallion engraved with the head of Alexandros, the same head that was on the golden drachma—the same profile, the same wavy hair, and the same ram's horns worn over the ear, twisting and turning, the symbol of his god-head. As if by instinct, Alex knew where to touch the medallion. There was a click and a great rumble; the stone lifted up, moved by some ancient mechanism that we did not understand. With fearful hearts we entered we knew not what.

We were in some room. The dim light caught the gleam of gold and the glitter of gems. In a long line on either side of the room were placed beautifully crafted coffins of goldwork, half-hidden in the gloom. The names of some of the most renowned of the ancient dead leaped out at us: the Ptolemies, and the Cleopatras, who had ruled Egypt three hundred years before the Romans. Stacked between the coffins were piles of valuable gifts given by the admirers of Alexandros. Here, too, were the golden Roman standards, bearing the names of Augustus, Hadrian, Caracalla, Trajan, and Diocletian. Though all of this was undoubtedly brilliant, something even more extraordinary now met our amazed gaze. What we saw were festooned garlands, Ionic columns, statues of the goddess Victory, and a golden temple. All of these were adorning the funeral catafalque that had carried the embalmed body of Alexandros from Persia to Egypt so many centuries ago. We stopped, dazzled by the sheer golden glory of the car, as the dim light played over the fabulous decorations and intricate designs. Under a golden netting, and sitting over another golden coffin, was a rock crystal dome, glowing and iridescent. Alex grasped my hand and looked into my face. Did we dare look? Did the Macedonian still rest in his golden coffin?

We slowly walked up the stairs to the alcove in which the car had been placed. Alex reached out, touching the gold netting that still hung around the temple. Originally, it had protected the body from profane onlookers when it was moved across the desert. Alex tested the ancient car to see if it would hold his weight. He drew back, expecting it to cave in, but nothing happened. Reassured, he put both hands on the car, lifted the netting, and reached out until he could touch the gold-embroidered purple funeral pall that was spread out around the rock-crystal dome. With extraordinary care he brought his knee up and lifted himself onto the car. Standing upright, his head near the vaulted roof of the temple, he looked through the transparent crystal into the coffin. "He's here and he looks alive. His . . . face is perfect; his hair is still a tawny gold color. There is no decay at all. It is as though I am looking into a mirror. It's me!"

"What?"

"I am Alexandros!"

"Here, give me a hand . . ." From faraway, inside and outside of the golden mausoleum, there was a rumbling sound, like distant thunder. The floor trembled. "The place is falling in! We had better get out of here."

Alex turned, looking at me through the shimmering netting, his eyes wet with tears, his face almost shining with religious awe. I seized him by the hand, for he seemed unable to move. "I am Alexandros."

"You'll be in here with him forever if you don't move. Come on!" I pulled him off the funeral car. He seemed to regain his senses on hearing the low thunder. Now fully frightened, we ran past the golden coffin and the Roman standards. Our torches showed us that the entrance stone was slowly moving downwards. "The stone is falling. We'll be trapped forever. Run!" We scrambled for our very lives. The ancient machinery made a rumbling noise that echoed throughout the chamber. The stone was nearly in place. Falling on our knees and scrambling on all fours, we slid beneath a moment before it sealed the chamber for all time.

We pulled ourselves to our feet. The same dim light as before caught the starburst and the medallion. But now sea water was seeping into the passage. More of it began to leak through the stones of the archway above us. The movement of the entrance stone must have jarred other stones loose. Nearby, a stone fell to the floor with an alarming clunk. Now the sea began to pour into where we stood. In a minute we were knee deep in swirling water. Soaked, our torches flickered and went out, leaving us in terrible darkness, while the passageway crumbled in around us, replaced by the Mediterranean Sea.

Screaming in terror we sloshed through the water and the darkness, our hands following the wall. The floor inclined upwards and we could feel the waterline falling as we ran up the corridor. Sea water close at our heels, we slipped, slid, and fell until our feet found the stairs leading upwards. Tumbling, scrambling, and dripping wet we fell upon the stairs and dragged ourselves up them. Ahead a dim light beckoned us to safety.

Scrambling on all fours, we fell into the entrance way just as the sea rushed up the stairs, washing away in its terrible velocity the stones of the ancient passageway. Exhausted and looking like drowned rats, we climbed out of the entrance way and fell into the mosque. We were pursued by a roaring fountain of frothy water which cascaded onto the dry, dusty stones. Then, with a thunderous clamor, the entrance stone dropped into place. The gilded star-burst of the Macedonian royal family disappeared behind the wall of limestone. Only puddles of sea water marked the entrance of the Tomb of Alexandros and the enormous treasures it held. Alex and I fell back, wiping the foul, saline water from our lips. We did indeed feel like river rats! Drenched and covered with mud, we sat for a long time looking at the prayer niche and toward Mecca. We had found the tomb and our quest had come to an end. The great door had closed, sealing and preserving the vast treasures for the rest of time. Until the Bay of Alexandria emptied, the Macedonian King would sleep his sleep of the centuries.

Dirty and exhausted we stumbled out of the old mosque, arm in 'rm, laughing with sheer joy. The driver looked greatly astonished as two crazy and insanely happy Englishmen fell into the carriage. to the hotel, driver," I commanded him.

"No, drive to the western gate," Alex said firmly, brushing the mud away from his clothes.

"We should change and get washed up."

"No, drive to the western Canoptic Gate." Alex ordered once again; the driver gave the nag a touch of the whip, and the carriage left the alley. Traveling along the main street, we soon passed beneath an old crumbling Roman archway marking the city limits. As far as we could see, the barren wastes of the Sahara desert stretched from horizon to horizon. The dreadful heat closed in around us. Asking the driver to stop, Alex jumped down from the carriage and walked to the edge of the sands. I followed him and we stood together for a long while. I looked into his eyes. He smiled. "You want to return to the monastery."

"Yes. I looked into the face of Alexandros, and I knew my destiny. For it was I who lay there, some twenty centuries after his death. We are the same. His city is gone forever, but a part of his legacy and his heritage remains. Perhaps in our lifetime the signs will show themselves. Man can live in peace, understanding, and tolerance. We can reveal then the marvelous treasures that we guard, and together we can make a better future. I'll only go if I have you at my side, beloved, dearest Edward."

"I cannot live without you. My life is meaningless and empty without you."

"I'm glad, Edward. Our love is immortal. Do you think we can find the monastery again?"

"Yes, Alex, together we will find it."